CALAMITY
IN
KENT

JOHN ROWLAND

With an Introduction by
MARTIN EDWARDS

D0185307

BRITISH LIBRARY

This edition published 2016 by
The British Library
96 Euston Road
London NW1 2DB

Originally published in 1950 by Herbert Jenkins

Copyright © 2016 Estate of John Rowland
Introduction copyright © 2016 Martin Edwards

Cataloguing in Publication Data
A catalogue record for this book is
available from the British Library

ISBN 978 0 7123 5783 8

Text designed and typeset by Tetragon, London

Printed in England by TJ International

To
Fytton Rowland

———————

in memory of holidays at a place
like "Broadgate"

CONTENTS

INTRODUCTION

The "locked room mystery" is a staple of traditional detective fiction, but in *Calamity in Kent*, John Rowland offers an unusual variation on the theme. The body of John Tilsley, who has been stabbed to death, is found in a locked carriage of a seaside cliff railway.

The setting is the resort of Broadgate, a name suggesting a fictional blend of Broadstairs and Ramsgate. Newspaperman Jimmy London, who narrates the story, is lodging by the sea, convalescing after a serious (but tantalisingly undisclosed) illness that has caused him to give up his job. Jimmy comes across a man behaving strangely; this proves to be the wonderfully named Aloysius Bender, operator of the railway, who tells Jimmy he has found a corpse in his cliff lift.

Jimmy, whose behaviour at times is a rather odd mix of the naive and the unscrupulous, is so keen to re-ignite his career with a sensational story that he interferes with the crime scene, and when Aloysius departs to fetch the police, he takes from the dead man's pocket a notebook containing "various queer combinations of figures", perhaps some kind of code. An enigmatic stranger comes on to the scene, claiming to be a local doctor. He says he knows the deceased, but makes a hasty getaway before the police arrive.

At this point, Jimmy enjoys a stroke of luck. The local cop, Inspector Beech, happens to be accompanied by the affable Inspector Shelley of Scotland Yard, John Rowland's regular detective, and an

old pal of Jimmy's. What is more, Shelley enlists Jimmy's help with
the investigation: "there are people who might talk to a journalist,
who... would not talk so readily to a policeman." Jimmy's investigations eventually lead him into danger, although it has to be said that
the cunning villain he encounters proves in the end to be almost as
obliging as Inspector Shelley; this is a light mystery with thrillerish
elements, rather than a cerebral whodunit.

The use of the cliff railway as a crime scene is an especially nice
touch, very much in keeping with the seaside backdrop. In Britain,
the hey-day of cliff railways was in the latter part of the nineteenth
century and the early decades of the twentieth; they were usually
to be found at resorts which boomed before cheaper air travel made
holidays in warmer climates more affordable. Twenty-five pre-war
cliff railways survive to this day. These include Ramsgate cliff lifts,
although the original cliff railway at Broadstairs has been supplanted
by the new Millennium Cliff Lift.

The "locked room" or "impossible crime" concept clearly appealed
to Rowland—the late Bob Adey's definitive study of the sub-genre,
Locked Room Murders, lists not only this title but also *Suicide Alibi*
(1937; "death by shooting in a room under observation") and *Death
Beneath the River* (1943; "death by shooting of a man driving a car
through a road tunnel"), in both of which Shelley also appeared.
One must concede, however, that the explanation for the locked cliff
railway carriage conundrum does not display the devilish ingenuity
that one associates with, say, the Americans John Dickson Carr and
Clayton Rawson, or Scotland's Anthony Wynne (whose *Murder of
a Lady*, another British Library Crime Classic, is a clever example
of the form).

The real life Wallace murder case, which dates back to 1930, is
mentioned twice during the story, a clue to Rowland's interest in

the famous Liverpudlian mystery; he had written a book about the case, published in 1949. According to John Gannon's much more recent *The Killing of Julia Wallace* (2012), the late Richard Gordon Parry, now widely considered to have been the real murderer, said he was approached by Rowland's agent while the book was being written. There is no way of verifying this intriguing but improbable claim.

Calamity in Kent was first published in 1950, and references to life in post-war Britain—newsprint rationing, the nationalisation of the coal industry, and black market scams—are scattered through the text. In spirit, however, this book has more in common with breezy popular fiction of the Thirties, when Rowland started writing, rather than with crime fiction of the Fifties, such as Patricia Highsmith's debut novel. *Strangers on a Train*, published in the very same year as *Calamity in Kent*, illustrated the shift in authorial preoccupations and readers' tastes since "the Golden Age of murder" between the wars.

John Herbert Shelley Rowland (1907–1984) seems to have recognised that the times were changing for crime novelists. Many leading writers of the Golden Age—examples include Dorothy L. Sayers, Anthony Berkeley—had already abandoned the genre to pursue other interests, and Rowland switched his focus. Those references to the Wallace case hint at an increasing interest in "true crime", and after 1950, he concentrated on non-fiction for the remainder of his career. He did, however, become a member of the Crime Writers' Association, which was founded in 1953, and his later output included further "true crime" titles and books on popular science. He became a Unitarian minister, and his son Fytton recalls that he spent each morning at work in his study—writing sermons, as well as such books as *Poisoner in the Dock* and *Unfit to Plead?* A likeable, unassuming man, he would no doubt be astonished that his long-forgotten crime novels are now finding a new readership in the twenty-first century.

MARTIN EDWARDS
www.martinedwardsbooks.com

CHAPTER I

In Which All the Trouble Begins

A S SOON AS I SAW THE FELLOW I WAS SURE THAT I WAS IN FOR some trouble. It was not merely that he was acting queerly; quite apart from the fact that he seemed to be drunk, or stunned, or shocked, there was something queer, almost grotesque, about his appearance. He had a shock of red hair which had not seen a comb for many a long day. Stray locks hung untidily about his forehead. The fact that he wore thick-lensed spectacles with heavy horn-rims added to the queerness of his appearance. And he staggered about the front at Broadgate as if he was drunk.

I took rather a dim view of this chap interrupting my morning stroll. I had come down to Broadgate, that pleasant little seaside resort in Kent, to convalesce after an operation, and I had no desire to be worried in the course of a before-breakfast walk. I had, indeed, been enjoying the luxury of a lazy ramble along the front, breathing in the air with real delight. But then, in the distance, just where the little cliff railway (commonly called the Broadgate Lift) ran from the top of the cliff through a tunnel down to the beach, I saw this odd-featured man staggering about.

It was all more than a trifle odd. "James London, my lad," I said to myself. "There is more in this than meets the eye." I had not spent some years in the service of sundry Fleet Street journals for nothing. The experienced journalist who has been running a column of comment, like my "London Calling," which used to be a feature in one morning paper, gets to know, by a kind of special sense, what is likely to be exciting news. And, in spite of the fact that I was supposed still to be a rather sick man, I felt my pulses racing at the idea that there might at this moment be breaking a news story which would be worth while. I was, in a sense, a freelance, since my illness had led me to resign from the post that I had occupied; but I knew that if this was anything more than a mere ten-days' wonder, any of the London dailies would be glad to appoint me, on a purely temporary basis, as a special correspondent to deal with the matter that was now attracting my attention.

I don't think that, in thus analysing my state of mind as I saw red-head staggering over the front at Broadgate, I am reading too many of my future ideas into my state of mind on that first day. I am pretty sure that what I have written went through my mind in quicker time than it has taken you to read it. And it certainly was a trifle odd that the man should stagger about in that way.

After all, it is only the most determined drinker who is drunk at a seaside resort at nine o'clock on a June morning. I did not believe that he was drunk. I had come down to Broadgate for a rest-cure; as I have said, I really took a poor view of this fellow upsetting my arrangements—I already felt that he might do that. But at the same time no journalist worth his salt can resist investigating a queer story that comes his way.

Therefore I walked briskly along the front until I came close to the red-headed monstrosity. He was now sitting on one of the seats. His head was held between his hands. He was leaning forward on the seat. I stood by him in silence for a moment. The very attitude of his body suggested shock or dejection or some great emotional crisis.

"In trouble, brother?" I said.

He did not reply. He did not even move. This, I thought, was queerer than ever. Surely my instinct had not been at fault? Surely this was not just an ordinary drunk, the only unusual part of the matter being the time?

I put my hand on his shoulder, and he jumped as if he had been shot.

"What is it?" he snapped. His voice was quiet, almost gentlemanly, if you know what I mean.

"In trouble?" I said for the second time.

He looked up at me. His eyes, I was surprised to see, had a greenish tinge. And at the back of those eyes was what I thought must be fear. Nothing else in the way of emotion would account for that queer glint in them.

"I don't know what to do," he admitted.

"Can I help?" I asked. My journalistic instincts were now thoroughly roused, and I felt sure that something extremely odd was going on. There was something very queer about this man and the way in which he was talking. I thought that it would be as well to try to calm him down a bit, so I sat down by his side, leaned back on the seat and crossed my legs. I got out my cigarette case, selected a cigarette, and held out the case to my companion.

"Have one?" I asked.

"Thanks." He accepted gratefully. I lit it for him, noting that his hand was shaking painfully. He inhaled the smoke and puffed it out spasmodically. I now knew for certain that there was some trouble ahead of me. I tried to struggle against it, but I did not struggle very hard. What journalist would?

"What's the trouble, brother?" I said.

"There's a dead man in my lift," he replied, in flat unemotional tones, as if he was merely making some remark about the weather.

"What?" It was my turn to be shocked, and, while I thought that I was pretty well shock-proof at my time of life, I was unable to stop myself shouting out this word.

"There's a dead man in my lift," he repeated, still without any kind of excitement in his tones.

"Where's your lift?" I asked.

He indicated the gate behind him, the gate which led to the entrance of the cliff railway. For the moment I had forgotten that it was usually called the Broadgate Lift.

"You are the operator of the lift?" I enquired.

He nodded.

"And when did you find this dead man?" I asked.

"When I unlocked the gates this morning." Red-head was thawing a bit now, getting almost chatty, I thought. It seemed that he had suffered from a pretty considerable shock, and the fact that I was giving him a chance to unburden himself was something that he very much appreciated.

"What time was this?" I asked.

He glanced at his wrist-watch. "About ten minutes ago," he said quietly. "During the season the lift starts working at nine o'clock. It finishes at night at half-past six."

I considered this for a moment. "Then you locked it up at half-past six last night?" I said.

"Yes."

"And the corpse was not there when you locked up last night?" I said. He shuddered slightly. "No," he replied.

"But it was there when you opened the gates this morning?"

"Yes."

"Were the locks tampered with in any way?" I asked. This seemed to me, at first sight, to be the obvious line of attack, though why on earth anyone should bother to get into a lift in order to die was something that it was not at all easy for me to understand.

"The locks hadn't been touched," he said. "I'd be prepared to swear to that."

"What sort of locks were they?" I asked.

He paused for a moment before answering that one. I got the feeling somehow that he was now at last realising that he was telling me a very queer tale. Indeed, I was already envisaging the headlines that the story would make. It seemed that my instinct when I had first caught sight of red-head had been true enough. This was a story that was going to hit the headlines all right. Just where it was going to lead it was impossible to say, of course; but that there would be some repercussions in Fleet Street and elsewhere I felt certain enough.

The man had not replied to my last question, so I thought that it might be as well to repeat it. "What sort of locks were they?" I said slowly, speaking as one might when speaking to a subnormal child.

"Padlocks," he said. "The bottom gates are locked from the inside. Then the lift is brought to the top, and the gates are fastened by means of a padlock on the outside."

I considered this. "What happens to the key?" I asked. It seemed to me to be as well to get all this clear before going any further in direct investigation—before, that is, having a look at the dead man who had appeared so mysteriously in the lift.

"I take it home with me," the man said.

"And it is certain that no one pinched it from you during the night?" I remarked.

"Quite certain."

"It had not been tampered with during the night?"

He shook his head with great emphasis. "The key is on the bunch in my trousers-pocket," he said. "I take the bunch out of my pocket and put it on the dressing-table at night. I did that last night, and the bunch of keys was still there this morning. Nothing unusual happened, you see."

I considered this. The fellow's story hung together. It was sensible and rational enough, except for the fact that this corpse had appeared in a place where it had no business to be. I found it difficult to believe. Yet I knew that in a moment I should have the evidence of my eyes to prove that what the man said was true. After all, no one would spin a yarn of that sort without foundation.

I was resolved to keep my mind clear; and I thought that the best way of doing so was to get all the facts straight before I allowed my mind to be complicated by the view of the body in the lift.

"Might I have your name?" I asked.

"Bender," he said. "Aloysius Bender." And the rather fantastic name seemed to go well enough with his undeniably fantastic appearance. He swept the long red hair away from his forehead with a weary gesture of his hand.

"And you live?"

"In King's Square," he said. "You see, I am a pensioner. I had a nasty wound in the war, which left me with a limp." He indicated his leg. Now I understood why he staggered. It was partly the effect of his war wound, which had left him with a really nasty limp.

I had been at the start almost repelled by the man's odd appearance. Now I was beginning to like him. The whole thing had clearly been a terrific shock to him, which was understandable enough. Now he was beginning to get over the first shock, and was therefore in every way more normal.

"This dead man in your lift," I went on. "Do you know who it is?"

He shook his head. "The man was a complete stranger to me," he said. "Never saw him in my life before that I know. But, of course, we get a lot of strangers down here during the season."

I nodded. "Got any idea how he got into your lift?" I asked.

"I can't think," he admitted.

I looked around me. The sea stretched out, blue and clean, before us. On either side stretched the quiet, peaceful promenade of Broadgate. And behind us the neat houses of the little Kentish town straggled up the hill. The whole situation seemed to be wrong. It was not here that one would have expected to find sudden death. Of course, I knew well enough the slogan of some famous journalist—was it Lord Northcliffe?—that the unexpected always happens. But the fact that such a thing has been said doesn't mean that we are any the less surprised when it comes off. And as I looked at the red-headed man by my side I reflected that this was yet again one of those things.

Trite enough, I suppose; but before I was finished I was to see that it was by no means one of those things—it was something queer and fantastic, something that was almost, if not quite, unbelievable.

Aloysius Bender was sitting quiet all this time. The chap had clearly been hard hit by what had happened. So much had the whole affair hit him that he was still, although more or less recovered from the primary shock, unable to take in much of what was going on.

I spoke again. The thing was, I told myself, to get as much as I could out of him now, before the police got on to him. I knew that, at any rate in theory, I should have reported everything to the Kentish police before I did anything in the way of questioning. But I was first of all a journalist; and the idea that I might well be getting on to a genuine scoop right away was something that no journalist could resist, even at the risk of getting on the wrong side of the law. And anyhow I knew that if the local police showed any signs of cutting up rough, my old friend Inspector Shelley of Scotland Yard would do something to pull me out of any spot of trouble in which I might manage to involve myself. In any case, a journalist, unless he is doing something really flagrantly illegal, will always let his news-sense get the upper hand.

So I asked Bender: "Any idea of how the man came to die? I mean to say, was there any sort of indication of whether he had had a fit or anything of that kind?"

Bender grinned. It was the first time, in fact, that there had been indication of emotion, apart from fear, in his face.

"Oh, yes," he said, "I know how the man died all right."

"You do?" This was better still, I told myself. I am not a ghoul, I should warn you, but I am a journalist, as I think I have mentioned more than once already.

"Yes. He was murdered."

I suppose that I should have been prepared for this, but as the words came out I felt a little shudder, partly of excitement, partly of alarm, run up my spine.

"Murdered?" I said.

"Yes. He was lying on his face, and the hilt of a nasty-looking knife was sticking out of his back."

Again the headlines flashed before my eyes. I really was in on something big here. As soon as I had had a look at the body I should really have to phone London. And I ran over in my mind the sundry news editors known to me, any one of whom would be prepared to appoint me as their special representative for the time, to send exclusive news of this affair. For the time being, I was well ahead of everyone else—ahead even of the police—on what might well turn out to be the crime of the season. The well-trained journalist gets, without too much difficulty, to recognise the crime which is going to hit the headlines, and to see that it is definitely of more interest than another murder which is worth only a paragraph on an inside page.

And if I knew anything about it, this Broadgate murder was one which was going to pack the headlines on the front pages for a good many days to come. And I had the incredible luck to be in at the start!

The fact that, technically speaking, I was still a sick man did not worry me unduly. I knew that I had made a good recovery, and that this little holiday at Broadgate was merely an extra precaution which my doctor had decided to take. In any event, sick or not, this chance of a scoop was the sort of thing that no worth-while journalist could possibly disregard. I resolved to take Bender in my confidence.

"Look here, Mr. Bender," I said. "I happen to be a journalist. This may be a great chance for me."

He looked a little scared. "You mean… you mean that the papers will print all about this?" he said.

"Well." I grinned. "It'll be one of the sensations of the century," I said. "After all, a man murdered in a locked lift. It's a real mystery, isn't it?"

"I suppose so," he admitted. But there was something a bit reluctant about his tone. I wondered if I had made a mistake by telling him who and what I was. Still, the damage was done now, if, indeed, it was damage. And the next job was obviously to see what I could about the dead man.

"Can I have a look at the body?" I asked.

"What about the police?" he responded. I had been wondering how long it would be before he got around to that. Still, I knew that I could handle him.

"If I come with you to the lift," I said, "that will be an extra witness. It will give you support if they ever come round to suspecting you."

"You think they might?" There was a real quaver about his voice now. There was no doubt that I had put some fear into his heart by suggesting that he might perhaps come under suspicion. I was sorry for the chap in a way. But I had to put my own future as a journalist first. This might well put me on the Fleet Street map again, after the long absence from newsprint which had been caused by my illness.

"I'll be a perfect witness to support you, Mr. Bender," I said. "Lead on to the lift! I'll see what there is to be seen, and then we'll fetch the police in. Don't worry; there'll be no trouble for you, no trouble at all."

I could see that his mind was not really at ease. He was more than a bit worried. Probably he hadn't realised, until I reminded him, that this was to become a front-page sensation in the press. But all the same he had enough sense to see that I might well be of some use to him, if he ever came under suspicion of this murder.

So, like a lamb, he led the way towards the lift. I was excited enough. The prologue, I told myself, was over. The first act of the play was about to begin.

CHAPTER II

In Which I Meet a Dead Man

I WAS NOT REALLY SURPRISED THAT ALOYSIUS BENDER WAS TO all appearances a trifle reluctant to lead on to his lift. The man was still nervous. He threw away his cigarette with a jumpy gesture, and his limp, as he walked slowly towards the lift gates, was very pronounced.

As for me, I was a bit excited. In my time I had been in on a few scoops. This, however, was the first time that I had ever had the inside story of a murder handed to me on a plate. And I knew that a recent increase in the newsprint ration meant that the papers would give a bit more space to the case, if it was truly sensational, than they had been able to do in years. I grinned savagely as I looked at the limping man ahead of me. What was he going to lead me on to? That it was going to be something pretty sensational I felt only too sure.

He fumbled in his pocket. I was consumed with impatience. Then I saw what it was. The lift-gates were still fastened. No doubt he had relocked them, in a more or less mechanical manner, as soon as he had made his horrifying discovery.

I looked at the lock with some interest. It was a massive padlock of an old-fashioned type, and it joined chains which in effect tied the two gates together. But I have known one or two crooks in my time, and I would have been prepared to wager that the lock could have been picked by any skilful man with a good bunch of skeleton keys.

The thing looked so heavy that the poor ignorant man in the street would have thought it to be perfectly safe, and the burglar, wishing to pick it, would have thought it to be the simplest job in the world.

Still, the chap now had managed to get a bunch of keys out of his pocket, and was struggling to insert one of them into the lock. His hands still trembled so violently that he found it a tough job. The key rattled against the lock, but did not go into the keyhole.

I lost patience. "Here, give the keys to me!" I snapped. I grabbed the keys from him and in a moment had the padlock unfastened.

Bender swung open the sliding gates. He then stood back, as if he was still too scared to go in. I glanced inside the lift, and stepped in.

There was no doubt that it was murder. The man was lying flat on his face, with one arm doubled under him in an unnatural manner. Sticking out of his back was the short hilt of a nasty-looking knife. It was, as far as I could see without touching it, one of those unpleasant weapons that they issued to Commandos during the war. It had clearly been driven in with pretty considerable force, just below the left shoulder-blade. And, judging by the blood, it must have struck an artery of some sort. The blood was pretty liberally spattered about the Broadgate Lift. I reflected that the dainty ladies who paraded the promenade from day to day would probably prefer to climb down the stairs for some days to come. If I knew anything about police methods, the lift, in any event, would not be in use for some time.

By this time Bender had followed me into the lift.

I looked at him with eyebrows raised. "Well?" I said.

"Well?" he replied.

"Have you looked at his face?" I asked.

"No."

"But you said that you didn't know the man," I objected.

"I don't."

I gently raised the body so that the face became visible. It was a handsome face, made in the classical mould. There was a black tooth-brush moustache, neatly trimmed. The hair was black and sleek. I should have placed the man at about thirty years of age, though that was, naturally, a mere guess. Anyhow, say he was between twenty-five and forty. That's near enough for the moment. I'd never seen him before to my knowledge.

"Still think you don't know him?" I snapped.

"I'm sure I don't," said Bender.

"Good enough," I commented.

I fished in the corpse's inside pocket. I know that, strictly speak-ing, this was not legal, but I had to get some information before the police arrived; otherwise, I knew, it wouldn't be easy to sell the story to any paper.

There was a wallet there. It contained about twenty pounds in pound notes. And there were a few papers there, too. I looked at them hastily. Letters addressed to Mr. John Tilsley, at the Charrington Hotel, Broadgate. And a bunch of visiting cards, inscribed with John Tilsley's name. No address, though. In fact, there was nothing to con-nect the man with anywhere outside the little Kentish town where his dead body was now lying.

I could see that Bender was looking at me pretty suspiciously. Indeed, I imagine that my behaviour must have seemed moderately odd to anyone not well acquainted with the ways of journalists. Still, I knew that I was in on a good thing, and I was not prepared to allow a liftman's suspicions to put me off. It was absolutely essential that I should do something which would make a good story for the Fleet Street market. I had got the name of the dead man; I had got his Broadgate address. That was a fairly promising start. No doubt at his hotel they would be able to tell me something about him. The main thing was that I didn't want to waste too much time. I knew that, if I took long, the police would have a few awkward questions to ask as to what I had been doing. And where the police are concerned, I like to keep a place discreetly in the background.

But, at the same time, I felt that I should do my best to get hold of some more information. I took one or two of the letters out of their envelopes. They looked commonplace enough. They were clearly personal letters of the most innocuous kind, signed "Bill" and "Sally." The addresses at the top of the letters were London addresses, and the letters were the sort of thing which most of us have written from time to time to friends on holiday. They merely expressed the hope that Tilsley was having a good time at Broadgate, and went on to give some scraps of what were obviously mere personal gossip about friends and neighbours, acquaintances and relatives. I didn't think that there was any question of there being any genuine revelations here.

I looked up at Bender. "Chap called Tilsley, it seems," I said. I tried to make my voice sound as casual as I could. It would not do to let this fellow develop all sorts of suspicions as to my interest in the case. He might tell the police too much about what was going on. Then any sort of journalistic material which I hoped to get hold of would be completely lost, and my chance to get back into the headlines would be gone.

"Tilsley?" he repeated, in a colourless kind of tone.

"Yes." I studied his face carefully, but it did not seem to me that there was anything resembling recognition there. I would have been prepared, at that moment, to swear that John Tilsley was a complete stranger to Aloysius Bender. And, anyhow, I didn't see why he should not be. A locked lift is a cunning enough place to hide a body—but it would not be so cunning if one had the only available key.

But was it the only available key? It was some indication of the speed with which the whole affair had taken place that this was a question that had not previously entered my mind.

"Mr. Bender," I said.

"Yes?"

"You said that there was a key —in fact, I've seen it—which remained on the bunch in your pocket all night."

"That's right."

"Is there another key anywhere?"

"Another key?" He stared at me stupidly as he said this. Again I felt my patience going. Of course, I told myself, this fellow had undergone a pretty nasty experience; it probably gave him a sense of shock, and it might indirectly be responsible for any sort of stupidity which he might show. And yet, even though I knew that this was reasonable enough as an explanation, it did not make it any easier for me to be patient with him.

"Yes, man," I said. "Somebody got in this lift last night, after you locked it, stabbed our unfortunate friend here, got out again, and relocked the lift on the outside. That is, of course, unless the murderer could manage to get through the iron gates without unlocking them. And I don't believe in that kind of dematerialisation."

"I see." He paused and looked at me. I thought that I could see signs of some spark of intelligence in those green eyes; but I had been mistaken. He simply relapsed into a lumpish silence.

"Well," I said. "Is there another key somewhere? There must be a second one, you know. After all, suppose you lost your key, the lift wouldn't just go out of action, would it? Or would it?"

He shook his head. "No, it wouldn't go out of action," he admitted.

"Then where is the other key?" I was getting completely impatient now, for I knew that in a matter of minutes I should have to tell the police about our discovery. I had wasted enough time already, time that I should find it mighty difficult to account for, if the legal gents should ever enquire into what I had been doing that morning.

"In the council offices, at the top of Manvell Street," he replied suddenly, as if he had abruptly come to life.

"Ah!" This was more the sort of information that I was after.

"It hangs on a peg inside the entrance to the offices, just above where the commissionaire sits," he went on. The man was getting quite chatty now, I reflected. It seemed that he was either getting over the preliminary shock of his discovery, or he was losing the mistrust of my motives which was only too obvious a little earlier.

"I see," I said. I had made no notes up to now, trusting to my moderately good memory. I knew that nothing was so likely to put off a reluctant talker as the fact that what he said was being written down. I suppose that the taking of notes, even by a journalist, savours a bit too much of the policeman noting evidence for most people to like it very much. However, I now thought that I had probably milked Mr. Bender of all the information that he was likely to be able to give me.

"Mr. Bender," I said.

"Yes."

"Do you know the police station?"

"Of course."

"Is it far away?"

"About ten minutes' walk, I should think."

"Would you go and fetch the police? I'll stand guard here and make sure that nobody interferes. It is important that we do that, and I think it would be better if you fetched the police, since you will know the way to the station far better than I should."

"All right." There was a kind of sulky acquiescence in his voice. I knew that he was not too willing to do what I was asking, but at the same time it was impossible for him to dispute the rationality of my suggestion. I was, in fact, kicking myself for not having thought of it a bit sooner. If I had only sent him off to the police before I searched the body I might well have been able to get the information without Bender knowing what I had been doing. And now he was sure to blab to the police, and I should have to do a bit of explaining.

Still, the damage was done. It was no good crying over spilt milk, so to speak.

Bender went off, leaving me in charge. I had another rapid glance at the body. I thrust my hand, with some reluctance, into the other pockets. One of the side-pockets of the coat contained a pipe, pouch, and a box of matches—nothing else. The other one had some loose change and a lighter. It was queer, I thought, that this man had little in the way of identifiable property—certainly nothing to indicate that he had had any sort of life before coming down for this holiday in Kent. His hip-pocket I was reluctant to examine, since I knew that it would never do if I got any blood on my hands, and there was blood in plenty in the region of the hip-pocket. Still, I managed to steel myself to the task.

I was rewarded. The pocket contained a small notebook. This, I told myself, might well be the personal property which would lead to something. It did, indeed. Inside its cover was scrawled: "John Tilsley, 25 Thackeray Court, S.W.5." I jotted down the address on the back of an envelope which I took from my own pocket. It might well be that this clue would lead to something. After all, I did not expect that this murder had its origin in Broadgate. It almost certainly originated from something in the man's own private life.

The notebook itself had nothing in it which conveyed much to me. It had various queer combinations of figures scrawled in it. It seemed to me that these were either some sort of gambling system or notes of mathematical problems. In either case, it did not seem to me that they could convey anything to the ordinary reader, or that they could have any sort of direct connexion with the man's death. That was, unless they were really some sort of private shorthand, written in a code which I, for one, was totally unable to decipher in the time which was likely to be at my disposal before the arrival of the police.

So, I slipped the little notebook into my hip-pocket. I knew that I might well have left fingerprints on these things, but I had no time to mess about, trying to remove them; and in any event I guessed that the police were not likely to try to see if there were any finger-prints on things safely stowed away in the pockets of a murdered man. They would not miss the notebook, anyhow. The weapon was what they were most likely to concentrate on. And I had been very careful to have nothing to do with that.

Now I had a look at it. I walked all round it, studying it from all angles. My first impression was confirmed by this detailed study. It was undoubtedly the knife that was issued to Commando troops during the war. Just how it had found its way here was, of course, a problem that I couldn't solve—not at the moment, at any rate.

Then the light in the lift changed. I had pushed the gates to, but hadn't locked them. Now they had been pulled to one side by some-one standing on the promenade.

"Hullo, hullo, hullo!" said a rich, unctuous voice. "And what has been going on here?"

CHAPTER III

In Which an Intruder Appears

I NEEDN'T SAY THAT I WAS A TRIFLE ALARMED. I HAD, OF COURSE, realised that there was quite a possibility of someone wanting to use the lift. But somehow there was something unexpected about this newcomer. I don't quite know what it was; but that there was something odd about him it was totally impossible for me to deny.

"I beg your pardon, sir?" I said querulously.

"My remark was 'Hullo, hullo, hullo,'" he said with a cheery grin. He was a tall, fat, red-faced fellow of sixty or so, and his face was wrinkled and happy.

"I heard that," I said. "But I am afraid that I must ask you not to get into this lift just at the moment, if you don't mind."

"This is a public lift, I take it," he said, still grinning, but with a suggestion, somehow, of steely strength behind the cheerful countenance.

"It is," I agreed readily enough, standing so as to guard the newcomer from a possible view of the body. I still thought that this corpse was, in a way, my property, and the fewer people that knew about it, the better I should be pleased.

"If it is a public lift," the newcomer said, the grin slowly fading from his red face, "can you kindly inform me why it is that you have the right to ask me not to get into it? On the other hand, perhaps you would be so kind as to inform me who you are, and by what right you debar me from taking my place in what is a public vehicle?"

The shutters were down now with a vengeance. The grin had completely vanished from the cheery face. It was, in fact, no longer a cheery face, but one which was grim and earnest. I saw that I should have to put up a pretty good argument to persuade this fellow that I was in the right. There was no doubt that he was, in his own opinion, entitled to ask for a ride in the lift. And short of telling him that there had been a murder (which was something that I was sturdily resolved not to do) I did not see what I could do.

"There has been an accident," I explained, temporising as far as I was able.

The grin returned. The man, it seemed, positively doted on accidents.

"What sort of accident?" he asked.

"An accident on the lift," I replied, somewhat obviously.

"You mean to say that the machinery of the lift has gone wrong, I take it?" he commented. This verbal fencing didn't really amuse me, but I didn't see what other course of action I could take.

"No," I admitted. "As far as I am aware, the lift is still in working order."

"Then why," he enquired, "am I not permitted to use it? And why, my dear sir, are you—whom I have never before seen in my life and who may therefore certainly be denounced as not the regular lift operator—why are you demanding that I should walk down about ten thousand infernal steps to the beach when there is a perfectly good lift available?"

I thought that there was little that I could do with this man. He looked like proving a confounded nuisance; there was no doubt, indeed, that I should have to tell him something about what was going on. I didn't really intend to reveal exactly what had taken place, but at the same time I felt pretty sure that unless I gave him some inkling, it would be impossible to get rid of him. And I had no desire that he should still be there when the police arrived on the scene. I knew that I should have enough to do in the way of awkward explanation, without having to do this in the presence of a stranger who had managed to attach himself to the party while Aloysius Bender was fetching someone from the police station.

"Someone has been hurt," I said.

"Badly?"

"Pretty badly, yes." No harm, I told myself, in admitting as much.

"Killed?"

"Ye-es." I was sorry that I had gone so far now, but having gone so far, I did not see that I could very well stop short, without involving myself in all sorts of other explanations which I wanted to avoid.

"Murder?" This was the one question that I had been fervently hoping he would not ask. I might, however, have known that it would come.

"I don't know yet," I answered.

"Police not here yet?" he went on, and by this time his grin had become something positively fiendish.

"No," I said.

"On the way?"

"Yes," I said. You will observe the way in which the chap had driven me, so to speak, into a conversational corner, so that it was well-nigh impossible for me to avoid telling him the very things that I had wanted to keep to myself.

"Mind if I have a look?" he went on, still grinning. He adroitly stepped past me into the lift. I had made up my mind not to tell him anything, or let him learn anything about what was going on. But he managed to get the best of me, and there was mighty little that I could do about it.

"Whew!" He whistled quietly to himself as he looked down at the body. "He got what was coming to him, didn't he?"

"Know the fellow?" I asked curiously. I was watching the newcomer carefully, and I was pretty sure, in my own mind, that he was not all that he appeared to be on the surface. I was, in other words, fairly certain that he had quite deliberately set out to see what was happening, that he had, in fact, some kind of knowledge of the murder. My instinct might, of course, be at fault, for I had no real knowledge of what had happened. But at the same time the instinct of a journalist with a nose for news is rarely at fault.

The man looked at me with a quizzical smile when I enquired if he knew the murdered man. "Do you know, I rather think I do know the fellow," he said, after a momentary pause. "In fact, I'm pretty certain that I have seen him a few times before the present sad occasion."

"Then who is he?" I asked.

"A somewhat bad lot, if I am not mistaken."

This was not quite what I had expected. Still, I knew that it would be as well not to show any sort of surprise. I merely raised my eyebrows slightly, and said: "A bad lot? What exactly do you mean by that?"

My companion grinned, but there was no humour about the expression. There was, in fact, a kind of savagery about it, which I by no means liked.

"He had a finger in many a dirty pie," was the reply. "He dabbled in all sorts of crooked games. In fact, he was a bad hat generally. By name Tilsley, if I'm not mistaken. And he seems to have upset someone pretty badly, for them to have dealt with him like that, eh?"

This was not quite the response that I had anticipated. Still, I was resolved to pick the man's brains, without giving away any kind of information on my side.

"Might I have your name, do you think?" I therefore asked him; though I thought, actually, that there might be a fairly considerable difficulty in persuading the man to tell me just who he was.

"My name is Watford," he said, "Cyrus Watford, to be precise. I have the pleasure—if pleasure is the correct word—of practising the science (or should I say art?) of medicine in this town. I have encountered the late lamented Mr. Tilsley in connexion with my profession."

This was straightforward enough, though I was by no means sure why a man who was apparently a perfectly ordinary doctor should come into contact with a man whom he knew enough about to describe as a "bad hat."

"And so," I said, "you got to know Mr. Tilsley well enough to know that he was a bad lot?"

"Yes." That was laconic enough, in all conscience. There was, I thought, a definite tendency on the part of the man to dry up as I showed signs of wanting to know a bit more about him, and about his acquaintanceship with the dead man. Whether Dr. Watford was all that he appeared to be on the surface, or whether there was more in his appearance on the scene of the crime than met the eye, was something that would have, I decided, to be investigated, and investigated soon. It would, in fact, take a pretty high position on the list of things that I had to study before I was much older.

"Did you want to get down to the beach, Doctor?" I asked, more with the aim of keeping him in conversation than anything else.

"I did want to," he replied, "but in view of the revelation that has met me here, I think that I shall change my mind, and just stick around, as our American friends so expressively say."

This suited me well enough. I thought that it would be of some value if the man could be induced to stay on the scene until such time as the police arrived. If I could contrive to hang about, it might well be that the man would be given the chance of giving himself away. And I was firmly convinced that this strange doctor was connected with the death of Tilsley more closely than he had himself admitted.

"Have the police been informed of this lamentable occurrence?" he asked.

"Yes," I said. "I already told you that."

"How?"

I smiled. "Another witness went to fetch the police," I explained. "They should be along here at any moment now."

The doctor looked at the watch on his wrist. "I think," he said hurriedly, "that it would be as well if I made a move."

"So suddenly?" I asked with a grin.

"I have patients whom I have to see, my dear sir," he replied, with what was doubtless intended to be a disarming smile, though it did not strike me that way.

"At nine o'clock in the morning, doctor?" I enquired. I didn't bother to try to conceal my disbelief. It was too clear for words that the man was anxious, if it were at all possible, to dodge seeing the police.

"A doctor's is a busy day, my dear friend," he said. "His work is never done, you might say. In fact, at all hours of the day he is at the beck and call of all and sundry—particularly if I may say as much without appearing to be in any way nasty, of those who fancy themselves to be much more ill than in actuality they are."

That speech sounded straightforward enough. But I couldn't get out of my mind the fact that the fellow had been quite prepared to go on talking to me until he recalled the fact that the police were likely to appear on the scene. When that got home in his mind, he was in a tearing hurry to get away without delay.

Still, it was, of course, impossible for me to detain him. I had, for one thing, no legitimate standing in the case myself. And even had I some standing, there was no reason that I could lay my mind to, which would enable me to keep Doctor Watford there. Yet there was a nagging suspicion at the back of my mind, a suspicion which refused to be quieted, and which suggested that there was something fundamentally wrong about the man. It was not that there was anything about his conversation which did not ring true; it was not even that his attitude seemed in any way incorrect. He might, I told myself, be everything that he held himself out to be. He might be a doctor who dealt with Tilsley as a patient, and who somehow had stumbled on some secret of Tilsley's which indicated that the man was a criminal. But there was something about him which to my mind suggested the fake and the phoney. Just what it was I could not for the life of me decide; but I made a mental note to study the doctor as much as I could. For the moment, it was certain, I had to let him go.

"So you are on your way, Doctor?" I said quietly, studying his countenance as I spoke. I'll swear that it was a look of the most intense relief that came over it as he began to realise that I was not going to try to keep him on the scene of the crime. This was, again, a reason for studying the man with great care in the future.

"Yes. I'm a busy man, sir," he said with a businesslike air. "My patients must come first, much though I would like to remain here and help the police in the investigations which must undoubtedly begin ere long."

And he was away, with long swinging strides that got him over the ground at a deceptively fast rate. I thought that I had seldom seen a man so delighted to be getting away; but I could not really make up my mind why he had been so pleased. That there was something more than a trifle suspicious about the doctor seemed to be an unavoidable conclusion; but what the suspicions really amounted to it was difficult to say.

I glanced at my watch. Things had happened so quickly that it seemed impossible that only about ten minutes had elapsed since I had sent Aloysius Bender in search of the police. Yet such was the case. All the argument with Doctor Watford had, in fact, taken only about eight minutes.

Still, Bender had said that he thought the police station was about ten minutes' walk. That meant that the police would be on the scene at any moment now—for it was sure enough that they would waste no time in coming along when once Bender had told his tale.

I swung open the lift gates and glanced cautiously up and down the promenade. It was still fairly peaceful; there were few people about. I supposed that most of the visitors were probably having their breakfast. Certainly it was a lucky thing for me that there were not crowds clamouring to be taken down to the beach. I should probably have found it none too easy to explain to them what had happened.

Then I saw a figure in blue in the distance. Slightly behind it was the limping man whose strange behaviour had first brought me into contact with this case. And behind him was a tall, spare man who seemed to me to be vaguely familiar, though I could not for the moment quite place him. Anyhow, there was no doubt that the police were coming. Now I had to face what might well be a trying cross-examination. Still, I had brought it on myself, and if I got into a jam or a tangle I had only myself to blame for it.

CHAPTER IV

In Which the Police Arrive

I SWUNG OPEN THE GATES OF THE LIFT TO ALLOW THE POLICE TO enter. And certainly Mr. Bender had told his tale well, for the limbs of the law had come along in force. There was a uniformed constable, a sergeant, and a grim-looking man with a military moustache, whom I soon learned to be Inspector Beech of the Kent County Constabulary. This was an impressive array of police talent; but in the background—that spare figure who had seemed familiar to me in the distance—was a man whom I was unfeignedly glad to see on the spot. If I had got myself in any sort of jam as a result of my excess of journalistic zeal he was undoubtedly the boy to get me out of that jam. He was, in fact, my old pal Detective-Inspector Shelley of New Scotland Yard. But just how he had contrived to get in on a murder on the coast of Kent within ten minutes of its discovery was something that I found difficult to understand.

"Hullo, Jimmy," Shelley said, holding out his hand in friendly fashion.

"Good-morning, Inspector," I said, only too delighted to have my credentials thus established early on in the case.

"You seem to make a habit of being in on the beginnings of murders, my lad," Shelley said. "Only last time it was in a London night-club. Still, don't go finding too many bodies for us, Jimmy. We have suspicious minds in the force, you know."

This was all said in an airy enough manner, as if the Inspector knew that I shouldn't take it too seriously. But I thought that behind it there might well be a hint not to assume that I should be quite beyond suspicion, merely because I was an old friend of the man from Scotland Yard.

I merely grinned. "Who are your friends, Inspector?" I asked. I was duly introduced. Inspector Beech gave me an unwinking stare that seemed to suggest he was not very impressed by me. I felt, under his glare, rather like a second-form schoolboy summoned to the headmaster's study.

It soon came out that Shelley had been staying with the Chief Constable, and, when my friend Bender had arrived at the police station, Shelley had actually been there, being shown round the premises by the chief, who was an old friend of his. He had forthwith rung Scotland Yard and had obtained permission to retain Shelley for a day or two, until it became clear whether this was a case which needed expert attention or not.

I thought that I could see more than a trace of resentment in Inspector Beech's manner. This was in many ways understandable, since he would probably not much like the idea of Shelley's being called in—though, naturally, he could not let Shelley see this.

Still, I thought that I should no doubt come under Beech's suspicious eye, since, as an admitted friend of Shelley's, I should more or less automatically be accepted as an unfriendly person.

I made up my mind to tell Beech the absolute minimum; any real confidence which I had would be reserved for Shelley.

But I now had the opportunity of witnessing the police at work—something which, in spite of some experience in my days as a cub reporter, I still found peculiarly fascinating.

Shelley and Beech, however, seemed to be working together well enough. That there may have been some psychological by-currents of which I was not aware was true enough; but outwardly they seemed moderately friendly. And I knew, from past conversations with him, that Shelley prided himself on handling the provincial policeman tactfully. It certainly seemed that he was doing that now.

Anyhow, there was something businesslike about the way in which the two Inspectors set to work. First of all, they moved the body over very gently; then they turned out the man's pockets, noting all the things which I had previously seen.

"Know the fellow, Bender?" Beech asked abruptly.

"No, sir. Never saw him before in my life," answered my red-headed acquaintance.

"Do you know him, Jimmy?" asked Shelley, looking at me with a quizzical eye.

"No," I said. "Of course, this is the first time I've ever been to Broadgate, so I might not know him, even though he may be a well-known local character."

"I don't think that he was a local character," Shelley replied, as he glanced at the letters he had taken from the man's hip-pocket. I wondered how much Bender had told the police about my searching the man, and consequently how much they knew about me. Of course, it was difficult for me to put myself in their place, and to decide just what they would think of the way in which I had acted. I'm sure that had I been in Beech's position I should have been very suspicious of a man who pushed himself into the case in the way in which I had done.

"Now, Mr. London," said Beech, when they had concluded their examination of the body, "I think that, before we go any further, we should like you to answer a few queries. What do you think, Mr. Shelley?"

"I entirely agree," Shelley said. "Of course, it so happens that I am an old friend of Mr. London's, and so I can, in a way, vouch for his character, so to speak. But at the same time I realise that he has a bit of explaining to do."

I grinned. Shelley, I saw, while he was entirely ready to do the correct thing, had not forgotten our old friendship and was prepared to make the course of events as smooth as possible for me.

"How did you come into this business, Mr. London?" Beech asked, producing a large notebook and hovering a pen over it, as if he thought that he could intimidate me into some admissions of criminality. At least, that was my idea; it may not have been his, of course.

I told my story frankly, explained that I had seen Mr. Bender, obviously on the point of collapse, and, being both a journalist and a human being, had come forward to see if there was anything that I could do to help.

Shelley, I could see, believed me; about Beech I was by no means convinced. He had a sceptical eye, that man, and he seemed to think that I was hiding something—as indeed I was, for I did not intend, if I could help it, to reveal the fact that I had searched the fellow's pockets, or that I had managed to get hold of some information which was rightfully the possession of the police.

"You're a journalist?" Beech said.

"Admitted," I grinned.

"On the staff of what paper?"

I explained that I was on the staff of no paper at the moment, having spent some months on my back after an operation which had not gone as smoothly as the doctors had hoped. I added that I was in the running for various jobs, and that I thought, as soon as my brief period of rest and convalescence was over, I should land something worth while.

Beech again did not look impressed. I thought that I had said my piece very nicely; but Beech had a truly suspicious mind, and did not seem to be prepared to accept me at my face value. This was a bit of a nuisance to me, though I could see that there was a certain amount of sense in his attitude—more sense, in fact, than he could know; unless he knew that I had been hunting through Tilsley's pockets.

"You won't be writing anything about this affair, then?" Beech said. I thought that I could detect a twinkle in Shelley's grey eyes.

"I can't guarantee that," I replied.

"Why not? You said that you were not at present on the staff of any paper?" objected Beech.

"Not at present. But I am in the running for various jobs, and I might land one of them at any moment. Then, since I am already to some extent on the inside of this case, so to speak, an editor might well ask me to cover the case officially for his paper," I explained.

Shelley chuckled. "If I know that unscrupulous journalistic mind of yours, Jimmy," he said, "you'll be on the phone within five minutes of our leaving you, ringing some London editor, telling him that you are on the inside of this case, and offering to cover it for him and give him a good deal of exclusive news into the bargain."

I grinned. "I must admit that such an idea had crossed my mind," I said.

"But can't we stop him, Shelley?" Beech asked indignantly. It seemed that there was something about a journalist which made him see red. I diagnosed that he had been badly reported at some time—perhaps when making a speech at a police dinner, or something of that kind—and that as a result he had ever after a dislike of pressmen.

"No," Shelley said cheerfully enough. "We can't stop him, and I don't see why we should try to. This case is certainly going to be pretty extensively reported in the papers, and Jimmy here is a fairly conscientious man, as journalists go. I mean to say, he takes a fair amount of trouble to get his facts straight; if he works for some London daily on the case, you can bet your life that he'll deal with it reasonably and fairly. And that's more than one can say of a lot of the news-hounds who are about nowadays."

I must say that I thought that was uncommonly nice of Shelley. His statement certainly appeared to impress Beech, who for a moment became almost human.

"You won't publish stuff without our permission, I take it, Mr. London?" he said.

"I won't publish anything you tell me without your permission," I amended his statement. "Anything which I manage to discover for myself I shall of course publish as I think fit. There is, after all, no embargo on news in this country—not as far as my information goes, anyhow."

I thought that he deserved that dig. After all, I had received an unsolicited testimonial from Shelley, and I thought that I could, at least, have been taken more or less on trust by a lesser light like Beech.

In all these exchanges we seemed almost to have forgotten the reason why we were all there. Even the body had passed into the backgrounds of our minds. But it was now recalled by the arrival of the police surgeon, a cadaverous Scot named Gordon.

He was as businesslike as the two policemen. He knelt beside the body, tested it briefly for *rigor mortis* by bending the joints of the arms, glanced at the knife, and then stood up.

"I'll have to have the body around at the mortuary, ye know," he said.

"I realise that, of course, Doctor," said Beech. "But can you give us any information now? I mean, can you indicate cause of death, time of death, and any other information which is likely to be of some value to us at this stage? It doesn't matter if it is only approximate, but we find every little indication valuable early on in the case. Of course, you know all that anyhow."

"Well," the Doctor said thoughtfully, and paused. He was clearly a naturally cautious man who did not at all like being pressed to commit himself to any sort of definite statement which he was not capable of proving. "Well, I wouldn't like to say too much until after the post-mortem."

"But you can tell us something?" There was an almost pleading tone about Beech's voice, and I saw that Shelley, who had had a long experience of reluctant medical witnesses, was more than a trifle amused.

"The cause of death I should have thought was obvious enough," Doctor Gordon said. He pointed to the knife. "Judging by the blood that spattered all over the place, I should say that the knife had severed a main artery somewhere. And a man with a main artery bust hasn't got much of a future, you know." He chuckled at his own macabre jest.

"And what about the time of death?" Inspector Beech was persistent enough. He was, indeed, like a bloodhound on the scent of something worth while in the way of food.

"I'd not like to commit myself very closely," the Doctor said cautiously, looking at his watch. "You know as well as I do, gentlemen, that *rigor mortis* is a very tricky and undependable thing. It varies so much from one case to another that it's by no means easy to base any sort of precise decision on it."

This little lecture in medico-legal practice was not too well received.

"Have a shot at it, Doctor," Shelley said—his first direct intervention since the doctor's arrival. "Give us some sort of idea of when you think the man died, if you possibly can."

Again the doctor peered at his watch. "Well," he said, "if I must give you some sort of estimate, I should say that the man died between seven o'clock and midnight last night. But even that is not much more than a guess, and it wouldn't surprise me in the least to learn that he died at five o'clock last night, or at three o'clock in the morning. If I have to give evidence at any trial, gentlemen, I shall refuse to be at all precise about the matter. I strongly distrust all definite statements based on *rigor mortis*."

I could see that Beech didn't like this; Shelley, on the other hand, was in no way put out. Personally, I thought that the doctor was being a bit pig-headed; but it had to be remembered that there had been cases when a medical witness, being too decided about the time of death, had been shown up in court by contradictory evidence, disproving what he advanced as a scientific estimate. Clearly Gordon was a cautious old boy who was not going to commit himself to anything which he did not regard as a cast-iron certainty.

Now he left, and an ambulance drove up. The attendants removed the mortal remains of John Tilsley. I thought, actually, that the whole thing had been quite skilfully handled. Few of the visitors who were now thronging the promenade could have had any idea of what had happened. The police managed the whole thing discreetly. Then Inspector Beech turned to Bender.

"What do you do on the odd occasions when the lift may get out of order?" he asked.

Bender fished in a locker underneath the seat that ran along one side of the lift. He produced a large sheet of cardboard. On it were printed, in large bold letters: "LIFT OUT OF ORDER."

"I hang that on the outside of the gate," he said. "There is a second one, too, for hanging outside the gate at the bottom, where it leads to the beach."

"Good." The Inspector was now all brisk efficiency. "You'll have to hang your notices out today, Bender," he said. "The lift will be out of action, I'm afraid, for a day or two—until we have completed our preliminary investigations of this affair, at any rate."

"As you wish, Inspector." Bender was ready to co-operate in whatever measures the police thought advisable. I could see that. But the red-headed man was now very much more the master of himself than he had been when I had seen him first, staggering across the promenade in a manner indicatory of the most severe sort of shock.

"And do you want me any more, Inspector?" I asked as inoffensively as I could.

"Want to get away to the nearest telephone without delay, Jimmy?" Shelley said with a light laugh. "Well, I don't know that there is much more that we want you for just now. What do you think, Mr. Beech?"

Beech, I could see, was not too pleased to agree; but there was little that he could do in the matter. In fact, there was really nothing that the police could do to hold me. They did not know, apparently, that I had done a bit of hunting around before their arrival. That, I thought, was just as well. But meanwhile the latest development meant that I was free to go my own way. It was good to think that I should soon be back in the old journalistic harness. I fingered the notebook in my pocket, and grinned.

CHAPTER V

In Which I Become a Special Correspondent

I KNEW THAT IT WOULD BE ONLY A MATTER OF HOURS BEFORE A bevy of newspaper-men arrived. As soon as this story broke it would be clear that this was one of the big murder-stories of the year, and every paper would be thinking out how best to cover it.

So I made my way to a phone-box at the end of the promenade. I had subconsciously noticed it that morning. There was no one in it. I fished in my pocket, found that I had some coppers, a couple of sixpences, and a shilling—that should be enough for a call to London—and turned my attention to a consideration of what paper would be most likely to pay me a sensible fee as a special correspond-ent, studying the new murder.

I really had to make up my mind which of my acquaintances among news-editors would be most likely to give me a job on my own recommendation. I decided, eventually, in favour of Mike Jones, news-editor of *The Daily Wire*. Mike was a tall, thin Welshman, with whom I had worked in prewar days. I knew that he remembered one or two scoops which, between us, we had in the past managed to pull off, and in consequence I thought that he would be more likely to appoint me to the post that I was after for the time being.

In a matter of a minute or two I was talking to him. I could picture him at his desk as he spoke.

"Jones here."

"Hullo, Mike bach," I said. "This is Jimmy London."

"Jimmy lad, and how are you after all these days? They told me that you'd been ill," Mike said.

"I have," I agreed. "But now I'm ready to get back in harness again."

"Good lad," Mike said. "Have you got anything particular in view, or are you just having a look round, so to speak, before deciding?"

"That's really why I rang you," I explained hurriedly. "I'm actually convalescing at Broadgate, but I've run into what looks like being a big, worth-while story."

"Trust your nose for news, Jimmy," chuckled Mike. "And what's the big story?"

"A murder," I said simply.

"We haven't had a good murder story for some months," replied Mike thoughtfully. "If this is a worth-while story, we could play it up pretty big. Is it a good one? I mean to say, has it got any romantic or mysterious aspects?"

"Don't know about romance, I haven't investigated it enough yet," I said. "But it's a variation on the old theme of the hermetically sealed room. A liftman locks his lift when he goes off duty one night. The locks aren't in any way tampered with; but when the doors are unlocked the next morning a dead body is inside."

Mike gave vent to a whistle of surprise. "You don't say!" he exclaimed. "Sounds like a worth-while story, Jimmy."

"Certainly does," I agreed. "So what do you say, Mike?"

"You want a job on the strength of this?" he asked with another chuckle.

"Not a permanent one," I said hastily. "I've got a lot of information on it. I know the name and address of the murdered man, and

I know a lot of the background. And Inspector Shelley of Scotland Yard, who is in charge of the case, is an old friend of mine."

"But what do you want?" Mike asked.

"A special commissioner's post," I said. "Make me the *Wire's* special commissioner or special correspondent in charge of the case. All my stuff to have my name on it. And you can pay me, at your best space-rates, for whatever you use. I'm quite content to justify my existence that way. I don't want a salary—not for the moment, anyway. I mightn't justify it."

"You justify it all right," answered Mike. "But if we pay you space-rates on what we use, and if this is the case that you say it is, you'll find yourself getting a good deal more than the union rate for a week or two, anyhow."

"And putting myself back on the map in the bargain," I reminded him.

"True enough."

"Don't forget the by-line," I said. "By James London, Our Special Correspondent. You may as well get that set up in pretty big type straight away, because you'll need it. This is going to be one of the greatest stories of the year. And you'll scoop every one of your competitors."

"Anything you can give us now?" Mike asked.

"Plenty."

"I'll switch you over to the news-room. Dictate whatever you've got to the shorthand-writer. And tell them that there will be more to come. We'll get your first story set up in time to go in the early editions; if you get more stuff through in time, well and good. But good luck, Jimmy bach."

So I found myself dictating a story to a shorthand-writer. Pretty hard-boiled most of the shorthand-writers in a daily paper's news-room; but I heard this chap gasp once or twice, which was a fair tribute to the stuff I was turning in. I made it as strong meat as I could, too. I laid on the adjectives and the mystery, made it look as if this murder was a cold-blooded piece of butchery (which, indeed, it was) but with the added spice of a genuine mystery story behind it. I rubbed in the fact that *The Daily Wire,* as usual, was first off the mark with the story, solving a puzzle which would eventually rank with Jack the Ripper and the Wallace Case as the greatest problems in the history of criminology. And I told the chap a tale about myself, in the hope that even the dreariest of sub-editors wouldn't be able to cut out all the build-up that I was giving myself, in order to re-establish myself in the world of London journalism.

As I left the phone-box, having spent all my available change in getting extra time to dictate my tale, I cursed myself for not having remembered to reverse the charges. Nevertheless, I was fairly pleased. What Shelley and Beech would say when they saw the paper the next morning wouldn't bear thinking of; but I had been perfectly frank with them, and I thought that there was little that they could say or do about the matter.

As I strolled along the promenade, whistling gently to myself, I almost bumped into Shelley. The man from Scotland Yard was standing by the railings, leaning on them and looking out to sea in a dreamy manner.

"Penny for them, Jimmy," he said as I passed him.

"They're worth more than that, Inspector," I replied with a grin.

"Sold your story?" he enquired.

"Yes."

"What paper?"

"*The Daily Wire.*"

"Well, that's better than some of the rags that you've worked for in your time, my lad," he said. "And now you're coming to a peaceful little restaurant with me to drink a peaceful little cup of coffee."

"What for?" I asked. I didn't altogether like his approach. There was, I thought, something slightly sinister about his expression, as if he had got something in for me. I had, as a matter of fact, never known Shelley try on any fast practice with anyone, unless, perhaps with an undoubted criminal; but all the same I felt a little uncomfortable at what he was now proposing to do.

Yet I had no reason whatever for refusing his invitation to coffee. Indeed, I was ready for a coffee myself. I suddenly realised that in all the excitement of the morning I had completely forgotten to have any breakfast.

"I'll not merely have a cup of coffee, Inspector, I'll have something to eat with it," I said. "I've just realised that I gave breakfast a complete miss this morning."

"Silly habit," Shelley said.

"Eating, you mean?" I enquired.

"No, missing breakfast."

And so we made our way up the steep main street of Broadgate to a little café in a peaceful side-street which Shelley had somehow discovered. There we seated ourselves in a corner and ordered coffee and toast. I felt positively ravenous, and wolfed down the toast as if I had nothing to eat for days. Actually, my last meal had been dinner on the previous night, and after about fifteen hours I was ready for something. I should have liked to have had something more; but I knew that Shelley had some sort of business up his sleeve. I knew, moreover, that he would not descend to talking business while I was engaged in the urgent matter of food.

Therefore I hastily finished my toast, caught the eye of the waitress, and then ordered another two cups of coffee. When these had been set before us, I looked the Inspector straight in the eye.

"Shoot!" I said.

Shelley looked puzzled. "I don't altogether understand you, Jimmy," he said.

"Don't talk nonsense, Inspector," I said with a laugh. "I know something about your methods now, and I'm sure that you didn't bring me in here merely for the pleasure of drinking coffee with me. You've either got something you want to talk to me about—some information which you imagine I've got hold of, and which you want me to share with you. Or, if that's not it, you've got some sort of proposition which you want to put before me. I'm not as green as you fondly imagine I am, you know."

Shelley smiled that deceptively quiet smile of his. "All right, Jimmy, you win," he said.

"And what's the proposition?" I asked.

He smiled and stirred his coffee thoughtfully. Then he got out his briar pipe, filled it with the rank weed he called tobacco, rammed it down with his thumb, and lit it. This was all done with a slow deliberation that I found positively maddening. But I knew well enough that he had tried to irritate me, and I was firmly resolved to show no sign of irritation.

"What do you know of John Tilsley?" he asked.

"Nothing, save that he was staying at the Charrington Hotel, and that his London address was 25 Thackeray Court, S.W.5., which will be either Kensington or Chelsea," I said. No point, I told myself, in trying to hide from Shelley what I had found out.

"You're a scamp, Jimmy," Shelley said seriously. "I guessed that, left alone with the body for ten minutes or so, you wouldn't let the time be altogether wasted. And I suppose that the man's name and address is already in type, ready for the *Wire's* first edition tomorrow morning?"

"The Broadgate address is," I admitted. "Not the London one; I was keeping that for my second story, to be phoned to them later in the day. It wouldn't do to give them the whole story in one chunk, you know. It's already a scoop, but I'm being paid space-rates, and I've got to do something to keep the story alive for a week or two."

Shelley grinned again, and this time his grin was very much more good-humoured than it had been before.

"I said you were a scamp, Jimmy, and I still think that you are," he said. "But then no journalist has any sort of conscience, anyhow."

I smiled. "But I'm sure, Inspector," I said, "that you did not bring me here merely to confirm what you already knew—that I'd picked up all the information that I could from Tilsley's pockets."

"No." He looked much more serious now. "What I wanted to say to you, Jimmy, is to suggest that we should be collaborators rather than rivals in this case."

"I don't quite know what you mean," I said. Actually, I knew well enough, but I wanted him to put his proposition into precise terms.

"Well," he went on, "you are no doubt going to do all you can in the way of investigation on this case."

"Naturally," I said. "I want to give my paper some good meaty stuff which they'll want to print extensively. As I said, I am being paid on space for whatever they use, and therefore I shall want to give them a good story each day. And since there is not much chance of getting anything good from the police, except the hand-out statement that all the papers will get, I am proposing to set myself to find out what I can about Tilsley and his background."

"Shall we pool our knowledge?" Shelley suggested in all seriousness.

"Have you got any?" I grinned.

"More than you think, perhaps, Jimmy," he said. "But the point is that I think it would be as well if we agreed to share the work of investigation. You see, there are people who might talk to a journalist, who, on the other hand, would not so readily talk to a policeman. Queer, no accounting for personal taste." That there was a sting in the last remark did not worry me. I was only too delighted at the proposition that he was putting to me. It meant that I should be in on the inside of the police case.

"Does Inspector Beech know anything about this idea of yours?" I asked.

"Inspector Beech is an excellent officer, able and capable," Shelley said. "But, like so many policemen, he is totally lacking in imagination."

I understood. Shelley was doing this completely off his own bat. It was good to know that I had, at any rate, retained his confidence, even though I had probably not impressed the local man as being in any way trustworthy.

"And how do you propose we shall begin?" I asked.

"Well, to begin with," Shelley said, "I think that you might go around to the Charrington Hotel, as a journalist trying to find out something about Mr. Tilsley's background. See if you can dig out any facts. Naturally, the police will also have made some enquiries; but it is quite possible that you will get hold of some information unknown to us. Are you agreed?"

"What about publishing anything I find?" I asked.

"You'll have a chat with me before phoning your paper," Shelley said seriously. "But I don't think that you'll find me in any way unreasonable, Jimmy. I'll not put an embargo on publishing anything unless I think that it is likely to put the murderer on his guard; and if I do stop you from publishing anything at any time, I'll undertake to let you publish it well ahead of any of your competitors. Is it a bargain?"

We solemnly shook hands. It was only when I had left Shelley and was making my way down the hill to the Charrington Hotel that I recalled that I had completely forgotten to tell him about the queer Doctor Watford or to show him the black notebook.

CHAPTER VI

In Which I Visit a Strange Hotel

I T WAS GOOD TO FEEL THAT I WAS NOW WORKING WITH SCOTLAND Yard. Even though the arrangement was strictly unofficial, and would doubtless be forcefully repudiated by Shelley if I claimed to be doing anything on behalf of police headquarters, the fact remained that an understanding of this sort was about as valuable as anything which could be possessed by a journalist in my position.

Shelley had suggested that the best thing that I could do as a first move on his behalf (as well, incidentally, as my own) was to visit the Charrington Hotel and see if there was any clue to the identity of John Tilsley there—or, for that matter, if there was any kind of background information about the man to be picked up.

I wasn't at all sure where the Charrington Hotel could be. The name was slightly familiar to me, so that I had probably seen it somewhere in my wanderings about Broadgate; but I couldn't make up my mind just where it was.

I went up to a policeman who was lazily waving slow-moving cars around a corner.

"Excuse me, officer," I said.

"Yes?" There was something sleepy about the way he spoke, almost as if life in a seaside resort did not make for any kind of briskness.

"Can you tell me where the Charrington Hotel is?"

He looked at me for a moment, almost as if he thought that there was something infinitely suspicious in such an enquiry.

Then he said: "Top of St. Peter's Street."

"Over there?" I asked, indicating what I thought I remembered to be the street of that name.

"That's right."

"Thank you very much," I replied.

"You're welcome," he said with what I thought was a rather surprising touch of humanity.

The Charrington, indeed, was only about a hundred yards from the spot on which I stood. From the outside it looked normal enough, the average small hotel in a small seaside resort. The open door led to an entrance hall in which stood a tall palm. I glanced in. There seemed no sign of life. Not a single human being was in sight. It was peculiar, it seemed to me, though there might well be an explanation.

Anyhow, there seemed to be no reason why I shouldn't go in and explore. I strolled carelessly into the hotel, more or less as if I had come there to meet someone. Then I stopped, irresolute. I thought I had better put on an act, in case someone was watching me through a peep-hole somewhere. That probably sounds a bit melodramatic; but I had got more than a trifle worked up over this business, and I don't mind admitting that at that moment I was prepared for anything to happen, no matter how fantastic it might seem.

At first nothing fantastic did happen, however. Indeed, nothing happened at all. The hotel lobby was silent, dead silent. I was just able to detect the ticking of a clock in some distant corner, out of sight. The general atmosphere of that hotel lobby was oppressive, almost eerie. There was something about it that I strongly resented; yet I was not at all sure what it was that I disliked, save the fact that there was no one to whom I could talk, and I had come prepared to talk in plenty.

Then I sensed, rather than saw, that someone had come in. I glanced around me, and at first couldn't see anybody. Then, behind the glass front of the small reception kiosk, I saw the woman.

She was more or less what I might have expected in this odd place. Yet I felt a sense of surprise as I looked at her. She was sitting down there, apparently more or less in a daze. Her face was dead white, and against that white the sleek blackness of her hair showed up with a sense of vivid contrast. Her mouth was a slash of scarlet across the white background of her countenance. Everything about her was contrasted. Her dress was of some kind of silky material, black, but with a sash of the same scarlet as her lipstick.

Suddenly the still lady came to life. She looked towards me, as if she had only just become aware of my existence on earth.

"Can I help you?" she said. And her voice completed the surprise. It was a musical voice, which seemed to belong to some attractive girl from the countryside—a dairymaid, perhaps—and certainly did not seem to be in the picture with this woman, sophisticated and blasé.

"I'm looking for a friend, whom I heard was staying here," I said. I had decided that this was the best method of attack.

"What is his name?" she asked. "I know most of the guests here, and even if I do not know him I can look up in the register and see if we have any record of his visit—tell you, indeed, if he is still here."

"His name is Tilsley, John Tilsley," I said watching her face with extreme care, to see if this name appeared to strike a familiar chord.

"John Tilsley," she repeated thoughtfully, her face expressionless. "I think that he has been a guest here; but whether he is still here I cannot for the moment recall. You see, we have about twenty-five letting bedrooms here, and one doesn't always remember who is still here and who may have left, to go on somewhere else. You will forgive me, while I go to look up our records, which are inside."

In a flash she was gone. There must have been some inner door, leading from the back of the reception kiosk into the inner recesses of the hotel. Again that eerie quietude descended. Again I was the sole inhabitant of that strange lobby. I looked around me now with added interest, however. I couldn't make up my mind what there was about the strange woman in the reception kiosk which seemed to me to strike a false note. It was not that she was unnecessarily polite. After all, if I was the friend of a guest in the hotel, it was only good business to speak to me in friendly fashion. No; it was no good. I shrugged my shoulders. Just what there was that was in some way out of the picture in that hotel I could not decide.

Then she was back. It seemed that she glided rather than walked. I did not hear her return. At one moment she was not there; at the next moment, when I happened to glance at the kiosk, there she was, as impassive and still as ever.

"You were enquiring after Mr. John Tilsley, I think," she said.

"That is so."

"Could you be so kind as to inform me what is your business with Mr. Tilsley?"

I paused. This was an unexpected check. Then I thought that before I gave in I would see if I could manage to get the better of the woman in a verbal encounter.

"Before I tell you that, could you be so kind as to tell me whether Mr. Tilsley is still in the hotel?" I asked.

"He is not in the hotel at the moment," she said. "But he is still on our books. His luggage is still in his room."

"Did he sleep here last night?" I asked. And now for the first time I saw a slight trace of emotion pass over the woman's impassive features.

"I am unable to answer that question," she said.

I snapped: "Do you mean you don't know, or you won't tell?"

"I mean that I do not know. We are not in the habit of keeping a watch on our guests, save to ensure that they pay for all the food and attention that they receive," she remarked. "If a guest desires to stay out for a night, that is no business of this hotel."

"Not even if he gets into trouble when he is out?" I said meaningly.

"What do you mean?" There was no doubt now about the tone of alarm. There was something that this woman was scared about. And yet her countenance was impossible to read. The heavy make-up disguised the emotions that must otherwise have become obvious in it.

"Even if a man gets killed when he is out?" I persisted. And this time it was clear that the thrust had gone home. The woman swayed slightly on her chair, as if she thought that she had almost lost her balance in the momentary shock.

"John murdered?" These words came in a horrified whisper. I complimented myself on the way in which I was handling the business. I didn't know how much of this stuff I should be able to use in *The Daily Wire;* certainly if I tried to suggest the sinister, eerie air of the Charrington Hotel I should probably have a libel action on my hands. But, even though I was able to use nothing of what I was now finding out, I felt no less interest in what I was doing.

"You knew him, then?" I said slowly.

She nodded.

"When did you see him last?"

"At teatime yesterday."

"In the hotel?"

She nodded again.

This was a useful piece of information, anyhow. Last seen at the hotel where he was lodging at teatime on the day of his death. That was the sort of concrete evidence that newspaper readers like. I thought that Shelley would like it too. There seemed to be no doubt that I was ahead of the police here. That surprised me a bit, I must admit.

Still, there is something to be said for leading a freelance existence. You do get hold of things that the plodding official, working within the limits of his job, may well miss.

"He had tea here yesterday?" I pursued, wanting to have careful confirmation of the information that I was getting hold of.

"Yes."

"In the dining-room?"

"No, in the lounge. We serve a fairly light afternoon tea in the lounge here, you see. And I actually had a cup of tea with him yesterday."

I thought that she was going to break down. She had looked hard-boiled enough in an odd way, but now she seemed to be on the verge of tears. The thought suddenly came to me: this woman had been very fond of Tilsley. Perhaps she had been in love with him. That might go some way towards accounting for the alarm she had shown at the news of his murder—not that the murder of someone that one knows is likely to be exactly ordinary news for any of us.

"You liked him?" I said.

She nodded, her face a picture of silent misery. I felt an urge of sympathy with the woman. This affair had obviously knocked her sideways. Still, I told myself, I should not help things along any by allowing myself to be overcome with sympathy. My job was to get at the bottom of the whole affair as best I could.

"Perhaps you were very fond of him?" I added quietly, studying her face closely to see what was her reaction to this suggestion.

She admitted it readily enough. "Yes, I loved him very dearly," she said simply. "I just don't know what will happen now. I feel as if the bottom of the world had dropped out."

"Then," I said, seeing that this was my chance to get in my spoke, "you would do anything you could to see his murderer brought to book?"

"Of course I would." Her face took on a look of earnestness that was almost savage. "John was, as I said, very dear to me. I'd do anything I could to see his murderer hang!" There was something that almost frightened me about the woman—a kind of controlled hatred that was more impressive than any hysterics would have been. I thought that she was a rather remarkable woman. Even more remarkable, in fact, than she appeared to be on the surface.

"Might I have your name?" I asked. "You see, I am a newspaper man, and my paper has given me the job of investigating this case. I have friends among the police, too, and I am working in with them on it." I thought that there was no harm in telling her where I stood. After all, I had a kind of semi-official standing that might tend to impress.

"My name is Skilbeck, Mrs. Skilbeck," she said. "I am a widow. John Tilsley and I were planning to get married within a month or two."

"I see." I nodded solemnly. I understood that to this odd woman the death of John Tilsley was a very real tragedy, which would have struck her down as if by a literal blow of a club.

"And you presumably know quite a lot about Mr. Tilsley's affairs?" I said.

"A certain amount," she admitted.

"What did he do?"

She looked a little taken aback at this. "What did he do?" she repeated after me.

"Yes."

"You mean, what was his job?"

"Exactly."

"Well," she said, speaking slowly and deliberately, "I didn't know much detail about his job, but he was a sort of commission agent. He represented various manufacturers of engineering apparatus and machinery. He used to travel around the country a good deal seeing buyers and other agents."

"I see," I said once again. This was the sort of vague job that might well tie up with a criminal background. I knew that there were various commission agents, tied up in the black market and concerned with defeating the various controls which governments had introduced in the effort to effect a sensible distribution of goods that were in short supply. This might, perhaps, provide the motive for the murder, which I was first of all looking for.

"You don't know the details of the job which he was doing?" I said.

"No."

"And therefore, I suppose, you wouldn't know if he had made any bad enemies in the course of his work?" I knew that this was likely to lead nowhere, but, nevertheless, it was a question that had to be asked.

"You mean," she said, and paused, as if she found it difficult to put her thoughts into words. "You mean"—and now the words came out with a rush—"that I wouldn't have any real suspicion of anyone likely to have murdered him."

I nodded.

"No," she said. "I really knew little about the details of his job. He wasn't the sort of man to talk much about what he was doing, you know."

"Then you have no ideas to put forward, which might help in leading us to the criminal?" I said.

"Not a notion," she said. Her face was still a picture of the most abysmal misery. Again I felt that sudden urge of sympathy. It might be that John Tilsley had been a crook. He might have been the worse kind of skunk, but the fact remained that this woman had been truly in love with him, if I was any sort of judge. And his sudden death had been the greatest tragedy that could possibly have come to her. Of that I was well assured.

"Is there any way in which you think that you could help us in our work?" I asked.

"I don't see that there is much really that I can do," she answered.

"You will know which was his room here," I said.

"Oh, yes."

"And you will, of course, be able to get hold of a key to it?"

"Yes, of course."

I looked at her steadily. "Will you trust me enough to let me have a look around that room, Mrs. Skilbeck?" I said.

"You think it would help?"

"I'm sure of it. And I should not be likely to upset things—either the contents of the room or the proprietors of this hotel—as much as the police would do."

"The police will come here?" She seemed to be a trifle alarmed at this.

"They're bound to, I think," I admitted.

"Well," she said, leaning back towards a board behind her. On it there were a series of hooks, each one bearing a key. "Well, you may as well come up to his room right away." She took down a key, and glided towards the main staircase. I followed quickly, you may be sure.

CHAPTER VII

In Which I Examine a Dead Man's Room

CLEARLY JOHN TILSLEY HAD BEEN IN SOME RESPECTS A favoured guest. His room was on the first floor, and seemed to be one of the best rooms in the hotel. Mrs. Skilbeck, true to her generally stoical way of looking at things (thus, anyhow, I had summed her up), showed no emotion as she inserted the key into the lock and opened a room which, since it had belonged to the man she had expected to marry, must have had some poignant memories for her. I thought that I had never known a woman so well in control of herself.

Still, it was time for me to forget her. My job now was to examine this room carefully, and make sure that I didn't miss anything of importance in the place. I had a good look around me.

The place was typical of a bedroom in a reasonably good-class hotel. Beneath the window was a divan bed, covered with a clean counterpane of green silk. A dressing-table stood opposite the light, and on the wall was a cupboard, with a mirror front—a shaving cabinet, in other words. A basin, with hot and cold taps, was underneath it. On the opposite side of the room was a chest of drawers—a massive piece of furniture made of mahogany.

This was all the furniture that the room contained, and there was a good deal of space. In other words, the place did not look in any way overcrowded. It was a good indication that the hotel was a reasonably well-run place. The effect of spaciousness, I have often thought, is the test of good taste in furnishing.

The walls were papered; the paper was, however, not one of those hideous patterned things with crawling roses that one often sees in hotels. It was almost plain, and its general principle was cream.

Thus I had taken in the general appearance of the room. It had, of course, little that one could call character; but what hotel room has? Certainly there was nothing about it that would enable one to come to any conclusions as to the type of man who had been living in it. There was, in fact, only one small indication that it had been occupied at all—a large studio portrait of Mrs. Skilbeck, which stood on the dressing table. This provided, at any rate, some superficial confirmation of her story.

"Would his luggage be here?" I asked her.

"The empty cases, trunks, and so on, are taken down into the basement when they are unpacked," she explained. "I imagine that all his personal possessions would be in the drawers of that chest, or of the dressing-table." She pointed vaguely at the two pieces of furniture in question.

I looked at her. She was still clearly holding herself in, not allowing any emotion to show itself. I thought that this must be a most difficult affair for her; she must, whether she showed it or not, be feeling very worried and almost distraught.

"Would you rather leave me to do my investigations on my own?" I asked. "I know that all this must be trying and distressing to you, Mrs. Skilbeck."

"If you don't mind," she said, "I think that I will go downstairs. If you find anything which you would like to question me about, ring that bell"—she indicated a bell-push in the wall, close to the dressing-table. "I will be up in a moment if you ring."

And silently as ever she glided from the room. I took a deep breath. Well, here I was! It was odd how I had managed to get right into the heart of this case, almost at the start of the job.

I wondered what Shelley would do, faced with this room to be examined. I glanced around me. I supposed that the first thing he would look for would be papers of one sort or another. But where would papers be hidden?

I made my way to the chest of drawers. Top drawer: handkerchiefs, collars, ties. No papers. Second drawer: shirts, underclothes. No papers. Third drawer: carefully folded flannel trousers. Nothing else; no papers. Fourth, bottom drawer: empty.

That had taken me only a minute or two. Perhaps the most promising piece of furniture in the room, from the point of view of being a possible hiding-place for papers, and I had drawn a complete blank. Still, I was not despondent. There were other chances yet. After all, the man must have had personal papers of some sort. No one, in these complicated days, gets on without having some kind of papers about. Letters, identity cards, and all the other paraphernalia of a complex civilisation—they must be somewhere. And even if the man had merely been on holiday, leaving most of his stuff in London, the fact remained that he would almost certainly have some papers with him in Broadgate. If, as Mrs. Skilbeck had said, he had been a commission agent of some kind, he would probably be doing some deals, even on his holiday. That sort of man is usually in some degree an adventurer, and as such never omits any chance of making some money. That, at any rate, was my experience of the fellows of the kind whom I had come across from time to time.

So the dressing table was the next thing to occupy my attention. It was a modern piece of furniture, with a huge curved mirror.

There were two small drawers at the top, one on each side of the mirror, and a nest (if that's the word) of three long drawers underneath.

I glanced at the big drawers first. I didn't really think that there would be anything of importance in them. And I was quite right. Two of them were completely empty, and the other had a few odd pieces of clothing—ties, a pair of braces, a belt, and some of those sundries which do not seem to be easy to classify, if you know what I mean.

Nothing there to interest me. But the two small drawers were more promising. As I opened the first one I whistled gently to myself. The drawer was absolutely crammed with pound notes. I took them out. There was nothing in the drawer but the money. I rapidly counted them. There were over a hundred and fifty of them. A hundred and fifty pounds in notes! That seemed to tie up well enough with my suspicion that the late lamented John Tilsley might be in some way connected with the black market in some commodity; after all, the average black marketeer usually deals in cash; cheques do not suit him as a rule.

I felt pleased at this discovery. Of course, I told myself, there might well be some other explanation; but, as a first guess at what was happening, it might be that my black market idea was a useful one.

It was with a real thrill that I turned to the other drawer. It was here that some papers might be found. And my guess was right. The drawer was crammed with papers. Letters, visiting cards, and sundry odds and ends. This was what I was after. I pulled the drawer right out, took it over to the bed, and tipped it up. Its contents spread over the bed. I rapidly sorted the stuff out.

There were about a dozen visiting cards. These I put into one heap. The letters I put into a pile by themselves.

The letters I thought the best thing to look at first. They were what seemed to me most likely to yield immediate results. And immediate results, which would impress Shelley, were what I was after at the moment. I knew that if I could give the man from Scotland Yard some information that seemed valuable and important well ahead of anything that his minions were able to get, I should be well in with him, and be all the more likely to have a share of whatever information he might have been able to collect in the same time.

The first two or three letters that I looked at didn't seem to be very promising. They were the same sort of thing that I had seen in the dead man's pockets. Just personal notes, saying that the writer hoped John was enjoying his holiday. They were, in fact, the sort of letters that most of us receive when we are on a longish holiday. The people who had been writing to him were living at various London addresses, mostly in the Chelsea and Kensington areas. There was one, I noticed, from Thackeray Court, S.W.5, which I recalled was the address from which Tilsley had come.

The contents of these letters, as I said, were of no real importance. I thought that the writers were probably mere friends or acquaintances of Tilsley's and probably had little to do with him in the course of his business. Or, if they had any business with him, their letters gave little indication of it.

About the fifth letter that I opened, however, was something a little different. It made me raise my eyebrows and whistle again.

This letter bore no address and no signature. It was typewritten on cheap paper. And it read as follows:—

"As usual, I suppose, see you on Wednesday, usual place, usual time. And this time see if you can bring along some of the real stuff, my lad. My folk are getting fed-up with the stuff that you sent last time. They said that it wasn't good enough for them. So I reckon that you'll have to watch your step in future, or you'll be running into a packet of trouble."

That was all. But it was a very suggestive letter, I thought. It seemed to go quite a long way to support my idea that Tilsley might have been doing something that was on the shady side of the law. Black marketeering might be the explanation; anyhow, whatever it was, that was a letter that Shelley would find interesting. I looked at the envelope. It was postmarked "London," and was dated a couple of days back. "You'll have to watch your step in future, or you'll be running into a packet of trouble." Well, Tilsley had run into a packet of trouble all right; I wondered if this letter had really had any influence on the murder.

I thought it at any rate possible that there was some real connection. Shelley might well be a better judge of that than I could possibly be. I pocketed the letter, with the idea to take it to him as soon as I had finished with the rest of the documents here.

The next thing to which I turned was a postcard. This was postmarked "Broadgate," I noticed, and was scrawled in a hand that was either naturally uneducated, or had been deliberately designed to look like the writing of an uneducated person. This certainly seemed as if it had some direct connection with the tragic events I was enquiring into, for it read:—

"Be careful. They're after you, Take my word for it, be careful."

Again there was no signature. I thought to myself that John Tilsley seemed to be getting rather a lot of warnings of one sort or another. Whether those warnings had any direct connection with the murder, it was, of course, impossible to say as yet, though, naturally, I inclined to the view that they had. But I hadn't really got enough experience of this sort of thing to be at all certain. I was glad that I had Shelley and all the powers of the police behind me; I knew that Shelley would

be only too pleased to have my information, and to let me know how
he interpreted it. But these two letters were, in a way, more than I
had expected to get. I had hoped for some lead as to the sort of business that Tilsley had been doing. As yet I had no kind of indication
on that point. But otherwise I was doing pretty well. I patted myself
on the back, so to speak. Then I turned back to the remaining letters.

There were two or three of the purely personal ones, which I
rapidly glanced at, and put on one side. There were one or two,
addressed to him from Broadgate to his address in London. These
were from Mrs. Skilbeck, who had, I noticed, the remarkable first
name of Phoebe. They did not express any deep emotion, though,
knowing the lady, I should not have expected them to do so. They
began "Darling John," and ended "Love, Phoebe," which was, I
imagined, as much as she would allow herself in the way of tender
emotions on paper. But the letters, like the picture of the lady on
the dressing table, provided some small confirmation of the truth
of the story which she had told about being engaged to Tilsley. In
fact, I had been quite impressed by the sincerity of Mrs. Skilbeck. I
thought that she was one of the most patently sincere people I had
ever met. I believed that she had told the truth; and if Tilsley had
been a crook of some sort, I was pretty sure that she had known
nothing at all about it.

I had now come more or less to the end of the letters. I had, it was
true, learned nothing about Tilsley's business, but I had found a little
about the way in which there might have been a basis for murder.
In fact, considering the fact that I had been there such a short time,
and had, really, only known of the man's existence for a matter of
an hour or two, I thought I had done very well.

I left the room and made my way down the stairs. I had locked
the door of Tilsley's room, and I handed the key to Mrs. Skilbeck,

who was still standing inside the little reception kiosk, as if nothing at all unusual had happened.

"Any luck?" she asked quietly as I handed the key over to her.

"Some," I said. "But there is nothing there to give any sort of indication of what exactly Mr. Tilsley's business was. You can't clarify my ideas on that point at all, I suppose?"

"Except what I have already told you—that he was working as a commission agent for various firms—I know nothing of the details of his business," she admitted, though I felt that she might be keeping something back.

"Do you know the names of any of the firms he was working for?" I asked.

She shook her head. It was clear that I was not going to get anywhere along these lines.

"Do you know of anyone who was threatening him, of any sort of danger in which he might be?"

She looked surprised. "Did you find threatening letters?" she asked.

"Well," I said, "not exactly threatening letters, but letters which suggested he might be running into trouble of some sort. You know nothing of that?"

"No."

"Well, that seems to be that for the moment," I said. "I shall be able to find you here at any time if anything else occurs to me?"

She nodded gravely, and I hared off to the police station. It was clear that I had to get hold of friend Shelley at the earliest possible moment.

CHAPTER VIII

In Which I Give Information... and Collect Some

S HELLEY SEEMED PLEASED ENOUGH TO SEE ME. I WAS, AS A
matter of fact, more than a little surprised to find him at the
police station. I had expected to find him with his nose glued to
some elusive trail. But he was sitting at a perfectly ordinary desk in
a perfectly ordinary room, which the Kentish police had put at his
disposal. Spread before him on the desk were a mass of papers. I
couldn't for the life of me think what they were, since this case had
been on only for a few hours, and I didn't think that much information
could yet have been assembled—not in manuscript form, anyway.
And somehow I didn't think that Shelley was the sort of man to put
on an act, to pile up the papers in order to impress any visitor who
might call on him.

"Hullo, Jimmy!" he said cheerfully, sweeping the papers together
into a folder and tying it up with a long piece of white tape.

"Good-morning again, Inspector," I replied. It was, indeed, now
only about a couple of hours since I had first been dragged, so to
speak, into the case, though it seemed to me to be about two weeks,
judging by all that had happened.

"Any news?" he asked.

"Yes," I said.

"Good lad! I knew that I could depend on you, though what the
good Inspector Beech and his comrades would say if they knew what

I was doing, in letting you come into the case, heaven knows!" Shelley looked almost ruefully worried at this, but I was pretty sure that he was not really perturbed about it. The man from Scotland Yard had handled enough cases in his time to be sure as to what he could or could not do. Yet, at the same time, I knew that he would have little hesitation in completely chucking me overboard if he felt that I was being indiscreet or not handling the matter just as he wanted me to do. Shelley, in fact, was a tough guy in his own peculiar way, though he would have instantly disclaimed the title if anyone had accused him of deserving it.

Still, I was glad to think that I had been able to do something to help; it would stand me in good stead for getting extra information for my paper. So I produced the two letters—or rather, the letter and the postcard which had seemed to me to be worth while in Tilsley's room.

"What do you think of these, Inspector?" I said, and chucked them across the table. He picked them up and studied them intently for a full minute, in complete silence.

"Interesting," he said.

"Does it mean that you have learned anything new from them, Inspector?" I asked.

"Yes… and no," he replied somewhat cryptically.

"Am I allowed to ask what that means?" I enquired.

"You are," Shelley said, and paused.

I waited for the revelation, but it did not seem to be forthcoming. Shelley sat back and puffed at his pipe, as if the clouds of rather rank smoke gave him some inspiration; but it seemed as if I might have to wait for a long time. I thought that it was time I gave him a mental prod of some sort.

"Well?" I said.

"I've managed to get hold of some genuine information about our friend Tilsley," Shelley said. "I think that it may give us some sort of lead as to the reason for his murder."

"Yes?" This sounded really interesting, and I awaited the new information.

"We believe he was engaged in some sort of transactions over black market petrol," Shelley explained. "He was tied up with a garage in London—near Kennington Oval—which was the centre of a racket for bleaching red petrol—specially coloured, for use in commercial vehicles, you know—and then selling it to ordinary motorists. It was a clever scheme, and it seems to have been run on quite a big scale. I don't know all the details yet; but our people in London are ferreting out all the stuff that they can get. I think that we've done pretty well to get what we have in a matter of two or three hours. But it seems that the Yard were already on his track, assisted by the enforcement staff of the Ministry of Fuel and Power. They knew that there was a big leakage of petrol in that district, and they were suspicious of this garage, which Tilsley had a big interest in. The whole thing ties up, and it may well be, as I said, that there was a connection of this black-market petrol with Tilsley's murder. I'm pretty hopeful that we shall be able to get the real tie-up worked out in a matter of a day or two. You see, I have told the folk in London who have been investigating the matter to pull in the garage men, and see if they can throw any light on what was going on."

This was quite a long speech for Shelley. I saw that he was excited. He did not normally reveal his emotions, but there was an under-current which I knew to be the sure signal of his pleasure at what was going on.

"How much of this can I publish?" I asked. That was what really interested me most at the moment. All these revelations were, of course, valuable, but at the same time I knew that they would not be of much use to me if I was not allowed to wire them to my paper.

"None, at the moment," Shelley replied. Then he thought for a moment, and added: "At least, you can hint at some sort of black-market transactions in the background of the case. But don't mention Kennington, and don't mention petrol. We don't want to give these gentry any sort of hint, until they are all safely in our hands. In any case the petrol business may not be all that is involved."

"I see." I considered this. It was, I suppose, good enough, though, indeed, I had already thought of the black market business as a general explanation.

"But what about the locked gates?" I asked.

"What about them?" he said.

"Any explanation?"

"Of how the body got there during the night?" Shelley enquired.

"Yes."

"No explanation at all as yet," the detective agreed somewhat ruefully. "Though I have hopes that the duplicate key in the Council Offices may give us some sort of clue as to what happened."

I thought this over. It did not seem to me to be very satisfactory, and I said as much. Shelley, of course, saw the weakness in the case as well as I did.

"The actual mechanism of the murder," he explained, "does not matter at the moment, though, of course, we shall have to do something about it before we manage to bring the case to court. Any good barrister could drive a horse and cart through the case, if we don't get some sort of explanation of how the body got there, the doors being still locked."

This was so obvious that I thought it didn't require any kind of explanation from me. Then I suddenly remembered something that I had completely forgotten.

"Inspector!" I exclaimed.

"Yes, Jimmy."

"Have you come across, in the case, a man called Doctor Cyrus Watford?"

Shelley shook his head emphatically. "Never heard of him," he said. "Why do you think he has something to do with the murder?"

"I don't know why on earth I didn't tell you before," I said, "but he butted in while I was guarding the body, before you arrived." And I went on to tell him about the interlude, when Doctor Watford had told me something about the man Tilsley.

Shelley looked thoughtful. "You say that he said he was a Doctor, and that he had to go and look after his patients?" he said.

"That's right," I said. "Actually I got the impression that he was in a bit of a hurry to get away. Personally, I was of the opinion that this had little to do with his patients. I got a distinct feeling that he was really anxious to get clear before the police arrived. I can't give you any genuine reason for this, but, at the same time, I think it was true enough."

Shelley considered what I had said; then he pressed a button on the desk. A bell rang outside. A policeman came in.

"Bring me a local telephone directory, please," Shelley said.

The policeman went out, and in a few moments came back with a slim red volume.

Shelley turned its pages rapidly. "Walton, Watson," he muttered. "No, Jimmy, there is no Watford here. Of course, he might be doing a locum's job, for one of the local doctors, but I doubt it. Still, that is pretty easily settled." He picked up the telephone.

"Put me through to Doctor Gordon, the police surgeon," he said.

In a moment I heard a murmur at the other end of the line. "Doctor Gordon?" Shelley asked. "I want to get in touch with a Doctor Watford, whom I'm told is practising in Broadgate. He is not in the telephone directory. I thought that he might be either a new man, or a man doing a locum's job for someone here, during the holiday season, you see."

There was a pause, and then Shelley turned to me: "You did say the man's name was Watford, didn't you?" he asked.

"Yes," I said. "Cyrus Watford."

"Cyrus Watford was the name," Shelley said, and paused. Then: "Well, thanks very much, Doctor," he added, and hung up the receiver.

"Well?" I asked. "Any verdict?"

"Doctor Cyrus Watford, whoever and whatever he is, is not a doctor in Broadgate," Shelley said. "Gordon has never heard of him."

"Then who is he?" I asked.

"That is something that I could bear to know," Shelley said grimly. "I'll have your description of him again, Jimmy, if I may. And make it as exact as you can, please."

I thought deeply before I replied. This was an unexpected development indeed. I hadn't thought that the Doctor was anything but what he had pretended to be.

"And oldish man—sixty or so," I said. "Tall, fat, red-faced. The sort of fellow that you would think of as the typical retired colonel."

"I see. I think that I get the general impression," Shelley commented.

"His face was wrinkled, but not in any elderly way, if you know what I mean," I went on. "In fact, he was a chap that I would have thought of as a man who was always laughing. He fairly radiated good-humour."

"That's a good point," Shelley said. "Bless you, for the journalist's eye, Jimmy. Few witnesses would have given us that point. If we hadn't had your observation, we shouldn't have known that—and, while you can't put that on a poster, it is the sort of thing that we can tell some of our people, and it will give them something to get on with, give them a hint of the sort of man to look for."

"You think that Cyrus Watford is of some importance in the case?" I asked.

"Pretty sure, I should think."

"Can I mention him in my reports?"

Shelley duly considered this. "Don't see any real reason why not," he said. "After all, he will be posted on the boards outside every police-station in the country from tomorrow morning onwards, if we do not succeed in pulling him in today. It's pretty certain that he is a man who knows something about the case. The fact that he told you he knew Tilsley, and that he said Tilsley was a bad hat, is a good indication that he was tied up with the case somehow. Though why he was indiscreet enough as to reveal that to you is something that we shall never know. I expect that he was so taken by surprise at seeing you there that he was somehow startled into revealing something that he would not have normally said."

"And what now?" I asked.

"What now?"

"Yes; what would you like me to do? After all, we are to some extent sharing this thing," I explained. "And it may well be that there is something else that I could do, which would be more or less outside your control. Then I could do a bit more investigation, and refer back to you this evening. I've already got enough to be able to phone my paper a fairly exciting story for tomorrow morning's issue."

Shelley thought for about half a minute before he answered. It was clear enough that he took our partnership quite seriously. I was glad about that. I knew that by keeping in with him I was likely to be well away with the paper. And to keep in with *The Daily Wire* was essential for me financially. I knew that my bank manager would take a poor view of any suggestion from me that he should extend my overdraft—and it was only by an extension of an overdraft that I should be able to eat, if I did not soon earn some money. And I am one of these queer people who find eating necessary.

"I think," Shelley said at last, "that the best thing you can do, if you don't mind going back to London for a few hours, is to have a look at our friend Tilsley's London background. Our people have made a few enquiries at his London address; but they have done very little in the way of delving into things. You see, if you play the poor innocent newspaper man, and see if you can get hold of anything, it might be helpful. You've got hold of something at the Charrington Hotel. Of course, our people would have got it before long, but if this woman whom you met had cut up rusty, it might have taken a bit longer than it took you to get the necessary information. Now, of course, we shall do a search which will be in many ways more expert than yours was—but I've no doubt that the two documents which you got were the important ones."

I thought that this was a great compliment, and said as much. Shelley grinned cheerfully. "I didn't ask for your help in this business without considering it, you know, Jimmy," he said. "Anyhow, off you go to London, with my blessing. There's a decent train at eleven-thirty, I think. It's got a dining-car, and it's due in at one forty-five. That should suit you."

CHAPTER IX

In Which I Go Back to London

ACTUALLY, I WAS NONE TOO PLEASED AT THE ASSIGNMENT Shelley had suggested as possible for me. It seemed to me that it was leading away from the centre of affairs. Yet, at the same time, it was obviously wise on my part to keep well in with Scotland Yard. I knew which side my bread was buttered, and I knew that any chance I might have of scooping my rivals in Fleet Street was really dependent on my getting hold of some genuine information, as a result of my friendship with Shelley.

Yet I knew that it would never do to let my editor know that I was leaving Broadgate and going back to London, even though it might be only for a few hours. Mike Jones, I knew, would take the line that anything in London could easily be handled by one of his regular staff, and would not justify the payment of space rates for material, which he could get easily by sending a man on a weekly wage around to collect it.

That this would be unreasonable of Mike was, of course, true enough. But people are not as reasonable as they should be. I thought that I should be able to get hold of something useful from Thackeray Court. But just what that information would be I could not guess.

Anyhow, I had plenty of food for thought as I sat back in the corner of an extremely comfortable third-class compartment of a fast train *en route* for Victoria. True, I paid four shillings and sixpence for a lunch which was eatable, though small in bulk. And I treated myself to a bottle of Bass, carefully preserving the bill for these comestibles, since I thought that, later on, I would put in an expense account, and I saw no reason why I should personally pay for things which I should not have bought had I not been working on this case.

Outside Victoria Station I hailed a taxi. "Do you know Thackeray Court?" I asked the driver.

He scratched his head. "Can't say I do, guv'nor," he said slowly. "Would it be one of them big blocks of flats out Hammersmith way?"

"I shouldn't think so," I said. "I think it's either Earl's Court or Kensington."

He slapped his knee with a resounding thwack. "I know!" he exclaimed. "Get in, guv'nor. It's a block not far from Gloucester Road station. I know it."

So we swung up towards Hyde Park Corner, and then down the long sweep of Knightsbridge. I felt a certain warmth of excitement about my heart. Forgotten now was my old worry that I might be missing something by coming back to London from Broadgate. I thought that I was actually getting near the heart of the whole business. After all, was it not likely that Tilsley's London home would contain something more, in the way of direct indications of whatever black market racket he was involved in, than his purely temporary lodging in Kent had done? Shelley had thought that it was a scheme for dealing in petrol off the ration, and it might be that I should be able to get hold of something which would definitely connect the man with the garage in Kennington that Shelley had indicated as the centre of the business.

The fact that the police had been here before me did not worry me at all. The eye of the journalist, after all, is a bit different from the eye

of the policeman. There might well be things which the police had
either overlooked, or had not thought of sufficient importance to be
investigated; and those things, with the special knowledge of the case
which was now mine, might seem to me to be of genuine value. That,
at any rate, was what I was hoping for as I drove along the streets of
South Kensington, with their tall, dignified early Victorian houses.

The taxi drew to a standstill. The driver fairly beamed with self-
congratulations. "There you are, guv'nor," he said. "That's the place."
He indicated a tall block of flats, built in that combination of brick
and roughcast typical of building in the 'thirties.

"Thank you," I said, and paid him off. I drew a deep breath. This
was perhaps the first really important moment in the case. On what
happened in the next few minutes might well depend my future
relationship with Shelley—and, by implication, the future of my
job with *The Daily Wire*. I was in no position to ignore the financial
implications of the whole affair. It was highly important to me to
re-establish myself in the crazy world of Fleet Street journalism, and
to do that I had to get every scrap of exclusive information that was
available in this place.

One thing I felt thankful about. I was in a good position with
regard to my competitors. As far as I knew no other newspaperman
even knew of the existence of Tilsley's London address. So I was a
good few steps ahead of everyone else.

I looked at the block of flats with interest. It was about eight
storeys high, built on a plain, severe, what I think is called "functional"
plan. In other words, there were no frills and decorations on it.

I went up to what appeared to be the main entrance. Here a
porter sat in a small alcove.

"Yus?" he said, fixing me with a stony glare.

"I'm trying to find out something about a Mr. John Tilsley who lives, or did live, here," I said. It seemed to me that there was nothing to be gained by hiding my reason for coming to the place.

"And who are you?" he retorted, glaring at me again. A most unfriendly chap, this hall-porter. I thought that the financial approach was definitely indicated.

I felt in my pocket and produced a couple of half-crowns. I slid these towards him, and thought that I could detect a sign of a thaw sliding over his grim visage.

"I'm a newspaper man," I said. "We are interested in Mr. Tilsley, and it will be worth your while to help."

He looked a bit more amiable. "Oh, I thought you was another of them cops," he said.

I raised my eyebrows, doing my best to simulate surprise. "Oh, have the police been here?" I asked.

"Have they been here?" He gave a short, bitter laugh. "Why, mister, they've been in and out of the place for hours this morning. It's not half an hour since the last of 'em left."

This was good news. If I found some of Shelley's underlings from Scotland Yard in possession I might well have found it a bit difficult to explain my presence, and what exactly I was after. Whereas, now that they had gone, it would be easy, I hoped, for me to find my way around the place and do what seemed to me to be necessary in the way of investigating the home of John Tilsley.

"Do you think that I could have a look at Tilsley's flat?" I asked.

"I don't know." He appeared very doubtful as to the wisdom of this course of action.

I guessed, however, at the reason for this hesitation. I fished in my pocket and produced another five shillings. These I slid, with an almost diffident air, towards him. This time there was a positive grin on his face as he swiftly pocketed the cash.

"The trouble is," he said, "that the police locked the flat and took away the key and told me that nobody was to go in until they gave me permission to let people in."

"Did they say why?" I asked.

"Yus. They said as Tilsley had been murdered." There was an almost ghoulish expression on the man's face as he said this. It seemed that he took a considerable delight in being even indirectly involved in a murder case.

"Did you give them the key, then?" I said, wondering how to get around this.

"Yus." But I thought that I could detect a definite sense of mischief (that is the only word for it) about his face. There was, I thought, something which he had done and which he did not intend to let out; something, in fact, which had been in some way a daring defiance of police orders.

That this was true enough soon became evident. "Is there, then, no way for me to get in and have a look at Tilsley's flat?" I asked. I guessed that this was the best way to get this awkward customer to tell me what was going on.

"Well, there is and there isn't, as you might say," the porter replied.

"What do you mean?"

"These flats have got a tradesman's entrance at the back," he said.

"Yes?"

"Yus. And the police took away the key to that door as well as the front one. But they didn't ask if there was any sort of master key."

Now I understood the crafty look which he had given me. "And you've got a master key?" I said.

"Yus. You see, it's got to be kept here, because some of the people in the flats are out all day. And they may order some stuff from the grocer or the greengrocer. And then it's part of my job to take the stuff in and put it in their flats. So I've got a master key to deliver the stuff with. See?" This was all said with an air of crafty confidence which is difficult to describe. I congratulated myself, however, on having established such terms of financial confidence with the porter earlier on. It meant that I should have little difficulty in having a view of the flat soon; I didn't quite know what Shelley would think about what I was doing: he would probably think it strictly unethical; that, however, didn't matter.

The great thing was that I was getting in, and I was now managing to acquire confidential information that would be of the greatest value in my work for *The Daily Wire*.

Within five minutes, indeed, I was in Tilsley's apartment. This was on the fourth floor, at the back of the building. It was an unpretentious flat—probably one of the cheapest in the building, I thought. But if Tilsley was actually involved in some black market racket it was highly probable that he would live in a comparatively unostentatious way. The super-spiv, driving a Rolls-Royce and wearing a fur coat, is for the most part a figure of fiction. The man who is living on the wrong side of the law is usually a man who is anxious not to attract undue attention to himself.

Certainly John Tilsley was a man who lived in a quiet, comparatively inexpensive way. His flat consisted of a living-room, with a gas-cooker hidden by a curtain in an alcove, and a bedroom. Neither of the rooms was big, and they were furnished with a quiet simplicity that spoke eloquently of the taste of the man who had bought the furniture.

"Are these flats let furnished?" I asked the porter, who had followed me into the room.

"No," he said. "This is Tilsley's furniture that you can see here, guv'nor."

I was impressed, I must admit. Somehow I had thought of the late lamented Mr. Tilsley as a rather flashy type. And the way in which this pleasant little sitting-room was furnished showed clearly enough that, whatever might have been his faults, a lack of taste was quite certainly not one of them.

I glanced around. It was no good to think of doing the orthodox things in searching. The police would have done all those things. First of all I did what I always do when I come into a strange room—I looked at the bookshelf. This was a tall, narrow piece of early Victorian mahogany. It had six shelves, crammed tightly with books. I glanced idly at them. They were, at first sight, the miscellaneous stuff that most vaguely literary people accumulate. There were a few nov-els—P. G. Wodehouse, Edgar Wallace, Aldous Huxley, George Orwell. A very mixed batch. I did not spend much time over these, however. My job was not to investigate the late Mr. Tilsley's literary taste.

The non-fiction shelves interested me more. There were a batch of text-books of chemistry. Not the ordinary school text-books, however, such as one finds in most households where books are not quickly disposed of when not any longer of use. These were advanced text-books, some dealing, I noticed with a feeling of some excitement, with oils and petroleums. There was even a book of the purification of petroleum and gasoline. There were also books on the alkaloids. It looked as if there might be something in Shelley's hunch that Tilsley was in the petrol black market. He was certainly interested in the chemical background of petrol and oil in a way which was, to say the least, unusual.

Actually, these text-books were the only indication of anything unusual. The other books, as I have said when I wrote of the novels, were a perfectly normal assortment of works, such as one found in any household of ordinary people.

But wait! I pulled myself up as I glimpsed a little black notebook. It was pushed down at the end of a shelf. I fished in my pocket. The book which I had found in Tilsley's pocket at Broadgate (and which I had kept to myself, thus, I suppose, not playing quite fair with Shelley) was an exact twin. And the scribbles in the Broadgate book had all been obviously written in some sort of code which I had, as yet, had no chance to try to decipher. I had carefully kept the original notebook in the background, and I now thought that in this new book I might well have the clue which would enable me to get to the real heart of the mystery.

I know that this was something in every way reprehensible. I ought not to have tried to keep anything to myself. But I salved my conscience by telling myself that Shelley had not told me by any means all he knew. That, indeed, was almost certainly so; but I knew that I ought to have told him something about these note-books. Still, I thought that if this new book gave me a clue which would enable me to find out something about the original book I should be able to go to Shelley in real triumph, a first-rate piece of work done.

The first glance at the pages of the new notebook gave me a sense of genuine exultation. I could see, since there were a series of names and addresses, with some cryptic signs and symbols opposite each of them. This was doubtless the clue to enable me to decipher the original book. I made a mental resolution to hand the two books over to Shelley when I got back to Kent. But meanwhile I should spend an hour or two over them, in the hope that I should be able to do something in the way of getting the information that they hid.

I became conscious of the fact that the porter was looking at me curiously.

"Anything else you want to see, guv'nor?" he asked quietly, as if he felt that I had been spending a long time over things that were totally unimportant.

"I want to have a look around," I explained. "But you need not stay, if you are busy."

"Can't leave you here on your own, guv'nor," he explained. "You see, guv'nor, I don't mean to insult you, but I don't know who you are, really, and if anything was missing after you'd gone, they'd say I was responsible. They'd say, I expect, that I'd pinched the stuff. And I've got my good name to consider. I've been working here for nine years, I have, and no black mark against my name in all that time. I don't want to spoil that there record, you see."

I did see. I knew that from the point of view of this man I was a pretty suspicious sort of character. Indeed, if I had been in his position I should have felt very doubtful about allowing any stranger to have a look around the place, And, to do him due justice, I think that the porter had felt pretty doubtful; it was only his natural cupidity, when he realised that I was prepared to pay for the privilege of examining Tilsley's apartment, that had overcome his natural suspicions of me.

So I strolled into Tilsley's bedroom, closely followed by the porter. There was, I soon saw, nothing at all here to deserve my attention. Well-kept and neatly-pressed clothes hung in the wardrobe. On the wall was a reproduction, nicely framed, of Augustus John's portrait of Suggia. On the dressing-table was a picture of the lady whom I had met in the Charrington Hotel at Broadgate. The personal background of the case hung together all right.

I made my way back to the sitting-room again. There was a small roll-top desk beside the window. I opened it (it was not locked), and looked for a few moments at the papers in it. These were piled up in a neat way that seemed to me to indicate that the police had been here before me.

Of course, it was pretty obvious that the police would tend to concentrate on the desk. There was the place where the men from Scotland Yard would expect to find the material they were after. I didn't think that it was really much good for me to go through the masses of papers that there were left. Anything that was of any real importance would have been taken away. No doubt at this moment—or very soon, anyhow—all the valuable stuff from here would be on Shelley's desk. And I should be able to swap my notebooks for whatever information Shelley had managed to extract from the papers.

I couldn't think how the police had missed the little black notebook. Probably they had glanced at the bookcase. They were, however, likely to be looking merely for the hidden document, folded inside a novel, or that sort of thing. The book which, to my mind, stuck out a mile, they would not notice, because they were not looking for that sort of thing.

So I thought that I had really obtained all that I wanted. The way in which I have described it here may make my search sound very perfunctory, but the fact is that I spent some considerable time in hunting there, but found so little of any real value that it seemed to me almost as if my trip to town had been almost wasted. Indeed, if it had not been for the notebook I should have thought that it was so.

CHAPTER X

In Which I Examine Two Notebooks

M Y LANDLADY AT BROADGATE WAS A PLEASANT OLD SOUL. She must have been completely mystified by my apparent disappearance. For, you must remember, I had set out that morning for a pre-breakfast walk, and had immediately got mixed up in this mysterious case. It was teatime when I got back, bearing the two all-important notebooks.

"Mr. London!" she exclaimed as she met me in the hall on my return. "I thought that you had got lost. I was thinking of going to the police about you."

I grinned rather shamefacedly. "I'm very sorry, Mrs. Cecil," I said. "You see, I met an old friend of mine from Fleet Street, and he rushed me off to London. It was a matter of a possible job, where I had to get there without delay. Only by getting there quickly was it possible to be sure that I should be considered. And I'm nearly well now, you know, so that I could go into the matter."

"And did you get the job?" she asked, looking at me, I thought, rather suspiciously. Indeed, my tale must have sounded rather thin.

"Yes."

"Oh, I am glad," she said. And she sounded as if she meant it.

"It's with *The Daily Wire*," I explained. Indeed, she must know soon, for the articles with my name at the top of them would very soon be appearing. There was no point in trying to keep the matter secret from her.

"I'm glad," she said again. "And when do you start?" I saw that what was worrying her was the matter of the room which I was occupying. She was mentally envisaging a "long let" suddenly drying up.

"Oh, I shall be doing the work from here for the moment, Mrs. Cecil," I said. "You see, it's a sort of special correspondent job. I shan't have to attend the office regularly, not to begin with, anyhow." I knew that the whole background of newspaper work would be completely foreign to her, and she would be compelled to take on trust what I told her. And anyhow it was sure enough that as soon as she saw the first of my contributions to *The Daily Wire* she would realise that I had only told the truth about my connection with the paper.

Now, however, my main concern was to get away from her, and do something with the two black notebooks that seemed almost to be burning holes in my pocket.

"Will you have some tea?" she asked.

"Do you think that you could get a tray sent up to my room, Mrs. Cecil?" I asked. "You see, I have some rather important work to do for my paper, and I can get on with it only if you can get my tea to me up there, so that I can have my tea while I am working."

"I'll do it, sir," she said. "But don't forget that you've been very ill. Don't overdo it; I've met too many people who have overworked too soon when they have left hospital, you know." And the old soul meant it, I knew. She really thought that I was an invalid, who should be looked after.

Still, I was not going to waste any more time over reassuring her. I had wasted enough time in conversation already. I knew that I should have to turn these books over to Shelley later in the day. And

I was determined to get out of them everything that I could before
I handed them over.

So I merely said: "Oh, I'll take care of myself, Mrs. Cecil," and
made my way upstairs.

In my room I got out the two notebooks and examined them
with some care. Externally, as I have already said, they were identical. They had black covers, made of shiny cloth. And they had about
a hundred pages each, of which only about a half had been used.

As I compared the two books it became increasingly obvious that
one was the clue to the other. This was correct even in some detail,
for, as I compared them page by page, it seemed to me that the pages
corresponded. For instance, the first page in the Broadgate notebook
was headed "H.K." Then there were a series of cryptic squiggles
and signs, with a few dates. The first page of the London notebook
was headed "Henry Kipling, 47 Warrington Road, Tooting." It then
went on to list a series of dates and sums of money. The suggestion
certainly seemed to me to be that this man Kipling had been buying
something from Tilsley, and that the dates and sums of money in
the London notebook gave a list of deals. The money involved was
pretty big, too. Sums of £100 and more were pretty frequent, and
there were one or two cases of £1,000. The dates extended over
about six months, and the total sum of money involved was over
£4,000. If that was really an account of some deals being carried
on, a turnover of over £4,000 for one customer indicated a fairly
big business. And the fact that the accounts were being kept in this
semi-secret way gave a good suggestion that the deals were on the
wrong side of the law.

I made a note of the name and address of Mr. Kipling. Then I
turned to the second page in each book. These provided an exact
repetition of the first, except that the initials in the Broadgate book

were "V.M.", and the name and address in the London were "Victor Mainwairing, 195 Paddington Terrace, Bayswater." The amounts of cash and the dates were, of course, different also, but I noted that the total cash over six months again ran into several thousands of pounds.

There were nearly fifty names and addresses in the book altogether. And in each case the sum of money involved was of the same sort of size. The biggest sum was £9,000, paid by Mr. James Jinks, of Brighton; the lowest was £900, paid by Mrs. Billiams, of Ealing. I reckoned that the turnover of the business, if that was indeed what we were to see in this book, was something like £150,000 in the six months covered. A business with a turnover of £300,000 a year is a pretty big business. And if it was, as we had more than a firm suspicion, an illegal, black-market business, the profits would be high. Here, in fact, was ample reason for the murder. After all, whoever was having anything to do with this affair was playing for pretty high stakes.

I spent some time looking at the two books. I had made a note of the names and addresses, though I realised that this was something that was too big for me. I couldn't afford the time to visit fifty addresses, extending from Brighton and Eastbourne in the south to St. Albans and Watford in the north. This business, whatever it was, had ramifications all over the Home Counties. And Scotland Yard would have to investigate it. The police organisation is so well planned that it can carry out a wide investigation of that sort and take it in its stride, whereas any individual like myself could not possibly undertake such a task.

Still, there were one or two addresses in Broadgate. I marked them down for future work. Curiously enough, the Charrington Hotel was not one of them, nor was Doctor Cyrus Watford, that queer intruder, mentioned.

The mysterious signs and symbols which were in the Broadgate notebook I was unable to understand. I had thought at first that the other book would provide the complete clue to the original one, but I now saw that this was a mistaken idea. No doubt there were some things in this affair so secret that they did not commit them to writing. If Shelley's original idea that this was a black-market petrol business was correct, no doubt those signs referred to gallons and coupons and all the other necessary matters connected with the petrol racket. But, even though I badly wanted to get in with the matter and to study this further, I realised that I really should have no time.

After all, I had probably put myself in wrongly with Shelley already, and the longer I hung on to these notebooks, the less he would think of me in future. So I wrote down the last of the fifty-odd names and addresses, put the notebook in my pocket, and hurried down the stairs.

Broadgate looked very pleasant as I made my way along the street to the police station. It was early in the season, but already gaily-clad holidaymakers were in the streets; on that east coast bathing early in the year is a matter for the more spartan souls only; but there were plenty of people who had been sitting on the sands, enjoying the early summer sunshine. I could not help contrasting their happy-go-lucky mood with the grim affair which was now obsessing my thoughts.

It was, indeed, difficult for me to realise that less than twelve hours ago I had been as happy-go-lucky as the best of them. Now I was so full of the matter of this murder that nothing else had any room in my thoughts. I was like a man who has just learned that he is suffering from some dread disease and is unable to get his thoughts away from his body, observing his symptoms all the time. Just as his disease haunts the unfortunate invalid, so the murder was haunting me.

In a few minutes I was at the police station, and was closeted with Shelley.

"Any news, Jimmy?" he asked.

"Not much," I said.

"Our people got in before you at Thackeray Court, I suppose?" he said with a smile.

"More or less," I agreed.

There was a distinct pause. Shelley presumably thought that his Scotland Yard colleagues had managed to get so well in ahead of me that there was virtually nothing left for me to find at the apartment which had been rented by Tilsley.

I smiled to myself. I knew that I had a bit of a bombshell for the Inspector, and I was more or less holding it in for a moment. Yet I was not altogether sure of myself, for I knew well enough that I had not played fair in not revealing that first little notebook a good deal earlier on. It might have led the Yard's cipher experts somewhere.

"The only worthwhile things," I said, "were these two notebooks."

I fished in my pocket, and slung them across the desk to Shelley. He picked them up, looking first at the one which I had found in Broadgate. He frowned over this for a few moments, then put it down.

The other one startled him. I could see that. He whistled softly to himself as he flipped over its pages. "Where did you get this, Jimmy?" he asked.

"In Tilsley's flat in Thackeray Court," I explained with a grin. This was my moment of real triumph.

"How did our men come to overlook it?" he asked. "This is quite the most important piece of evidence we have come across yet. Unless I am mistaken, this gives us pretty well all the men who may be involved in the racket. Congratulations on having got it, Jimmy, though, for the life of me, I can't think how our men in London overlooked it."

"Perhaps you should employ people who are not altogether illiterate," I said with another grin.

"What do you mean?"

"I mean that it was only because I had a look at Mr. Tilsley's literary effects that I found it. It was, in other words, pushed down the end of the bookcase," I explained.

Shelley smiled. "Well," he said, "there is, perhaps, something to be said in favour of using a literary man in a case of this sort. He may well find things that would otherwise escape attention."

"Thank you for those few kind words," I said.

"But you do realise, Jimmy, the importance of this find?" Shelley asked. "It may well save us weeks of hard work, digging out the names and addresses of the people involved. And, judging by the cash payments made, the sum of money in the business is pretty big, too."

"I make the turnover about £300,000 a year," I said.

"Oh, so you've had a good look at the notebooks?" Shelley grinned.

"What do you expect?" I said.

"Anything which puzzled you?" he enquired.

"I can't make out the mysterious signs and squiggles in the other notebook," I said.

"Some sort of code, I expect," Shelley replied. "I'll turn the whole thing over to our code and cipher experts. They'll dig it all out in a matter of a few hours, I think."

I had my doubts on that point, but probably Shelley knew more about the capabilities of his own experts than I did. Anyhow, I was glad that he had greeted my discoveries with so much satisfaction.

"Have you got hold of anything worth while during my absence?" I asked.

He shook his head. "Nothing publishable, anyhow, Jimmy," he said. "Scotland Yard is a mighty machine, you know, and a fairly slow-moving machine at that. It gets there in the end, as many an over-confident crook has known to his cost. But to get results from a machine of our kind is something that often takes a long time. We can't go on individual hunches and inspirations as a lone wolf like yourself can do."

"Then what would you suggest I should do next?" I asked. I had, somehow, come to take Shelley's advice on these matters.

"I've really got no suggestions for you just now, Jimmy. I should say just nose around and see if you can dig out anything. That old news-hunter's nose of yours is sure to lead you to something worth while before long."

I didn't know if this was altogether a good compliment, but I put on it the best face that I could for the moment. I had, after all, a couple of Broadgate addresses which would bear investigation. To see to them would probably be enough to keep me going for the rest of the day. I did not think that I was in any way bound to share with Shelley exact details of what I was proposing to do. After all, he had advised me to go nosing around and finding out what I could. And if he had any sense he would know that I had made a note of those Broadgate addresses that were in Tilsley's book.

So I bade the detective a strictly temporary farewell, after promising to come and see him again the following morning. I had no very great confidence that I should be able to get hold of anything worth while from the two addresses, but they were at any rate worth trying. And it was only when I was walking down the street from the police station that I remembered that Shelley had not asked me where I had found the original notebook. My little bit of deception had gone unnoticed! I smiled happily. I was still well thought of by Shelley.

CHAPTER XI

In Which a New Witness Appears

I GLANCED AT THE LIST OF ADDRESSES WHICH I HAD NOTED DOWN before handing Tilsley's little books to Shelley. Well, there was something to be said for the fact that I had a chance of making two contacts in Broadgate. I still felt that Broadgate was the real centre of the whole affair, and that it was in this Kentish resort that the solution would eventually be found. This was, of course, a wholly unreasonable feeling, but I have often had an irrational hunch which has, in the end, turned out to be justified, even though it is not, strictly speaking, arguable.

Anyhow, here were the two addresses: "Miss Maya Johnson, 135 Brunswick Terrace, Broadgate; Henry Margerison, 77 Cecile Road, Broadgate."

They were the two people I had to meet; I could not make up my mind which one to look at first. I took a coin out of my pocket. Heads the lady; tails the man. I tossed it, and it came down heads.

Miss Maya Johnson—the name sounded a queer mixture of the exotic and the banal—lived at Brunswick Terrace. I wasn't quite sure where that was, so I asked my landlady.

"It's on the top of the hill, behind the town," she said. "You know, sir, one of those long, rambling terraces that run out towards the North Foreland."

Indeed, I knew them. In the early days of my convalescence in Broadgate I had often walked out that way, never quite succeeding in getting to the white lighthouse that stood on the North Foreland. But I was very conscious of the long, rambling terraces that ran out towards it. So Miss Johnson lived out in that direction, did she? Well, I should have to go and see her.

I climbed up the steep hill that led from the harbour to the terraces where Miss Johnson's home was situated. I was now very clear that this was something that was not easy to deal with. Previously I had been on pretty safe ground in that I was investigating a place that was directly connected with Tilsley. But now I had to feel my way carefully, since I was not aware of what was the connexion between Miss Johnson and the dead man. Still, the connexion did exist, and I had to find out its details.

I glanced at the names of the streets that I was passing through. Mrs. Cecil had not been very clear as to just where it was. I thought myself that it was a considerable distance out towards the North Foreland, and my opinion was soon shown to be true. I walked out some half-mile or so before I saw the name of the terrace I was looking for. Then I spotted it. Good, I told myself; now the great moment was at hand.

I looked for Number 135, and soon saw it. The house was entered by a massive door, decorated by wrought-iron twisted into strange shapes. I walked up the short path that approached the door, and looked at the door itself. The house had obviously been divided into a number of flats, since there were several cards on the door, each bearing a name and each under a bell-push.

Yes; Maya Johnson was one of the names to be seen. I made up my mind that I would put a bold face on it, and let the moments of conversation with Miss Johnson bring their own decisions. To improvise in such a matter might seem to be foolish, but I thought that foolishness might be the better part of wisdom.

I boldly pressed the button which worked the bell connected to Miss Johnson's flat. I must confess that I felt a little nervous, though I hoped that I did not show my feelings too obviously.

The door opened. I drew my breath with surprise, for facing me was one of the most beautiful girls I had ever seen. Her hair was an ash-blonde so fair as to seem almost white; her eyes were the clearest blue, and her skin was that pink-and-white colour so often seen on magazine covers and so rarely met with in real life. She was wearing a long dress of royal blue, relieved by a bow of some white milky material at the neck. I was almost knocked off my feet by her absolute breathtaking beauty. I'm in some ways, I think, a fairly hard-boiled individual—anyone who has got on in the journalistic world has to be so—but I had never seen a girl who created such an impression on me at the first glance.

"Miss Johnson?" I managed to say.

"Yes. And you are…?" She spoke in a quiet, extremely musical voice. I thought that her voice well matched her general appearance.

"My name is London," I said. "I want to have a word with you, if I may, on a rather important matter. It is also rather private. So perhaps…" I paused.

"Come in, Mr. London," she said. She stood aside and I stepped over the doorstep into the house. She then shut the door and led the way to the stairs.

Her flat was on the first floor. The sitting-room was tastefully decorated. It was obviously a woman's room, yet it had not that fussiness of which so many women's rooms may be convicted. In fact, its very quietude seemed to me to be its most satisfactory character.

"Sit down, Mr. London," Maya Johnson said, indicating a comfortable-looking armchair, and seating herself in a chair opposite me.

"Thank you," I said, and sat down where indicated.

"Now," she said, in brisk, businesslike tones, "what can I do for you, Mr. London?"

"It's rather a difficult question," I admitted, wondering just what would be the most satisfactory way of approaching the matter of John Tilsley.

"So it would seem." She smiled and gave vent to what in a less charming woman would have been called a giggle.

"I really want to know if you can tell me anything about a man called Tilsley—John Tilsley," I said, taking the plunge with what was really a sudden decision.

She looked thoughtful. "On what grounds do you ask me such questions, Mr. London?" she asked. "I mean to say, who are you and why do you ask these things?"

"I am a newspaperman," I said. "And I ask you questions because I think that the police will soon be asking them. And I think that you might find it easier or more pleasant to answer me than to answer the police."

She looked serious at this. "The police?" she said, in what was not much more than a whisper. And I thought that her face had become definitely paler, as if the very mention of the police had put some strange fear into her.

"Yes, the police," I said, watching her carefully.

"But why?"

"Because John Tilsley is dead," I said. I knew that this was a brutal way of blurting out the fact, but I did not know what connexion with the crime this woman might have; and to take her by surprise was the only way in which I could manage to get hold of the sort of information that I was after. I had certainly taken her by surprise, all right. Her face now went several shades paler.

"Dead!" she exclaimed in a sort of horrified whisper.

"Yes."

"How did he die?"

"He was murdered," I said, again being purposely brutal.

"Murdered? Oh, why did he do it?"

This was said in a whisper, and I got the sensation of listening to the woman's thoughts. She was probably in no way aware of what she had said, or even that she had said anything aloud. She was merely so horrified at the news that her thoughts were expressing themselves in words, almost without any sort of intention on her part.

"Can you tell me anything, Miss Johnson?" I asked.

She got a grip on herself somehow. "Tell you anything about what?" she asked.

"About Tilsley."

There was a distinct pause, as if she was collecting her thoughts. I was afraid that the moment of shock was over, and that there was now considerably less chance of getting out of her the sort of information that I deemed likely to be useful.

"I know very little about him," she said.

"But you paid him a lot of money," I reminded her. After all, the names of everyone in those little notebooks were connected with large sums of money that had changed hands.

"Me? Oh, no!" This was said with such emphasis and with such open-eyed surprise that I felt, in spite of all my suspicions, that she was telling the truth when she denied having any kind of financial dealings with the dead man.

"But in his accounts he showed considerable dealings with you, Miss Johnson," I pointed out. "Well over a thousand pounds had changed hands within the last six months or so."

"No!" This was even more emphatic than her previous denial. "I have never paid John Tilsley a penny. I can't understand my name appearing in his accounts. I met him socially, but only on one or two occasions. I did not know him at all well."

"Where did you meet him?"

"At a friend's house."

"In Broadgate?"

"Yes."

"Could I have the friend's name? This is rather important, you see," I pointed out. "We are trying to discover what was Tilsley's reasons for coming to Broadgate at all. And it is only by following up all possible connexions here that we can find why he was here."

"You say 'we' are trying to discover things, Mr. London," she said rather sharply. "Could you tell me who 'we' are?"

"Primarily myself and my paper," I said. "But I have friends at police headquarters, and, naturally, if I find anything worth while which I feel may be of value in solving the puzzle of the man's death, I should naturally feel bound to pass that information on to them."

"I see." She seemed again to be digesting this statement, a little puzzled as to what was her wisest response to it.

"Well?" I said, seeing that she now had to be more or less jogged into saying something.

"My friend lives a few doors away from here," she said. "In fact, he keeps that garage at the bottom of the street. He knew Tilsley in connexion with his business. In fact, I gathered that Tilsley was an agent for some firm of manufacturers—either a car firm or a firm making car components or accessories. I never had the facts, nor, in fact, was I very interested in the details. You see, my friend didn't talk to me much about his business. We were friends in a social sense, if you like; we had no business connexions, since I haven't got a car, and never have had one."

This seemed sensible enough. But it still didn't explain one obstinate fact—the fact that in Tilsley's little notebook this woman was down as having paid over a thousand pounds in the past six months.

"What is your friend's name?" I asked again, thinking that there should be nothing now to prevent her giving it, since she had already admitted that he was a garage proprietor not far away.

"Foster," she said. "He is called Timothy Foster, and as I said, he keeps the garage down the street. I am sure that he would be pleased to tell you all that be knows about Tilsley if you go along and see him. Tell him that I sent you, that I suggested you should call on him."

What she was saying seemed to me to be open enough and friendly enough. Indeed, she was to all appearances perfectly frank and co-operative. But something gave me pause. There was something which she was keeping back. I don't know what it was that made me feel this. I sensed somehow that there was a feeling of tension in the girl's mind. Something had happened since I came into this charming room which did not ring quite true. I thought swiftly over the conversation, trying to make up my mind what it was that made me feel suspicious of the girl. Then I suddenly remembered. When I had told her that Tilsley had been murdered, she had said: "Oh, why did he do it?" The point was, you see, that she had clearly thought of someone as the murderer. At least, that was how I interpreted that remark. And it had been, in a sense, forced out of her under a momentary mental shock.

Afterwards, when she had been able to recover her mental balance, she had been perfectly normal and straightforward, as I have said. But in that first moment the truth of her feelings had come out. Nothing that she could say afterwards could altogether efface that.

And who, I asked myself, was the "he" she had referred to, but this man Foster? Who indeed? Perhaps they were due to get married. Perhaps Tilsley had been blackmailing Foster. Perhaps Maya Johnson knew in actuality what were the deals in which Tilsley and Foster had been involved, and thus jumped to the conclusion that Foster was the murderer. Perhaps... All sorts of wild conclusions came into my mind. I knew that there was little that I could do, for the moment, to solve these problems. And in any case I should have to see Foster, and should then have to go back and do a bit of real hard thinking. But that some part of the mystery would be settled out here near the North Foreland I was becoming increasingly certain.

"Do you think that the dealings with Tilsley which your friend had might account for as much as a thousand pounds in about six months?" I asked. I knew that this was only a kind of verbal fencing, but these were questions that I had to ask, even though the answers to them might be in some sense quibbles and evasions.

"I really don't know," Maya Johnson answered, opening her blue eyes widely and innocently.

"You don't know?" I repeated, hoping that I made myself sound at any rate a trifle sceptical.

"No," she said. "You see, Mr. London, as I have already explained to you, I know very little about Mr. Foster's business affairs."

"Do you think it is possible that Mr. Foster might have used your name in some way in connexion with this business?" I went on to ask.

"What do you mean?"

"Well, your name, as I have said, was used. There's no doubt about that. Otherwise I shouldn't be here."

"Yes, I see that."

"It has occurred to me that there may have been some business which your friend Mr. Foster was not too keen to have made public—we all have such things, on occasion—and therefore your name appeared in the deals." I thought that I had done this with some skill.

She at once agreed with my suggestion. "Yes," she said, "that is quite possible. Indeed, I think I remember Tim telling me that he had given my address to some dealer, and telling me that I might get an occasional letter, really meant for him, or addressed to him care of me."

"Did he explain why?" I asked. Some of this story of hers might be lies, but that there was a substratum of truth in it I was very sure.

"It was something to do with income-tax," she said. "After all, most people try to wangle their income-tax a bit if they can, don't they? I imagine that he was doing some deals for cash, and he didn't want any sort of documentary evidence at his garage in case the income-tax people got too curious."

Superficially this might have seemed to be quite a convincing yarn; but I was in no way taken in by it. I knew enough about the ways of the income-tax men to know that they would not search through a man's correspondence providing his books were convincing. And if Timothy Foster was as cunning as his girl friend was suggesting, I thought that he would have very little difficulty in so "cooking" his books as to take in everyone but the most highly skilled. Still, I didn't show my scepticism this time. I let Maya Johnson think that I was fully convinced of the sense of what she was saying.

"And did you receive any letters for Foster here?" I asked.

"One now and then."

"And how many altogether, in the course of the last six months or so, say?" I asked.

"I really don't remember," she said with a shrug of her shoulders. "I don't suppose it's more than a matter of half a dozen altogether."

This was not as convincing as it might have been. I wished that I had kept a note of the dates and amounts which stood opposite Maya Johnson's name in Tilsley's notebook. Still, I supposed that I could consult these in Shelley's office at any time when I wanted to do so. And I knew Shelley would be extremely interested with what I had to tell him, when I got back to the police station. But that lay in the future; for the moment my job was to get hold of all the information that I could and not to be too suspicious. The suspicions could be sorted out later.

"You don't happen to remember any of the dates, I suppose?" I said quietly.

"No; why should I?"

"I thought there might be something which stuck in your mind, as sometimes happens," I explained. "You know, one which came on somebody's birthday—that sort of thing."

"No; the letters just came, and next time I was going down the street I dropped them in to Tim at the garage," she explained.

And that, it seemed, was that. I was not sure if I was any further forward. But at least I had hit on something slightly suspicious.

CHAPTER XII

In Which I Visit a Garage

A S I LEFT MAYA JOHNSON'S FLAT I WONDERED IF IT WOULD BE too late to call at the garage that evening. After all, it was now about half-past six. If Timothy Foster was there, there would be nice time to have a chat with him before I went back to my boarding-house for dinner.

I was relieved to see the lights in the garage. "Foster" shone in red tubular letters above the entrance, and, just inside, a man in dirty overalls was wielding a grease-gun.

"Mr. Foster about?" I asked.

The man jerked his thumb over his shoulder, indicating an inner office. I told myself that I was to some extent in luck, anyway. I only hoped that Foster's girl friend hadn't phoned him up while I was walking around. I didn't want him to be forewarned as to my arrival.

I tapped on the office door. "Come in," growled a deep voice. I shoved the door open and walked in. Seated behind the table was a massive-looking young man. Thick black hair, plastered down with cream, surmounted the large head. His coat hung over the back of the chair. He was sitting in shirt and trousers, and was working over a pile of papers that were on the desk in front of him. He looked up at my entrance, apparently a little taken by surprise.

"Who are you?" he growled.

"My name is London, James London," I said. "And I want a chat with you, if you can spare a few minutes, Mr. Foster." I saw that a businesslike air would pay with this fellow.

"I don't know what you can want with me," he said. I sensed a touch of tension in the air. Foster felt, I was sure, vaguely uncomfortable, and I should like to have known what was worrying him.

"It's with regard to the late John Tilsley," I said, watching him narrowly.

"The late?" That answer, I thought, came just a little too promptly, as if he was more or less prepared for it.

"Yes; didn't you know that he was dead?"

"Hadn't the least idea," Foster said. There was a slight air of bewilderment about the man's face; but at the same time I thought that his denial didn't ring true. I would have been prepared to swear that he had known of Tilsley's death, though he had been taken by surprise by my approach to the matter. Indeed, I think that he had been surprised by the fact that anyone had come to question him about it. The mere fact that he had not asked me what right I had to query him regarding the matter was a strange fact. I know that if anyone came to me and started asking me questions about a friend of mine who had died, I should want to know his credentials before I started to unburden myself. The fact that Foster did not do so was something slightly suspicious—though where that suspicion might be expected to point I was not at this moment prepared to say.

"He was murdered, you know," I said in as matter-of-fact a manner as I could command. And this time, though he winced, I would have been prepared to swear that he was not in any way surprised at the news. Of course, this might not really have been in any way suspicious; it may merely have been an indication of the fact that his girl friend had rung him and told him the news, by way of warning him that I was on the way to see him.

"I wonder if you could tell me anything about the man," I said.

"I shouldn't think so."

"But you had some dealings with him, didn't you?"

"Nothing of any real importance."

This seemed to me to be extraordinarily unconvincing, and I think that I let Foster see that I was in no way impressed by his statement.

"Nothing of any real importance?" I repeated. "Come, my dear Mr. Foster, that won't do."

"What do you mean?" he blustered. "And anyhow, who are you to come asking me questions like this? Do you come from Scotland Yard?"

It was a bit late in the day for him to start to put up this sort of bluff, and again I let him see that I was in no way impressed by what he was saying.

"I'm not from Scotland Yard," I said, "though I have some good friends there."

"Then where do you come from?" he asked.

"I come from Fleet Street," I said.

He grinned sardonically. "A newshound, eh?" he said.

"Precisely," I agreed.

"And what exactly do you want to know? What right have you got to ask me questions about John Tilsley? What can you do if I flatly refuse to answer the questions about him that you ask me?"

There was almost a whine about the man's voice now. I saw that, whatever else I had succeeded in doing, I had managed to put some fear into this man. He was badly scared. I thought that there could be little doubt about that—though I was not at the moment prepared to say what it was that had scared him so.

"I can do nothing," I said, "except tell the police what I have found out already about yourself... and about Miss Maya Johnson."

He almost yelped. "You keep her name out of this," he said. "She knows nothing about what was going on. You've no right to drag her into it."

"But what about the deals in her name, Mr. Foster," I said. "What about the hundreds of pounds which Tilsley had received from her? You see, I have seen Tilsley's account books, and I know that on paper, at any rate, she had been in various business deals with him."

"She never had any business deals with him." This was said in a kind of surly snarl; as soon as I heard that tone come into his voice I was pretty sure that I had Mr. Timothy Foster just where I wanted him. A man who adopts that kind of tone is usually, in my experience, a man who needs only a little careful handling to produce just whatever information one is after.

So I said: "Well, she may have some difficulty in convincing the police of that."

There was a sort of pathetic eagerness in the way in which he now rounded on me. Soon, I told myself, the man would be absolutely eating out of my hand.

"You think that the police will soon be questioning Maya?" he asked.

"I'm sure of it."

"Why?"

"Well, I thought I had already explained that she was featuring pretty prominently in the books kept by our friend Tilsley. And when a man has been involved in some fairly shady deals—deals, mark you, which may have infringed various laws, and which, in some way, lead to his death—the police are naturally enough interested in everyone who has been in any way involved in those details. That, of course, is not to say that everyone eventually comes under suspicion of having anything to do with the man's death; but there is a natural feeling on the part of the police that it is among the man's business associates that the explanation of the man's death is most likely to be found. I hope that you follow what I am trying to say."

I hoped, too, that I had not laid it on too hard and strong. I thought that in some respects I might have done so, but I knew, now, that I had the man in a sense on tenterhooks; and when you are trying to get some information out of a man, and have got him into the right stage of nervousness, there is something to be said in favour of rubbing things in good and hard. It is only thus that the proper use can be made of the nervous condition.

It didn't seem, at any rate, that I had in any way overdone things. Foster just gulped and looked at me with wide open eyes.

"You mean to say," he gasped, "that they may be suspecting Maya Johnson of killing Tilsley?"

"I didn't quite say that," I corrected him. "I merely said that, in common with all the others whose names and addresses have been found in Tilsley's books, she will sooner or later be called in for questioning by the police—that is, unless someone can definitely prove that she really had nothing whatever to do with the man."

"All right," he said, "you win. I'll tell you all I know about the business if you will undertake to keep Maya's name out of this investigation."

"I can't undertake that," I pointed out. "But I can undertake that if she is genuinely innocent I can give my friends at Scotland Yard all the particulars that I know of her innocence. And, knowing them as I do, I don't think that there is much doubt that they will agree to forgo anything more than the most formal of cross-examinations."

He nodded. This, it seemed, satisfied him. I was glad that I had played my hand pretty high. Once or twice I had thought that I was tending to overdo the friend of Scotland Yard stuff; but it had obviously paid in the end.

"And what is it that you've got to tell me?" I asked.

"I think that Tilsley was a crook," he began, and I grinned broadly.

"That's no news," I said. "But what particular sort of crookery do you think that he specialised in?"

"I'm not at all sure."

Again I grinned, but a little more savagely this time. "You had dealings with the man, and you're not sure?" I said with some scepticism. "Come, Foster, you don't really expect me to believe that, do you?"

"The deals I had with him were more or less above board," he explained.

"Yes?" I tried not to sneer.

"Yes. It was a matter of various spare parts and components, things which are in pretty short supply. He told me that he could let me have them at a price—usually a pretty high price. But since I have some customers who are prepared to pay a high price themselves he argued that I should be able to make money out of them. The real trouble is that the makers have standard prices for all spares, and they take a poor view of anyone who sells above those prices. It is a sort of black market; it doesn't break any laws except the unwritten laws of the motor industry. But if the makers knew that I was doing that sort of thing they would probably close down my sources of supply. And that would put me in a jam."

"Is that why you had Tilsley send his letters to you care of Miss Johnson?" I asked.

"Yes."

"Nothing illegal—in the sense of breaking the law of the land—was going on?"

"Nothing."

I must admit that this was a bit of a facer for me. I had been so sure that something to do with a black market had been going on, involving some sort of infringement of the raw material controls, that this revelation that it was only an infringement of the rules set up by the motor industry staggered me. Of course, there was a definite possibility that Foster was lying. But, as I have already indicated, I have a fair knowledge of human nature. I've mixed with most types in my time. And when a man is telling lies I usually have a pretty good idea of the fact.

And I was sure that Foster was telling what, at any rate, he believed to be the truth.

"You see," he said, as if he could read the thoughts that were running round my head, "other people in the industry might feel that I was doing them down. Especially in view of the fact that the prices I had to charge were very high. Tilsley never sold anything at less than about ten times the official market price for any of the spares."

I whistled gently. "That's a bit steep, isn't it?" I said.

"Yes, but if your car is out of action because of a broken part that should cost a pound, you'd probably rather pay ten pounds than have the car laid up for six months," he said. I had to admit the justice of this.

"And that is all that you knew of John Tilsley?" I said.

"Absolutely all."

"You knew nothing of any business which he might be doing outside this racket in spare parts for cars?"

"None at all."

And this time again I was prepared to bet that the man was telling the truth. But it was a real staggering revelation. I wondered what Shelley would have to say about it.

"Where did you meet Tilsley originally?" I asked.

"In here."

"In this garage, you mean?"

"Yes."

"Did he just come and offer you the spare parts?"

"Oh, no. He brought his car in for repair. Something quite small had gone wrong—he'd broken some little bolt somewhere. I told him that it would take a week or two, as the makers wouldn't supply such parts under three months, and I should have to have the thing specially made."

"And what then?" I asked.

"He told me that he could lay his hands on various parts, but only if they were ordered in advance, and only if I was prepared to pay a pretty high price for them. He couldn't guarantee to supply anything and everything; but most spares for most of the more popular makes he thought he could do."

"And has he done so?"

"Oh, yes. What happens, you see, a customer comes in here with or without his car. He will point out that something is broken, or will let me have a look at the car to find it out for myself. Then I have to tell him that it is out of stock, get in touch with Tilsley in London, and in a couple of days it will be delivered here. He's let me down from time to time, but as a rule it's perfectly reliable. The only annoying thing is that the times he's let me down almost always turn out to be an old and valued customer."

I grinned. "It always turns out that way," I said. "But you did say, Foster, that you thought the man was a crook. There may be something slightly unethical about this story that you have told me today, but there is nothing really crooked about it, is there? I mean to say, there is nothing which is a direct breaking of the law."

He paused and smiled sourly. "Well, no," he said. "But, you see, I always keep asking myself: where did Tilsley get all these spares? They're not so easy to come by in these days, you know. Especially when they come from some popular car of twelve years or so back—a car of the age which is always tending to break down in one way or another."

"And what is your answer to that pretty little riddle?" I asked.

"I think the spares are stolen," he said. "In other words, your friends at Scotland Yard might find themselves holding me as a receiver of stolen goods. Mind you, I never had any sort of definite proof that they were stolen; if I had I wouldn't have gone on dealing with the man. That sort of game is too dangerous to keep up for long. But I think in my own mind that he has got a gang of confederates in a lot of the car factories, salting away spare parts. Then he has a store of some sort in London, and he's probably supplying a lot of small garages like mine with the stuff their customers want."

"It's possible," I had to admit.

"It's only a suspicion of mine," he said, "but I think that there's a lot to be said in favour of it. And if he has been doing that, well, some of us might be for it. That's why I was a bit scared, I don't mind admitting, when you came in."

And that was all that I could learn from him. I was not altogether convinced by his argument. But at the same time I was pretty well as sure as I could be of anything in this case that Foster himself believed in the argument which he had been putting forward.

CHAPTER XIII

In Which We Compare Notes

A S I LEFT FOSTER'S GARAGE I SUDDENLY FOUND THAT I WAS hungry. This was not really surprising, as I had had little to eat all day—nothing, indeed, since a fairly inadequate lunch on the train. And it was now about the time that Mrs. Cecil in my digs would be serving dinner. Still, before I did anything to satisfy my hunger I should have to get in touch with my paper. They would expect something good and strong for the last edition, I thought. So I hunted out the nearest phone box and sent off my report. I said nothing, of course, about my latest investigations; but I gave them a good deal about Tilsley, described in discreet terms the Charrington Hotel, where he had been living at Broadgate, and provided his London address—though without giving any suggestion that I had already visited Thackeray Court. My job, after all, was to spin my material out so that I was able to give them sufficiently sensational stuff each day to ensure front-page importance.

When I had finished my dictation over the telephone I felt fairly well satisfied with what I had done. I was sure that Mick, my editor, would not be regretting having made me his special correspondent.

So it was with a happy mind that I went in to my dinner. It was a dull meal. Stew, made of some unidentifiable meat, with potatoes and washy cabbage, followed by a steamed pudding that originally set out to be a marmalade pudding and finished, I thought, half marmalade and half syrup. Still, I was hungry enough to enjoy anything, and I had no difficulty in disposing of the fairly liberal helpings which Mrs. Cecil dished up for me.

"I hope that your job is going well, Mr. London," she said, during a quiet interval.

"Quite well, thank you," I said politely, mentally cursing the woman for bringing the matter of my job to the attention of my fellow-guests. While I was staying at this boarding-house I had taken little notice of the other people there. To begin with I had been too intent on recovering my health, and later on I seemed to develop so many other interests in the place that my fellow-guests did not interest me at all. And now that I was in the throes of this murder investigation I was in no way inclined to spend any of my energy in making myself polite to a crowd of nit-wits.

Fortunately, however, Mrs. Cecil's enquiry seemed to pass unnoticed. No one made any comment on it. I finished my dinner as soon as I could, hastily drank down a cup of not very good coffee, and hurried out. I thought that it was high time that I told Shelley what I was doing. Besides, he might by this time have some information that would be of use to me.

I washed, put on a clean collar, and then made my way round to the police station. The walk up to the station was by this time a pretty familiar route to me. A sergeant whom I had not seen before was seated at the desk in the outer office of the police station.

"Yes?" he said in an unpleasant growl as I entered.

"I want to see Inspector Shelley," I announced.

"Why?" This was another growl.

"Because I have some information for him. Will you tell him that Mr. London is here?" I fairly snapped this out. I was annoyed to think that this jack-in-office of a sergeant was more or less keeping me away from the one man in the world who seemed likely to be of value to me—and at the time when I had some information to give him, too.

With a grumble the sergeant climbed down from his chair and made his way into the inner office. When he came out he held open the door into the inner office, and gestured me to come in there. It was clear that he did not altogether approve of a man from outside the magic ranks of the police force being on apparently familiar terms with one of the high and mighty from Scotland Yard. Still, since I had no doubt that Shelley had dealt with him fairly sharply, there was nothing that he could do about it save take me in.

"Good man, Jimmy!" Shelley exclaimed as I entered. "I hope that you've got something for me. I've been wondering all evening how you were getting on."

"Well, I've done a fairly useful piece of work this evening, I think," I told him.

"Good! And where have you been?"

"I've been investigating a garage out on the North Foreland road," I said.

"H'm?" Shelley's eyebrows rose alarmingly. This, it seemed, was not what he had anticipated hearing.

"It is kept by a man called Foster," I explained.

"Foster? Foster? That name hasn't cropped up in this case previously, has it? I can't say that it is in any way familiar, anyhow," said Shelley with a rather puzzled frown on his expressive face.

"No; he's a new one. But he's engaged, I think, to Maya Johnson," I said.

Shelley pulled the little black notebook towards him. It had been lying on the desk before him. He rapidly flipped over its pages, and the frown cleared from his forehead.

"So you made a note of these addresses, Jimmy?" he murmured. "You're a bad lad, but I suppose that I should have expected it, after all."

"I didn't think it would do any harm," I said. I was, above all, anxious to keep well in with Shelley.

"I don't suppose that it has done any harm," the detective agreed readily enough. "But anyhow, tell me, Jimmy; what have you found out about Miss Johnson and Mr. Foster?"

I gave him a quick account of what I had discovered out by the North Foreland. Shelley listened with the closest attention, now and then nodding, as if he approved of what I had done, and now and then pursing up his lips, as if he was not at all sure that my actions had been all that they might have been.

When I finished he grinned. "I think that you've done pretty well on the whole, Jimmy," he said. "There were many things that you have found which would only have been found by our people in a day or two's time. And time gained in a case like this is always something very well worth while. But now what I want to know is something which you have been very careful not to commit your-self about."

"And what's that?" I asked, though, in actuality, I was moderately certain what he was going to say.

"What do you really think of these people? Do you think that Maya Johnson is really as innocent of all knowledge of the affair as she makes out? Do you think that Foster was merely a dealer, buying things from Tilsley which were dearer than the price set by the manufacturers? Or was all this merely a screen behind which was hidden some darker deal? I know that what you say on those points will be only surmise, but you're a pretty shrewd judge of character, Jimmy, and I think that you will know a lot about these people. What do you really think about them? That's what I want to know. You will be talking off the record, as they say, and I want your really candid opinion. That is what I shan't get from any of my people whom I might send around to interview them."

I paused. This was in some ways rather a tall order, though it was the sort of query that might well come from an editor if I had interviewed some people in the course of my job as a journalist.

Then I said: "I think that Maya Johnson is genuine. I think that she is innocent of anything connected with the crime, or with any crooked business that has been going on. That is my impression anyhow. But there is one thing about her that I fail to understand."

"What's that?" Shelley fairly pounced on my admission, which I think had more or less taken him by surprise.

"That is that she is scared. She suspects someone of the murder."

Shelley looked interested. "Who do you think she suspects?" he asked.

"Who but Foster?" I asked in return.

"You think that because of her remark when you told her about Tilsley's death," Shelley remarked.

"Yes. She said: 'Oh, why did he do it?'" said I. "And who could 'he' be but Foster? After all, if I'm any sort of judge, that couple are deeply in love. They are, I think, planning to get married. They didn't tell me so in so many words, but one or two remarks suggested it. And if she thinks that Foster killed Tilsley she is naturally scared stiff for him. But why? Why does she think that he is a murderer if she really knows nothing of what was going on? And yet I got the impression that when she said Tilsley was a dealer of some sort whom she had merely met in a social way, and that she knew nothing about the details of his business, she was telling the truth. That's what rather puzzled me."

"I see that," Shelley said. "And what did you make of Mr. Foster? Did you think that he was everything that he appeared to be on the surface?"

"I'm not so sure of him," I admitted. "I thought that his explanation of the dealings which he had had with Tilsley sounded a bit thin here and there. And if he was merely improvising, making up some sort of explanation on the spur of the moment, it would not have been easy to get hold of something which would hold water."

Shelley looked tolerably impressed at what I had said. "I'm not disappointed in you, Jimmy," he said. "I thought that you would give me a pretty shrewd summary of these people—and, by Jove, you've done it. I seem to know those two folk as well as if I'd met 'em."

I smiled. "Glad to be of some use to you, Inspector," I grinned. "And now, what sort of information have you got for me?"

He looked thoughtful. "Well, this is definitely not for publication, Jimmy," he said, "but I have the feeling, from the information that is slowly trickling in, that there is something behind this even bigger than the black-market petrol racket which we originally thought provided the motive for the crime. That some illegal dealings in petrol have been going on, and that this man Tilsley had something to do with it, seems to be pretty certain; but I think that there was something bigger still which he was involved in."

"And what is it?" I asked.

"That I don't know as yet," Shelley admitted. "After all, we have only been looking into the crime for about a day or so. But we are getting reports on all the people whose names and addresses appear in these notebooks—and, taken all in all, they're a fairly shady lot. Some of them have been involved in fencing—dealing in stolen goods—one or two have been suspected of drug-smuggling, and others have been thought to be responsible for all sorts of other troubles. Not one, I might say, has been convicted. But the suspicions of the police, in matters of that sort, are not usually without foundation, even though there is not enough evidence to get a conviction. I'm collecting the evidence now." He indicated the mass of papers that lay on the desk before him.

"As I've said before, Jimmy, my lad, Scotland Yard is really a vast machine. It is only on rare occasions that a detective can, so to speak, play a lone hand. The man like myself, in charge of the case, has to assemble information from all sorts of sources, and try to tie it together into a coherent whole. Or, if you like, he has to put together the pieces of jigsaw puzzle, and decide what the final picture is like."

I had previously heard Shelley philosophising in this manner, and had at first thought it interesting. Now, however, I knew that it was often his way of side-stepping a question he was rather anxious to avoid, and I wondered just what it was that he did not much want to tell me.

"Any connexion with the people we know in Broadgate?" I asked.

"Not with Miss Johnson and Mr. Foster," Shelley said. "As a matter of fact, Jimmy, it never occurred to me that you might be going to see them. I was keeping Miss Johnson to myself, and I was going to go round and see her tomorrow morning. Now, I suppose, though I shall still have to do that, I shan't get anything new from her—after all, you've got all the information that is available from there."

"And what about that mysterious figure, Dr. Cyrus Watford?" I asked.

Shelley, for the first time during our chat, looked annoyed. "He's the one unsatisfactory figure in the whole case," the detective admitted.

"Why?" I asked.

"Well, he has just completely disappeared. Of course, Cyrus Watford is probably not his real name, but I've not been able to trace the man at all. He must be in some way tied up with this murder, and I want to know why and how."

"What makes you think that he must be tied up with the murder in some way?" I asked.

"Well, if he was innocent, he would come forward. After all, he was the first—or nearly the first—on the scene. His actions were tolerably suspicious, anyhow. And then to slip away in the way he did—well, I don't think much of the way it worked out, anyhow. In fact, he's the one man that I want to have a chat with. I'm pretty sure that he'd be able to tell us something worth while."

There was no doubt that Shelley was more than a little annoyed at the complete disappearance of Watford. But I didn't think there was much that I could do about that, unless I so happened to time my walks that I met the man in the street or on the promenade.

"Nothing more at the moment then, Inspector?" I said.

"Nothing, I'm afraid. There may be something more tomorrow, when I've had a chance to go through all this material," he said, indicating the pile of papers on the desk in front of him. "But, meanwhile, the best thing that you can do, Jimmy, is to go to the pictures and then go home and sleep the sleep of the just for about ten hours. Then you'll be fit for all the problems that'll no doubt be facing you tomorrow."

I grinned. Then I thought that I would take his advice, but with one difference. I called at the Royal George, that fine old hostelry, and had a pint of their very delicious bitter before I went to bed.

CHAPTER XIV

In Which Everything Happens Again

WHEN I WOKE THE NEXT MORNING THE JUNE SUNSHINE WAS flooding into my bedroom. I stretched lazily in my bed. Everything seemed to be well with my world. I thought that it was good to be alive, at the seaside, in an English June.

Then I remembered, suddenly, that I was a newspaperman, given the job of investigating a highly unpleasant murder. Even the sunshine seemed to lose some of its tonic quality. I got up, had a hasty bath, shaved, and dressed. I wandered downstairs, glanced at the clock in the hall, and cursed as I saw it was a quarter of an hour short of nine. That meant that I shouldn't be able to do anything in the way of breakfast for at least twenty minutes. Mrs. Cecil served breakfast officially at nine o'clock, but it was invariably five to ten minutes late.

I might as well go for a stroll in the sunshine, I told myself. The newsagent at the other end of the promenade opened at half-past eight, and I could get a copy of *The Daily Wire,* and see what sort of a show Mick was giving me. Since I was being paid space rates, the amount of my stuff that had escaped the attention of the subs was what would determine my pay for the week.

And he had done me well. There was a flaming headline on the front page, with a personal note about me, stating that James London, well known as a criminologist, would be reporting the crime. The murder they described as the most mysterious affair since Jack the

Ripper—which seemed to me to be pulling it a bit strong. Personally, I could think of several in recent years that might be in the running for the mystery stakes. Still, who was I to grumble? The thing gave me a good build-up, and enabled me to get well and truly back on the map. I sat down on a seat on the promenade and read the stuff through. As far as I could remember, they had used pretty well everything that I had phoned through. Probably Mick's orders were that they should use as much as possible of what I was sending; and thankful I was that they were doing it.

Then I heard a sudden shout from behind me. I wheeled round and looked in the direction from which the shout had come. I had been so interested in the paper that I had not really noticed just where it was that I had sat down. I now saw that I was just opposite the lift. And for a moment I had a nightmare feeling that, by some magical art, I had been transported back twenty-four hours in time.

From the little path that led to the lift a man was staggering along. It was the ginger-haired lift attendant whom I had seen on the previous morning. And Aloysius Bender was pale as death. It was obvious, as on the day before, that he had suffered a pretty considerable shock. He staggered over to me, and a gleam of recognition came into his bloodshot eyes.

"Oh, it's you!" he gasped, rather obviously.

"It's me, brother," I said. "But what on earth's the matter with you?"

"It's happened again!" he said.

"What has?"

"There's another dead man in my lift!"

"What?" I fairly yelled. This certainly seemed to justify the headlines in *The Daily Wire*. "Another? Who is it?"

"I don't know. Never saw him before." Bender seemed to be recovering his poise now. I suppose that even the discovery of corpses is something which may become more or less normal if it happens often enough.

"Were you going to open up?" I asked.

"Yes. The police gave me the keys back last night, and said that they had done all that they wanted to do with the lift, and I could restart and run as usual today. And now this has to happen!"

I got to my feet. Once again I was in at the start of the case. But this time, I thought, I should have to get Shelley.

"You know the police station?" I asked, rather obviously.

"Yes."

"Go there, and ask for Inspector Shelley. Tell him that I sent you. Say that there has been another murder, and get him to come along here without delay. That'll be easy, anyhow. Once he knows what has happened, you won't be able to keep him away," I said.

"I'll go," he said, and made his limping way off.

"Just a minute," I murmured.

"Yes?"

"Did you lock the lift up again?"

"Yes."

"Good."

I think that the next ten minutes were the longest ten minutes I ever spent in my life. I re-read my story in the paper time after time. I even descended to reading the advertisements, but scarcely took in what I was reading. All the time I had my eyes fixed on the end of the street down which I knew Bender and Shelley would come. I suppose that had I been unscrupulous enough I could have taken the keys off Bender and had the chance of examining the dead body before the arrival of Shelley, but I thought that the man from the

Yard would probably take a poor view of it if I tried again to get in ahead of him. And it was now getting doubly important that I should keep on the right side of Detective-Inspector Shelley.

After all, I was now in a specially privileged position, and since the second murder made it sure that this was to be one of the greatest criminal cases of the century, I thought that it was as well that I should firmly establish myself as the expert writer on it. Mick would be pluming himself on having on the spot the man with inside knowledge. And when the case was over, I should more or less be able to pick my job on Fleet Street.

In spite of these thoughts—pleasant thoughts, most of them— which went through my mind, I found the waiting a difficult business. But I knew that Shelley would be on the spot in the fastest possible time. And I was a good enough friend of the detective to be certain that he would be in the police station by nine o'clock in the morning. He had, indeed, probably been there since eight.

Now I saw him coming, and I rose to my feet, my heart thumping in my chest. Not for the first time in this case I felt an almost unsupportable sense of excitement.

"Hullo, Jimmy." Shelley was calm and quiet as he approached.

"Good morning, Inspector," I replied. I hoped that I did not show the overwhelming excitement which was possessing me.

"You seem to be in on the violent deaths in Kent, don't you, Jimmy?" Shelley said with a savage sort of grin. I had to admit that it seemed as if I was one of the born witnesses in a case of this sort. But I didn't think that there was any sort of *double entendre* in what Shelley was saying. Indeed, I was pretty sure that he was merely saying something which would give him a chance of talking, while he gave all his attention to the matter in hand—that is, a second murder, which must have come to him as a pretty severe shock.

"Can I have your keys, Mr. Bender?" he asked of our red-headed friend. Without a word, Bender produced the keys and handed them over.

Shelley walked slowly and steadily towards the lift. No sort of excitement was visible in his manner. I thought that I had seldom seen a man so completely master of his environment.

The detective looked carefully at the padlock. "When you opened it this morning, Mr. Bender," he remarked, "there was no sign that it had been in any way tampered with?"

"No sign at all, sir," said Bender in a trembling voice. I thought that the liftman was still suffering from shock as a result of what he had gone through.

Shelley inserted the key in the lock, and soon removed the padlock from the staples in which it was inserted. Then he swung back the gates.

I peered over his shoulder. I was to some extent prepared for the sight which met my eyes. The body of a tall, massive man was lying inside. A knife, similar to that which had been used to kill Tilsley stuck out of his back in almost the same position as that which I had seen in the previous case. I could not see the man's face, for he had clearly pitched forward as he had been stabbed.

Shelley stepped inside in a meticulously careful fashion.

"Come in, Jimmy," he said. "But be careful where you step. There is a lot of blood in here, and I don't want us to mess it up with our footprints. There may be some clues here for the footprint experts, if we manage to keep clear of the blood ourselves."

I was only too pleased to follow the man from Scotland Yard. This was getting exclusive news with a vengeance! I looked at the prone figure that lay there. The murderer's victim was a man, I thought, of middle-age. His hair was greying around the temples, and his figure was that of a man in his 'fifties. A gold watch-chain, with its watch attached, had fallen out of his waistcoat pocket as he had been struck down, and it lay across the floor of the lift. Obviously robbery was no motive in this crime.

Shelley bent down and deftly removed the fat wallet from the dead man's hip-pocket. He opened it. It contained what, at a glance, I should have estimated as being more than fifty pounds in pound notes. Again, no sign of robbery. I said as much to the Inspector.

"No, Jimmy, robbery had nothing to do with these crimes," he agreed.

"Any sign of the man's identity?" I asked. Shelley was now turning out the contents of the wallet.

"That's just what I'm trying to find out," the detective said slowly, as he turned out various papers from the wallet.

Then he looked up at me. "Does the name Margerison, Henry Margerison, convey anything to you, Jimmy?" he asked.

"It strikes a chord somewhere," I said.

Shelley grinned. "Your memory is o.k., is it?" he asked.

"Yes," I said.

"Well you remember the people whose names were included in the little notebook that belonged to Tilsley?" he said.

"Yes."

"There was one Broadgate address—Miss Maya Johnson's, you know," Shelley murmured.

"I know," I interrupted him, "and the other was Henry Margerison."

"Quite right," Shelley said. "Well, we shan't get any information from Mr. Margerison, I fear. I don't know what his connexion with the first murder may have been, but to my mind it is quite clear that there was some direct connexion. That must account for his death."

While he was saying this, Shelley was still running through the papers in Margerison's wallet.

"There you are, Jimmy," he said after a few minutes. He held out a piece of paper. It was a receipt, and recorded the payment by Margerison to Tilsley of the sum of a hundred pounds. Here, at any rate, was confirmation that the two men were connected.

"In the racket, you think?" I said, but Shelley gave me a warning glance, with a side-glance at Bender. He obviously thought it a trifle indiscreet to talk in front of the liftman, though I thought that Bender hadn't enough commonsense to be in any way dangerous. Still, I knew that Beech, the local man with whom Shelley was presumably working in this case, would very much disapprove of any outsider knowing about anything, just as, in fact, I was aware that he strongly disapproved of my getting in on the case. And, while Beech was not present at the moment, no doubt he would be told the truth of what went on, even in his absence—that is one of the troubles about living and working in a small place.

And now Doctor Gordon appeared, that lean Scot, who seemed somehow to thrive on murder and sudden death. Police surgeons seem, in fact, to be a race to themselves.

"I don't think I'll use this lift any more, Inspector," he said with a sardonic grin. "Unhealthy sort of thing, judging by its recent customers."

Shelley smiled. "Have a look at him and give us a rapid verdict, if you can, Doctor," he said.

"Speed, that's all you policemen think about nowadays," the Doctor retorted. "How you expect a man of science to do his work soundly, I don't know. Anyhow, what do you want me to tell you that you don't know already?"

"How the man died, when he died, and where he died," said Shelley. "That'll be enough to begin with."

The Doctor snorted. I had already realised that he was not exactly an easy man to get on with. He was obviously a man of very strong opinions, and he was not prepared to compromise in any way.

"Where he died is something for a detective to settle, not a Doctor," he said. "In fact, it's your pigeon, as they say in the civil service. As to how he died, well yon knife sticking out o' the poor fellow's back should be good enough as a cause of death. And as to when he died, well I gave ye a good lecture on *rigor mortis* and the tricks it plays yesterday. I'll no commit myself to anything very close, I warn you of that."

Shelley smiled. He had had enough experience of crusty old Scots not to let Gordon put him off his stride.

"Give us an estimate, Doctor," he pleaded.

The doctor had been examining the body meanwhile, flexing muscles and bending arms and legs.

"I'll say about the same thing as I said about the other body I saw yesterday morning," Doctor Gordon replied. "Between seven o'clock and midnight. That's as close as I could get to it; and even there I'm maybe being a bit more exact than I should be. Maybe the margins should be extended a wee bit."

Shelley made a grimace of distaste. "Can't you get it any closer, Doctor?" he asked.

The doctor shook his head emphatically. "No," he said. "It's a very tricky business, settling the time of death, and I'll no do anything which hasn't strict scientific sanction."

I could see that Shelley was irritated; but there was indeed nothing that he could do about it save accept the doctor's word on the matter. It would, he knew, be no use at all to try to force the doctor to a decision in which he did not believe. And that is what it would have amounted to had he tried to pin the man down any more accurately.

"Well, that would appear to be that, then, Doctor," Shelley said.

"That's so." The doctor's mouth closed with a decisive snap.

"The ambulance will be here shortly, I expect," said Shelley. "We shall want a post-mortem done, of course, though I don't anticipate that you'll find anything of any importance at it. That knife-wound is only too obvious as the cause of death, and I don't expect that you'll find the man was drowned or poisoned."

With a final snort the doctor left us, and Shelley stood silent for a moment, gazing down at the recumbent body.

"Do you know, Jimmy," he said at length, "I've just thought of something a little odd."

"What's that?" I asked.

"We've been concerned with Mr. Margerison for about an hour now; but we haven't even seen his face. It is, after all, possible that he is someone who is known to the police in some way. I might even know the man myself—you never can tell."

"That's so," I agreed, though I did not think it at all likely that there would be any truth in Shelley's suggestions. It was, to my mind, only too obvious that this man Margerison was one of Tilsley's gang; and Shelley himself had said that they were known to the police only as people of ill repute—not as people who had been found guilty of anything.

Still, I knew that if Shelley had an idea in his head nothing would get it out. So I helped him to turn the body over, so that we could get a view of the face.

"Inspector!" I gasped, when we had succeeded in doing this.

"What is it, Jimmy?" He could see that I had received a real shock.

"I believe you knew!"

"I knew what?"

I pointed at the face of the dead man. "That Henry Margerison," I said slowly, "was the man whom I had met as Cyrus Watford!"

CHAPTER XV

In Which Surprises Follow

THIS WAS A BIT OF A FACER, I MUST ADMIT. I HAD ANTICIPATED that I should meet Cyrus Watford some time again, but had never for a moment thought that he might turn out to be the second victim of the murderer. I had not, for that matter, even thought that there might be a second victim.

Shelley, I now realised, as soon as I had got over my initial surprise, was questioning Bender.

"Have you ever seen this man before, Bender?" he asked, indicating the body.

"Never, sir."

"Sure of that?"

"Absolutely sure, sir. Never saw him in my life before."

I for one was prepared to believe that the red-headed man was telling the truth. There was an air of earnestness about his denial which made it, at any rate for me, completely convincing. Shelley's impassive countenance gave no indication of whether he believed the man or not, but I was inclined to think that he did.

"Have you ever heard the names of Cyrus Watford or Henry Margerison?" Shelley next asked.

"No, sir." The man shook his head in helpless fashion, and I could see that Shelley was getting more than a little impatient at the way in which the fellow was proving useless as a source of information.

This, I thought, was a little unfair to Bender, as he could not well claim access to information which was not really in his possession.

"This is a pretty kettle of fish, Jimmy," Shelley said rather mournfully.

"This took you by surprise, eh?" I said.

"Yes, I don't mind admitting that it did," Shelley said. "Of course, in a murder case there is always the possibility that the criminal will think he cannot put himself in any more peril by committing a second murder; but somehow I didn't think that this was the sort of crime likely to lead to a second one. It seemed to me to be so obviously a crime committed for a specific purpose—even though as yet we don't know with any certainty what that purpose was."

"Still, the second murder may stem directly from the first one," I said.

"Almost certainly," Shelley agreed. "Probably our friend Watford or Margerison, whatever his name is, knew a little too much about the first crime. And as a result he had to be bumped off. I've no doubt that will be the verdict when we know a bit more than we do now. But meanwhile we have to have a look at Margerison's home life. Coming, Jimmy?"

Naturally, I didn't need a second invitation. I really was amazingly lucky to have got so well in with Shelley. Rarely can a newspaper man have been so well connected in a murder case under investigation. I didn't, however, remember Margerison's address, though I had it in my notes at the digs. For once my memory let me down. Shelley, of course, remembered it.

"Where is Cecile Road?" the detective asked.

"Don't know," I replied. "Do you, Bender?"

"One of the new residential roads, to the south of the town," Bender said. "Out on the opposite side to the North Foreland Road."

"Far away?" asked Shelley.

"No. You'd walk there in a quarter of an hour or so," said the liftman.

"Good. We'll walk." Leaving in charge of the lift a constable who had arrived unobtrusively, and giving him full instructions of what to do when the ambulance arrived, Shelley led the way.

"I've got your address, Bender, haven't I?" he said.

"Yes, sir."

"Well, there'll probably be further questions to ask of you later on," Shelley remarked. I thought that Bender winced, as if he did not look forward with any eagerness to the new bout of questioning. Still he said nothing, but took his dismissal with comparative scepticism.

I always remember that walk out to Cecile Road as one of the few pleasant interludes in what was becoming almost a nightmare adventure. The sun was mounting in the sky; the sea stretched below us, blue and clear; the white-flecked waves shimmered in the sun. Out on the horizon a steamship moved lazily along, its smoke trailing behind it.

But this was only an interlude. Soon my mind was to be recalled to the matter on hand. Cecile Road was a long and straggling thoroughfare, lined on either side with sizable houses of the modern villa type. It was clearly a place which had grown up after the first world war. The houses were pleasant enough places, and I could envisage their inhabitants as living somewhat self-centred lives, their whole interests concentrated on their gardens and their golf. Yet somehow tragedy had struck incongruously in this pleasant street. There is, I always think, something a trifle odd when a murder occurs among ordinary people. We are accustomed to murder in high places. When a Mussolini or a Gandhi dies it seems to be such a mighty tragedy that it appears almost ordinary—or, at any rate, something which might be anticipated. It is when tragedy appears in the lives of people more or less ordinary in their everyday attitude that it seems queer and incongruous.

Still, there was No 77 Cecile Road. It was a house just like the others in the road. Its front garden looked attractive enough. There was a small lawn, surrounded with a border in which white carnations rioted. Tall lupins stood at the back, and various other flowers—purple, blue and red—which I did not know were interspersed between those which I recognised.

Shelley did not seem to be noticing these horticultural details. He was, however, studying the house. Then he came towards me: "Remember, Jimmy, you have no official standing. So keep quiet and just listen. Let me do all the talking here," he said in what was not much more than a whisper.

I nodded. I was too conscious of my luck in being here at all to want to butt in on what I knew was Shelley's job of cross-examination of whoever might be found in the house.

The detective strode up the concrete path that led from the little wooden gate to the front door. On the doorstep he hesitated for a moment, and then pressed firmly the bell-push in the middle of the door.

There was a breathless pause. Again I was conscious of the underlying drama of the case. Then the door opened, and a rather nervous looking little maid, her hair unkempt and her apron awry, peered out at us.

"Good morning," said Shelley politely. I was interested to study his technique in this situation—one in which I had never previously observed him in.

"Good morning, sir," she said, with an odd little bob of a bow.

"Is Mr. Margerison in?" Shelley asked.

"Will you please wait a moment? I'll find out," the maid said, and disappeared into the interior of the house.

Then we had another wait. I thought that the life of a detective was not unlike that of a soldier in wartime—sudden spurts of activity, interspersed with long periods of comparative boredom. Still, soon the maid came back.

"Will you come in, sir?" she said. "Mr. Montrose will see you."

We had no time to ask ourselves who on earth Mr. Montrose might be. We were ushered into a pleasant little sitting-room, where we were left by the maid.

"Mr. Montrose will be with you very soon, sir, if you'll kindly wait here," she said.

She went out, shutting the door quietly behind her. Shelley and I looked at each other with a mutual grin. This was, somehow, a completely unexpected reception. We had anticipated a weeping widow or even a cheerful son; but to meet with a maid and a man whose name, even, we had never previously heard was so completely against all our anticipations that I think we were absolutely taken by surprise.

In a few moments, however, before we had time to overcome our first surprise, the door opened again. There entered a tall, distinguished-looking man, with glasses and a moustache in what used to be called the military style. He held out his hand.

"I'm afraid I don't know you gentlemen," he said. "But we must introduce ourselves. My name is Montrose, and my friend Margerison, for whom you are asking, lives here with me. He is, however, out at the moment, and I thought that perhaps I could do something to help, since we have been involved in various business deals together, and I presume that it is some business matter that you have come here about."

This was all said in a friendly tone, and Shelley took the out-stretched hand.

"My name is Shelley," the detective said, "and this is my friend Mr. London."

Montrose solemnly shook us both by the hand. "I am pleased to make your acquaintance, gentlemen," he said. "And now, perhaps, you will be so kind as to let me know what I can do for you."

"Can you tell us when you last saw Mr. Margerison?" Shelley asked, and I could see that the detective was aware that this was rather a ticklish situation, which had to be handled with some care.

Montrose thought carefully. Then he said: "Well, I saw him at tea yesterday. I didn't see him at dinner, since I was dining out myself last night. I came home late, and went straight to bed, so I didn't see him then. Yes; teatime yesterday was the last time I saw him—say, five o'clock. But what is the meaning of this question? I trust that nothing untoward has happened to Margerison?" The rather precise, old-fashioned diction suited the general appearance and attitude of Montrose.

"I'm afraid I have rather a shock for you, Mr. Montrose," Shelley said slowly.

"Yes?"

"Yes."

"Well, go on, man! I'm not a child; I have enough willpower, I hope, to be able to stand whatever it is that you have to say to me."

"I'll ask one more question first, if I may," said Shelley.

"Go on."

"In your business deals with Margerison did you ever come across a man called Tilsley?"

"Yes."

"You know that Tilsley was murdered yesterday?"

"I saw something about it in the paper this morning. Shocking business!" exclaimed Montrose with a mournful shake of the head. "But what has that to do with Margerison—or myself, for that matter?"

"I don't know that it has anything to do with you, sir," Shelley said. "But it might have a good deal to do with Mr. Margerison. You see, Mr. Margerison is dead."

I'd have sworn that the look that crossed Montrose's face was one of mingled amazement and consternation.

"Dead!" he almost shouted.

"Yes."

"But I didn't even know that he was ill," Montrose said.

"He was not. I am an officer from Scotland Yard," Shelley explained, "and I have been given the job of investigating his death. I don't think that there is any doubt about it, Mr. Montrose—your friend Margerison was murdered, probably by the same hand as that which murdered Tilsley."

"But this is terrible," murmured Montrose. "I can't think what can be the explanation. I should have said that Margerison hadn't an enemy in the world, unless…" His voice faded away into a tone of indecision and doubt.

"Unless what, sir?" Shelley was now the sleuth, his nose well on the scent.

"Unless it had some connexion with what he told me about the death of John Tilsley."

This was just the sort of thing that Shelley was after, I could see. Anyhow, it looked as if it might lead somewhere.

"What did he tell you?" Shelley asked.

"He told me that he had seen the lift, just after the body of Tilsley had been found. He said that this was going to be a terrific problem for the police to solve. And he added that he thought he had solved the problem."

Shelley thought this over for a moment. Then he said: "You mean, he thought he understood how it was that a body could get in the lift, although the gates were still locked, and the locks had, to all appearances, not been in any way tampered with?"

"I presume that is what he meant," Montrose said.

"He didn't go into any details?"

"No. I asked him, naturally, what he meant; but he said that it was only a sort of hypothesis, though he was sure that it was correct. He said, however, that he was going to see if he could do something to prove it. And, when he had got some proof, he was going to the police with it. But, until that proof was available, he thought that it was as well to say nothing at all about it."

"I see." This, once more, was something that took a little digesting, I could see. Naturally enough, it agreed with what we had decided were the facts of the two murders. It meant that Margerison had discovered something about the death of Tilsley, and that he had proposed to do something in the way of investigation on his own. It was then only necessary to assume that the murderer had obtained some knowledge of Margerison's suspicions, when it would obviously become necessary for Margerison to be eliminated. Such a reading of the course of events was what now became clear enough. But the trouble was, of course, that it gave us no sort of idea of the identity of the murderer. I suppose that it was too much to hope that such information might be forthcoming at this stage; I had, however, had an idea that there might have been a short cut at this point.

Not so, Shelley. With his long experience of crime investigation, the man from Scotland Yard had learned that there are very rarely short cuts in the work of a detective.

"There is one other matter, Mr. Montrose," he said.

"Yes?"

"You said that you had known something about Tilsley in connection with your business deals with Margerison?"

"Quite so."

"Could you give me any idea, in confidence, what those business deals were concerned with? I don't, at this stage, want anything in the way of detail. But it would be helpful to know just what sort of deals they were—I mean, if they were deals in any sort of raw materials, say."

Montrose looked a trifle dubious at this request. It seemed that he did not know if it was altogether wise to reveal anything of what had been going on. Then he drew in a deep breath, and I realised that we were going to get a little more of the background of the mystery.

"I don't know that I should really reveal this," he said, "since a good deal of it was really shared between Margerison and myself. But Margerison is dead, and there can be, I suppose, little harm now in telling you about it. I don't mind admitting, however, that I feel some doubt about telling it, even now."

"It is your duty to tell it, sir," Shelley said sternly. "You may well be helping to bring a murderer to justice if you let me know exactly what happened."

"That's true," Montrose said. "Well, Margerison was engaged in the metal market. He worked as a buyer for a firm dealing largely in the precious metals—particularly gold and platinum."

"Quite so." Not by so much as the blink of an eyelid did Shelley reveal that he felt any surprise at this, though the information was, of course, totally unexpected.

"Some of the precious metals are rather difficult to get hold of in any quantity, and it so happened that Tilsley had some unexpected sources of supply. His prices were high, but he could let us have quantities of gold and platinum when it was not easy to buy them on the open market."

"How long had this been going on?" Shelley asked.

"Two or three years, I should think," Montrose said. "I had been involved in it only for about eighteen months or so."

"And, if I may ask, sir, what was your function in it? Where, if I may put it so, did you come in?"

"I was merely a sleeping partner. My interest in the thing was purely financial. I had known Margerison for years, and he came to me a year or eighteen months ago, pointed out that he had this unexpected source of supply of these metals, and then said that he was a little short of capital. He suggested that I should back him, and that, as a result, there would be a good return for any fluid capital which I might have available. It so happened that I had between two and three thousand pounds available—the nationalisation of coal had thrown some of my investments back to me, so to speak—and I lent it to him."

"Results satisfactory, sir?" asked Shelley with a smile.

"Oh, quite; the return was more than one could possibly have got in the normal course of investment. Naturally, there were occasions when I felt doubtful, and I'm wondering at this moment just how I stand. I'm not at all sure where the cash is now, in view of poor Margerison's death."

"It had to be fluid capital, I think you said, sir?" Shelley remarked.

"Yes. You see, Tilsley always insisted on being paid in notes. He would not take a cheque. That is the only point that made me a trifle dubious about the whole thing. I wondered if there was some infringement of the law somewhere. One always feels suspicious, I think, of the man who wants to be paid in cash for the sort of thing that would normally be paid for by a cheque. And this is particularly true of things like precious metals, where a comparatively small bulk of the material may well be worth some hundreds of pounds."

This was reasonable enough. I was quite favourably impressed by this man Montrose, and I thought that Shelley was equally so. Indeed, the fellow appeared to radiate simple honesty—one of the few among the many people we had met in this case who did not seem to have anything to hide, and who seemed to be in every way open and above board.

Shelley had little more to say to him, and in a few minutes we were strolling down the road once more. Shelley turned to me with some interest, I thought.

"Well, what's your opinion, Jimmy?" he said.

"My opinion?" I repeated.

"Yes; your opinion of our friend Montrose."

"Seems sensible enough, and straightforward enough, too," I said.

"I'm inclined to agree with you," Shelley said. "But there's one very odd thing, you know."

"What's that?" I asked.

"Well, I can't see any straightforward connection between a man who deals in spare parts for cars and a man who deals in gold and platinum. And yet it seems that our Mr. Tilsley was both of those, rolled into one. It's odd." Shelley relapsed into a thoughtful silence.

"Unless they were both stolen," I said.

"Yes, but that, somehow, doesn't ring quite true," said Shelley. "A thief, like other crooks, tends to be in a way a specialist. I don't mean to say that he wouldn't steal anything stealable; but there is nothing in common between motor parts and precious metals. They wouldn't be handled by means of the same technique, if you know what I mean. Still, that's one of life's little oddities, and no doubt it will be settled at a later stage in the case. If we knew the solution of that puzzle just now we might, I think, be somewhere near the solution of the whole affair—of the murder, I mean. Still, we don't know it, Jimmy, and we shall just have to go on plugging away until we do. I only hope that we shan't take too long over the job, or there may be some even more nasty consequences."

"What do you mean?" I asked.

"Our friend the murderer has already dealt with two victims," Shelley said in solemn tones. "In other words, he has put his head pretty effectively into the noose if we are able to lay our hands on him."

"True enough," I agreed.

"And if he thinks that another murder will make him safe, then you can bet your boots that murder will be committed," Shelley said. "So you'd better look out, Jimmy!"

There was a grin on Shelley's face as he said this, and a tone of gentle bantering in his voice. But when I thought of the banner headlines in *The Daily Wire,* and the fact that my name was going to appear each day as the well-known criminologist who was investigating the affair, I felt more than a trifle uncomfortable.

CHAPTER XVI

In Which I Talk to the Liftman

I T SEEMED, FOR THE MOMENT, AS IF WE HAD COME TO A DEAD end in our investigations. I knew that to get any really fresh information I should have to await the collation of the material that Shelley was getting from Scotland Yard. Only thus could I hope to get hold of new stuff.

But now that I was fairly launched on my career as a special investigator for the Press I could not bear the thought of inaction. Only a couple of days before I had been a convalescent, lazing away a few weeks on the Kentish coast. But thought of returning to that status now seemed to me to be hopeless. I had been plunged into such exciting events that to get back to the old routine of meals under the eagle eye of Mrs. Cecil, walks on the promenade, and an occasional decorous bathe seemed to me to be the most completely feeble way of getting on with life. I wanted to feel myself involved in uncovering facts, revealing unexpected connections between the people in the case, and finding out what I could do.

And Shelley's warning had some influence on me as well. I had no intention of giving any murderer a sitting target. But it was true enough that I was in some danger, especially if the murderer thought that I might be revealing something of what he was doing. The sooner the man was caught the sooner I should be safe. Thus my professional interest was reinforced by the personal interest of my own safety.

Yet I did not see what more I could do. Shelley had not suggested anything further that I could carry out in the way of investigations— and I knew that I had now established myself well enough in his confidence to be asked to do anything which I could. It was thus clear enough that there was nothing that he considered could usefully be given to me to do at the moment. Yet, as I've said, I was not content. I wanted to do something, even though I wasn't sure what it was.

I sat on the old familiar seat on the promenade. I cast my mind over all that had happened in the case. I wondered who there was who might be able to help. Naturally, sooner or later we should have to see how the death of Margerison had affected all the odd people who had come into the case earlier on. But meanwhile I thought that there must be someone who had not been as fully investigated as probably would pay.

At the back of my mind, like the nag of an aching tooth, was the thought that there was someone whose background had not been looked into as much as it should have been. Then I recalled who it was. Of course! Aloysius Bender. I had not spoken to him much since the second murder. Everything had happened in such a rush, Shelley had come on the scene so swiftly, that, apart from the first words with him when Margerison's body had been discovered, I had had no converse with the liftman.

I remembered that I had a note of the man's address somewhere. Since he was not working the lift (it was still closed, by police instructions), it was highly probable that he was at home. I remembered jotting down his address on the back of an envelope during the early stages of the case. I turned out the contents of my breast pocket, and found the envelope. There it was: "Aloysius Bender, 196 Peter Street." I wondered where Peter Street was. Then I remembered. The Broadgate Parish Council, for the benefit of visitors, had erected further along the promenade a map of the town. If I had a look at that I should be able to spot the street.

I strolled along to the big oak frame that contained the map. At first I found it difficult to find Peter Street, but eventually spotted it. It was a narrow, twisting alleyway which straggled from one side of Broadgate to the other, running roughly parallel to the sea front, about half a mile up the hill that led inland from the sea.

It took me only about ten minutes to find the place. I soon spotted 196. It was an unsavoury-looking cottage. I rapped on the door with my knuckles, since no bell or knocker was anywhere visible. A slatternly-looking woman opened the door and greeted me with a stony glare.

"Yes?" she snapped.

"Does Mr. Bender live here?" I asked.

"He does. But he's out."

"Do you know where I might be able to find him?" I said. "It's rather urgent."

"Where would you find him, but in the boozer?" she snapped back at me.

"Which one?" I asked.

"Out on the High Street. Place called the Seven Bells. He'll be swilling in the public bar," she said, and slammed the door loudly in my face. I wondered if this was Mrs. Bender, venting on me her wrath at the fact that her spouse was drinking. Then I thought that this was not very likely. If this woman had any real power over Bender she would not be the sort to allow him to go drinking at all. She was more likely his landlady, annoyed because money was going in beer which should have been devoted to paying her rent.

Still, I made my way to the High Street, where I soon saw the Seven Bells. It was a quiet little pub, not unlike the sort of place that must have made Broadgate attractive in Edwardian days, before the advent of chain stores and char-a-bancs introduced the ordinary Londoner to the Kent Coast as "London by the sea." The saloon bar entrance was on the main street, and there was an arrow painted on the front, pointing down a side alley and indicating that the public bar was tucked away there.

As I strolled in, I soon saw my friend Bender. He was seated on a wooden form against the wall, propped up and with a pint of bitter on the table in front of him. The place could not have been open more than half an hour (I was a bit hazy about the times of opening in Broadgate), but it seemed that Bender must have been going the pace pretty well. There was a glazed expression about his eyes that suggested he had already imbibed a few pints—unless the beer was a good deal stronger than it usually is in these degenerate days.

I bought myself a pint and made my way to his side.

"Good morning, Mr. Bender," I said. "Trying to drown your sorrows, eh?"

He squinted at me, obviously finding some difficulty in focussing his eyes.

"Oh, it's you, Mr. London," he said at last.

"That's so. Here's good hunting to Scotland Yard," I said, raising my tankard and taking a sip.

"D'you think that they'll find him?" Bender said.

"Find who?" I asked.

"The man who's been killing people in my lift," he replied. "After all, it'll never do if this goes on. The council'll shut the lift down altogether if it does."

He chuckled in a drunken, almost obscene manner, as if he thought this was a witticism of the most extreme brilliance. I thought that his condition was really a lucky break for me. If he really had much knowledge of what was going on; if he had any kind of information as to the man who was committing these murders, if, even, he had any inkling as to how they had been committed, he was now in a very suitable condition to be persuaded to unburden himself of his weight of knowledge.

"It would never do if that happened," I said. "You'd be out of a job, wouldn't you?"

He leaned forward over the table, an untidy lock of his red hair dangling over his eye. He put a dirty forefinger alongside his nose, and winked meaningfully.

"I'll never be out of a job, Mr. London," he said.

"No?" I said. "And why not?"

"Because I've got influential friends," he answered, stumbling somewhat over the difficult adjective. "They won't let poor old Bender starve."

This was interesting. It might be mere idle boasting, however, I thought. I didn't quite know how to get out of him the information that I was after. I now had him in an affable mood, and I didn't want to say anything that would make him in any way suspicious. I felt tolerably sure that if I aroused his suspicions in any way—if I made him think that I was trying in any way to ferret out information—he would shut up like an oyster, and the chance of getting hold of something useful would at once be gone, and quite likely gone for ever.

And there was something about Bender's manner which suggested that he had some very useful information, a suggestion of infinite knowledge. Of course, I knew that this might be mere drunken fantasy; but at the same time it was possible that there was a genuine foundation for it. The position was ticklish in the extreme. I wished that Shelley had been there to advise me how to tackle it. But then it was quite likely that, given the presence of Shelley, the man would have had nothing at all to say. After all, a newspaperman is not a policeman. And to a suspiciously-minded individual a policeman is a kind of licensed Nosey Parker to be avoided at all costs.

"So you know something, do you, Mr. Bender?" I said, trying to make my voice as pleadingly knowing as possible. I thought that the confidential air was what was most likely to go down in Aloysius Bender's present condition.

"I know more than most people think," he said, with a revolting grimace that was, I imagined, meant to be a knowing wink.

"I'm sure of that," I said.

"In fact, Mr. London, strictly between ourselves, I'm not sure that I'm not the most important person in the whole thing." He looked immensely satisfied with himself. "If the police knew all that I know... well, they'd know a lot more than they do just now."

This was intensely irritating to me. These vague hints were all very well. They might mean a lot, or they might mean nothing at all. It was totally impossible, without something more definite in the way of statement, for me to say whether Bender really knew anything about the mystery.

"And what do you know, Mr. Bender?" I asked.

"Ah, that would be telling!" he exclaimed, with another of his horrible grimaces.

"My paper would make it worth your while, you know, if you told us anything that was really exclusive," I said. "You know what a scoop is, don't you?"

"A scoop?" He looked puzzled. "Oh, you mean when one paper gets in ahead of all the others, gets hold of some news that the others don't know anything about."

"That's it."

He grinned. "And what sort of scoop do you think might come out of this case?" he said.

"Well," I temporised. This was the most ticklish spot in a very ticklish conversation, I thought. "You have been telling me that you've got some special knowledge," I said. "If that knowledge is as special as you seem to think, my paper would, I know, be prepared to pay good money for it."

"Would they?" I thought that there was a gleam of cupidity in the man's eye. The suggestion that there was good money in the information which he had at his disposal seemed to be coming to him as a new idea. For a few moments I thought that I really had got hold of something worth while. Then the gleam in his eye appeared to fade.

"But," he said, looking immensely knowing, "there's a thing called libel, isn't there?"

"What of it?" I asked.

"Well, your paper wouldn't pay for information that might lead somebody to say they'd been libelled, if you printed it," he objected. I wondered if I had over-estimated the state of the man's drunkenness. This seemed to be a very sober argument. Still, now that I had gone so far, it was more or less impossible for me to withdraw.

"The libel attitude does complicate things a bit," I admitted. "But still, you can't libel a man by telling the truth about him, you know. And I suppose that you wouldn't find any difficulty in proving the truth of what you know."

"I don't know." For the first time during the curious interview Bender's attitude of certainty and knowingness seemed to desert him. "You can know a lot of things about a man without being able to prove it."

"But can't you give me some sort of idea of what it is that you could tell?" I pressed him. "After all, this isn't a matter of a cross-word puzzle. This is a murder case; a serious matter. If you've got any sort of information that might lead to the discovery of the murderer it is, after all, your duty to pass on to the police what you know. It might well prevent more murders, after all."

His eyes gleamed with malice. "You mean that you think there may be more murders," he said. There was a gloating attitude about the man, something almost ghoulish, which I much disliked.

"There might," I agreed. "After all, if a man has done two murders, he'll have nothing to lose by committing more—especially if he thinks that other murders may mean the death of those who might get him convicted of the first ones. Why"—and here a new method of attack occurred to me—"you might even be in danger yourself, if this knowledge of yours is as important and valuable as you think it is. The murderer presumably knows that you have it; you haven't shared your knowledge with anyone, and if you were killed it would never get known to anybody. The murderer might take that line. If he did so, then he would see that killing you would at once eliminate any chance that you might give him away to the police."

I thought that this threat would be likely to cast fear into his heart, but it seemed to make no impression at all. Bender merely leered at me in a drunken fashion, and said: "He won't kill me, oh no! I know too much."

"But that's the very reason why he might kill you," I argued with some irritation and heat. "The fact that you know such a lot is the very reason why he would be likely to put you out of the way."

But he wagged his head with annoying confidence. I saw that he was in what I took to be a condition that I could only describe as of alcoholic stupidity. Still, I thought that I would have one last effort at getting some information out of him. After all, even though he may have had too big an idea of the value of his information, I thought it was as well to see what it was that he knew.

"Can't you give me some idea of what your knowledge is, Mr. Bender?" I said. "Don't mention any names, but just give me an idea of what you have been hinting at this morning."

He grinned. "It's the keys," he said.

"The keys?" I was puzzled.

"The keys to the locks of the lift," he explained.

"And what about them?" I asked.

"I know of another set."

This, I told myself, was the right sort of information; it was the very sort of clue which would make Shelley want to jump for joy. I only hoped that I should be able to find out something more.

"But I thought," I said, "that there were only two sets—the set in your possession, and the other set that hang in the council offices."

"Ah," he said, winking again, "that's what everybody thinks. But I know better."

"And who has the other set?" I asked.

"A certain gentleman," he said. "He asked me, months ago, to let him take plaster casts of my keys."

"And you allowed him to do that?"

"Yes; he paid me well to do it."

"And what reason did he give for taking impressions of the keys?" I asked.

"So that he could play a joke on someone."

This seemed a pretty feeble effort, but I supposed that it might well be the sort of explanation which would get past a man as stupid as Bender appeared to be.

"Won't you tell me who it is?" I asked.

He shook his head emphatically. "What I know I believe in keeping to myself," he said.

And there I was compelled to leave the matter.

CHAPTER XVII

In Which Accusations Are Made

I KEPT *THE DAILY WIRE* FAIRLY SATISFIED BY PHONING THEM A sensational account of the second murder. I provided a little character cameo of the man Margerison, hinted at his double identity (though I imagine that the character of Cyrus Watford was made up on the spur of the moment to keep me quiet), and suggested that further sensational results were pending, as soon as the police had carried out certain routine checks of information that was already in their possession.

That last, in fact, is always a safe card to play. The average reader of newspapers never seems to realise that the suggestion that the police are on the track of something big is the normal "come-back" of the crime reporter stuck for something to say.

Still, I thought that I was keeping things up pretty well. I was as sure as I could be of a big splash on the front page for the second day running. I had probably already earned enough to ensure my being able to pay for my stay in Broadgate. And I intended to slap in a fairly heavy expense account soon. After all, I saw no reason why the paper shouldn't pay for some of the entertainment which I had done.

That evening I thought that the time had come to relax a bit. It was all very well, I told myself, to concentrate on the job in hand. But everyone needs to relax at times. My mood of the morning, when I had felt impelled to action, had passed.

I craved some sort of entertainment. And entertainment, with me, usually involves beer. I am no soaker, mind you, but I hold that the national beverage of the Englishman is something which provides a useful sideline to any other amusement which may be on the way.

So I wandered around Broadgate, wondering which of the many pubs I should honour with my custom. There was the Hartfield, that huge erection at one end of the promenade. It had a sort of dive-bar, which could be reached either from the promenade or from the beach. I had found that a pleasant spot in the past. But it was expensive, and the beer was often luke-warm on a really hot evening. So I gave that a miss. Then there was the Royal George, the big residential place on the front. The saloon bar there kept some first-rate draught beer; but again it was likely to be hot and crowded. I thought that I would like something smaller and, if possible, quieter.

I remembered the Brewer's Arms, an unpretentious little pub, originally, no doubt, intended for the fishermen. It was down almost on the quay, on the side of Broadgate which was still more or less like it had been in the old days. You got a few of the visitors here, plus some of the artists and writers who had settled in the town. But on the whole it was a peaceful little pub; and in my present mood a peaceful little pub was just what I craved.

To the Brewer's Arms I therefore went. I bought myself a pint of bitter and settled in a corner to study humanity. I often think that a strange pub is one of the best places in the world to do that.

As I settled down I glanced around me to see if there was anyone I knew in the place. I did not expect that any of those with whom I had come into contact in connection with the case would put in an appearance; somehow it did not seem to me that the type of people I had met up to now were quite the sort who would find the

Brewer's Arms just a congenial spot. But in a few minutes I realised that I was wrong.

I was conscious, in the way in which one often is, that I was being stared at. Then I glanced around to see who it was who was looking at me. Soon I saw. In the opposite corner of the bar were seated two moderately familiar figures—none other than Maya Johnson and Timothy Foster. I caught the man's eye and he smiled in a half-hearted sort of way. I was not going to miss any opportunity of improving my knowledge of the case, so I got to my feet, strolled across the bar, and stood by them. They were, after all, in a public place anyhow, so I didn't reckon that I should be spoiling their *tête-a-tête* by speaking to them.

"I hope I'm not butting in," I said. And I really don't think that I was. Probably these two had been so consumed with a combination of curiosity and anxiety that they were only too glad to find someone to whom they could talk about the murders. Of course, I didn't know what Shelley and his minions might have said to them already; but I thought that I could rely on my sense of atmosphere to be pretty sure that I didn't say anything too stupid, put my foot in it too openly.

Anyhow, I was sure that I was welcome there at first. For Maya Johnson moved along the old wooden settle thing on which the pair were seated, smiled, and indicated that I should sit down with them.

I accepted the implied invitation with alacrity. I knew that here I might be getting myself a little involved, as I had done earlier with Bender; but after all I had no official standing at all in the case, and it was up to me to get such information as I could by whatever method I liked. I didn't worry at all that some people might have frowned on my methods of getting the information; nor did it worry me that my methods were not exactly those which Shelley might have chosen.

I was not Detective-Inspector Shelley, with all the might of Scotland Yard behind me. I was a mere pressman, working on my own; and whatever seemed to me the most satisfactory way of getting information, as long as I did not go too far on the wrong side of the law, it was in every way open to me to use. That was how I looked at the matter through the whole course of the case; and I think that the sequel showed that I was right. As to that the reader will be able to judge when he comes to the end of this narrative.

"Any news, Mr. London?" Maya Johnson asked eagerly as I sat down.

"Well, that depends, in the words of the well-known broadcaster, on what you mean by news," I said, stalling for all I was worth.

"Have they caught the murderer yet?" asked Foster.

"No." That was an easy one to answer. But I resented the fact that I was being asked questions. I had intended to do all the asking, and let them answer my queries.

"Any ideas on the subject of the murderer's identity, Mr. London?" asked Maya Johnson. There was a slight suggestion of bantering in the tone of these people, but at the same time I was well aware of the seriousness of their position. I was assured that they too didn't feel themselves to be in a position of a hundred per cent safety.

"Well," I said, "everybody has their theories in these matters, you know."

"And what is yours?" asked Foster.

I recalled a remark of Bender's earlier in the day. "Well, there is a law of libel in this country, you know," I said. "One can't be too outspoken in such affairs as these, or one may find a prosecution for criminal libel hanging around one. And that is something which I have no ambition to undergo."

"We think that we know who did it, you know," Maya Johnson said seriously. I studied that beautiful face with added interest.

"Really?"

"Yes; you see, we knew Tilsley and we knew a little of his affairs. Not that he talked about them very much, but now and then he let something slip. Tim and I have been exchanging ideas since we saw you yesterday, seeing how our memories of Tilsley tallied, and we both agree on the point of the man in Broadgate who is most likely to have been responsible for Tilsley's death."

"Really?" I didn't dare to do anything in the way of mental jogging here. If these young people were to share with me the idea that had come to them, the sharing would be a matter of their own free will, and nothing that I did or said would make very much difference.

"Who do you suspect?" I asked. "I'll not take any advantage of what you say. I'll only undertake to pass on to the correct quarters whatever seems to me to have some sort of factual basis. And I'll see that there is some sort of protection against the libel laws, if such protection is possible—which I think it will be."

They exchanged glances. I could see that they were in two minds, doubtful, not knowing me well enough to judge if I could be really trusted. I didn't know what I could very well do to increase their trust, but I knew that the best thing that I could do was to let the couple have their head, and hope that they would be able to tell me what they knew, without in any way straining whatever good will I had managed to build up for myself in their minds.

"Did you ever hear of a man called Margerison?" asked Foster at length.

"The name is familiar," I said realising that they had not seen an evening paper, and so did not know anything about the second murder that had taken place in Broadgate.

"He is a dealer of some sort—I'm not sure what sort—but we think that there is something more than a little crooked about him," Maya Johnson explained.

"And what does that mean?" I asked.

"That we think he murdered John Tilsley," answered Foster.

I smiled. "I'm afraid that you're barking up the wrong tree there," I said.

"Why?" they exclaimed simultaneously.

"Because Margerison himself was murdered late last night," I said.

"What?" This was almost a roar from Foster.

"I assure you that it is true," I said. I took a folded edition of an evening paper from under my arm, and pointed to a headline on the front page.

Foster fairly grabbed the paper from me. He spread it out on the table before him, and he and Maya Johnson devoured its contents eagerly. There was no doubt that this revelation had taken them by surprise.

Now I was becoming conscious that there was a sudden increase in the tension of the atmosphere. I am sensitive to these things, and I was aware that something was happening. I looked up and drew in my breath with a sudden hiss.

Standing in front of us was another of the odd figures who had already come into the case—Mrs. Skilbeck, the pale woman from the Charrington Hotel. I was very surprised to see her there. Her face was distorted with grief and rage. Something had happened, I could tell, to cause a real emotional crisis in this normally stoical woman.

"Mr. London!" she gasped. "I saw you come in here, and I watched and followed."

This surprised me somewhat. "Why?" I asked. "Have you got something to ask me or tell me?"

"I thought I had something to tell you," she said, "and that is why I followed you in here. Now I'm not so sure that I have anything which I should care to tell you, when I see the company which you are in." Her eyes flashed fire as she glanced at Maya Johnson and Timothy Foster.

This was so surprising to me that I did not quite know how to respond to it.

"I'm afraid that I don't understand you," I said. "These people are friends of mine, and they were friends of Mr. Tilsley. They have been kind, in trying to help me towards solving the mystery of his death—a mystery in which I thought you too were interested."

I was a little consciously on my dignity; but, honestly, I couldn't for the life of me see what the woman was getting at.

"You won't solve the mystery of his death by talking to these people if you talk to them till doomsday," she said. "And you say that they are friends of yours and friends of John Tilsley's. They may be friends of yours—I don't care if they are or not—but they were certainly never friends of his. I knew him too well to swallow any such story as that. Of course, you never knew him, or knew anything about what he was doing, so I cannot answer for your opinion of them."

This was a completely unexpected speech, and I didn't know what to say about it. Certainly Mrs. Skilbeck was an odd woman, and she had some queer mental attributes. Maya Johnson had been gazing at the newcomer with wide-open, astonished eyes. Now she spoke to her.

"We were friends and business acquaintances of Mr. Tilsley," she said. "I don't know who you are to say that we can't help Mr. London, here, to solve the mystery of his death. We have certain ideas about the matter. They may be mistaken ideas—I wouldn't know about that—but they are at least sincere, and you have no right, no right whatever, to say that we do not mean everything we say."

"I don't know much about you, Maya Johnson," replied Mrs. Skilbeck. "One thing, however, I do know about Timothy Foster here. You might be wiser, if you are fond of him, not to ask me what it is."

Maya Johnson looked completely mystified. I certainly shared her feelings.

"I don't understand," she said.

"I thought you might not," Mrs. Skilbeck replied, and her face took on an expression of determination. She looked like some grim avenger as she stood there.

"But what do you say that you know about Tim?" Maya Johnson asked quietly.

"I know what John Tilsley used to say about him—he said it to me repeatedly."

"And what was that?" It was curious, I reflected, that this scene of complex drama could be played out in the saloon bar of a little Kentish public house without anyone else becoming aware of what was going on. None of the other drinkers in the bar seemed even to notice that anything was happening which merited their attention.

"What did John Tilsley say about Tim?" repeated Maya Johnson. Timothy Foster laid his hand on her arm, as if he would restrain her from going any further in the matter, but she shook his hand off in an irritated fashion.

"No, Tim, I want to know," she said.

"You shall know, if you want to, and much good will it do you," said Mrs. Skilbeck. "John always said that he would be murdered, and that Tim Foster would be his murderer!"

There was silence. Then Mrs. Skilbeck, with that uncanny glide-like walk, made her way out of the bar, while Maya Johnson collapsed over the table, her head on her arms, in a helpless storm of tears.

CHAPTER XVIII

In Which an Emotional Crisis is Surmounted

I DON'T KNOW IF YOU'VE EVER SAT IN A FISHERMAN'S PUB OPPO-
site a woman in tears, a woman, moreover, whose fiancé has just
been accused of murder. If you have you will know that I felt about
as uncomfortable as a man well can. The fact that Mrs. Skilbeck had
left us had slightly cleared the atmosphere; but there was no doubt
that a feeling of great emotional tension existed, a feeling not at all
easy to dissipate.

Foster leaned protectively over Maya Johnson, his hand resting
lightly on her shoulder.

"Come on, snap out of it!" he counselled her. "What does it
matter what the woman said?"

Maya Johnson raised her head. Her eyes were red and her face
already considerably tear-stained. "But she said that you had killed
Tilsley," Maya said.

"What does it matter what she said?" asked Foster for the
second time.

"It matters a lot!"

I could see that this remark shook Foster considerably. He sat up
and looked surprised.

"In what way?" he asked.

"Well, if she goes around saying that sort of thing it will sooner
or later come to the ears of the police!"

"And what if it does?" I couldn't help admiring the sheer pudding-headed obstinacy of the man, unwilling even for a moment to admit that such an accusation of murder could in any way hurt him or have any sort of effect on his life. Still, I personally thought that Maya Johnson's attitude was the more sensible one. It would have been foolish to deny that the slinging about of murder accusations is a dangerous business, especially when the police are to all intents and purposes stumped by a case. If enough mud is slung at anyone, as the old proverb has it, some is likely to stick. I thought it was high time I took some part in this argument, and tried to make this obstinate young man see some sense.

"Look here, Mr. Foster," I said, "you must realise that there is a lot of sense in what Miss Johnson is trying to say. If a woman as bitter as Mrs. Skilbeck slings about accusations like that there will be plenty of people who will believe that she is telling the truth. You know—there's no smoke without fire, and all that sort of thing."

"But I don't care what people believe. I know that I didn't kill Tilsley, and that's enough for me." He set his jaw obstinately. I could have kicked him. It is all very well to be firm, but firmness eventually becomes stupidity, I think.

"It isn't what you know, Mr. Foster," I said. "It's what the police think that will eventually settle this case, and we don't yet know what Mrs. Skilbeck may be telling the police."

"You think that she will tell the police what she told us?" This was Maya Johnson, and the nervousness in her tones made it clear to me that she was very deeply in love with Timothy Foster. I had, indeed, for long thought that this was so, but her response to this threat to him made it clear to me that her feelings were deep.

"I don't think that she will have any option," I said. "If the police hear of these accusations—and they're bound to do so sooner or later—they will at once pull her in for questioning. They'll have no option in the matter, either. They would be fools to ignore it. This case is a real mystery, and anyone who makes an accusation which seems to have some factual support is bound to be listened to with considerable respect."

The people in the pub had by this time ignored us. When Maya Johnson had first collapsed over the table the barman had made a move towards us, as if he thought that this was a case of a drunken customer who would have to be requested to leave; but since she had apparently settled down quickly he had changed his mind.

What I had said seemed to impress the lady fairly considerably. Even the obstinate Foster appeared to see that there was much good sense in what I was saying.

"You do see, don't you, Tim?" Maya Johnson said earnestly. "This is not something that you can just laugh off—you've got to take it seriously. Your life may depend on what happens in the next day or two—and if your life doesn't matter to you, it matters a lot to me."

I was impressed by this girl. She was amazingly beautiful, but, unlike many beautiful girls, her face was not merely a brilliant façade with nothing behind it. I thought that she was a very intelligent woman, with a lot of good sense in her pretty head.

"All right," he said. "What do you want me to do about it?"

"I've got a proposition," she said, and paused. The emotional crisis appeared to have passed, but I was still conscious of some tension in the air.

"What is it?" I asked.

"You are investigating this case, aren't you?" she said. "I mean, you are reporting it for your paper, and you're trying to see if you can get hold of any fresh information which will give you a chance to beat the other papers to it."

I nodded. "That's so," I said.

"And you believe that Tim is innocent?"

"I do." This was nothing more than the truth.

"Well, will you do your best to clear Tim of this accusation that Mrs. Skilbeck has made?"

"Well, in a sense I'm doing that already," I said.

"What do you mean?"

I smiled. "Well, I'm doing my best to find out who is responsible for the death of Tilsley, and if I do manage to find out who it is, that will clear Tim, won't it?"

For the first time since Mrs. Skilbeck had entered Miss Johnson smiled. It was not a very strong smile, but nevertheless it was a big improvement on the strained expression which had previously filled her face.

"Will you come back to my flat with us?" she asked. "I feel that we should have a further chat about this, and a place like this doesn't seem to me to be at all suitable for such a discussion."

"O.K.," I said, draining my glass.

So in a few minutes we were installed in Maya Johnson's comfortable flat. I sat on the settee under the window, and Maya Johnson and Tim Foster occupied cosy armchairs on either side of the empty fireplace.

"Now," she said with an air of determination, "I think that this is a sort of council of war." It was odd how this beautiful woman had, in a sense, taken control of the situation. I was slightly amused. Actually, there was no doubt which of the two young people was the stronger personality. I had no doubt that they would have a happy married life; equally I had no doubt that the big decisions would be hers and not his.

"Well," I remarked, "there is one thing which might be settled right away, and you can settle it without any difficulty at all, I should think."

"What is that?"

"That is whether either or both of you have an alibi for last night."

She looked puzzled. "Why *last* night?" she asked. "Tilsley was killed the night before."

"True," I explained, "but you forget that Margerison was killed last night, and there is obviously a connection between the two crimes. Personally, I don't think that there is any doubt at all that whoever killed Tilsley also killed Margerison. The police, I know, share that opinion."

They looked at each other. "What time was it that you left here, Tim?" she asked.

"About ten o'clock," he said.

"You were here from some early hour until ten?" I asked.

"I shut the garage at about half-past six," he explained, "and came straight around here. Maya cooked us a meal, which we ate at about half-past seven. I was, as I said, here until about ten o'clock. Then I went home."

"See anyone you knew on the way?"

"Not a soul."

"Anyone see you enter the house?"

"No. It's a service flat that I've got, and there is no porter on duty after nine. All the residents have a front-door key and let themselves in."

"H'm." I thought this over. It did not seem to be too promising since it was clearly in no sense an alibi.

"When was Margerison killed?" asked Maya Johnson. She was now icy-cold and clear. The trace of hysteria which I had seemed to sense in the pub had now gone.

"The police surgeon is playing for safety," I said. "All that he will say is that it was some time between seven o'clock and midnight last night. The sensible doctor, in these cases, will not commit himself too closely, you know."

Maya Johnson looked a little scared. "Then Tim hasn't got any sort of alibi," she commented.

"Not for the latter part of the period, anyhow," I admitted. "And even for the earlier period, they will probably think that your evidence is biased. They do not accept without considerable reservations the evidence of a fiancée for the man to whom she's engaged. From the police point of view after all, that's good sense. You might well be lying, and, supposing that Tim was guilty, you might be expected to lie if you thought that you could save his life."

She nodded gloomily. "Yes, I can see that they would argue that way," she said. "But it means that we shall have to find some other method of attack."

I agreed. "It's no good, I think, to try to work this case from the angle of trying to prove Tim's innocence," I said. "He can probably *not* be proved innocent. I mean to say, if he were arrested, his counsel at a trial might find difficulty in getting him off."

"But what do you think we should do?" asked Miss Johnson, a trace of hysteria again creeping into her voice, though I could see that she was doing her level best to control herself.

"I think that, since it is impossible as things are to prove him innocent, the angle of attack is to prove someone else guilty," I said.

"But who?"

"That's the problem," I admitted.

"Can't you think of something?" she asked. "If we don't move, that Mrs. Skilbeck will be spinning her yarn to the police, and then we shall be in a real jam, you know. After all, Mr. London, you admitted a few moments back that it might be very difficult, if Tim were arrested, to prove that he did not commit the murders."

Tim Foster grinned. "Nice callous pair you are," he said. "The way you talk you might think that I'd already got the rope around my neck."

"Tim," I said solemnly, "the point is to make sure that we do something *before* the rope is around your neck. If we wait until the police have decided that there is something suspicious about you, and that it is time that they considered an arrest, we may well be too late—or we are, at any rate, making our job of getting you off doubly difficult. That's what I'm anxious to avoid—and that, I think, is what Miss Johnson here is also anxious to avoid."

"That's right," she said eagerly. "Now, Tim, think! Can you think of any valuable information which we might not have given to Mr. London?"

He shook his head. "I told him everything that I knew," he said. "After all, your questions were pretty exhaustive when you called at the garage yesterday, you know."

I had to admit that this was true. Yet I felt in my bones that there must be something which could be done. In a short time I had become quite friendly towards this couple. Indeed, I was in a way very fond of them. I thought that they were the sort of folks one would be glad to help, and I knew that they would be able to do some worth-while jobs in the world, given the opportunity. It is, after all, not every day that one has the chance to do a really good turn to a well-disposed couple, to make their lives happier. I thought that I was lucky to have the chance. But that I should have to have a bit more information than had yet come my way in order to do so I felt certain.

"Tilsley is the king-pin in this game," I said. "The murders spring in some way from the life that he has been leading. And only if we get to know something more about his activities and where they led shall we be able to get some concrete evidence of the sort that we're after."

Maya Johnson looked worried. "But won't the police be able to do all that far better than we can hope to do?" she asked.

"They're doing it already," I said. "And fortunately Inspector Shelley from Scotland Yard, who is in charge of the case, is a good friend of mine. I've already been able to help him a bit, and so he keeps me fairly well posted with what's going on. He knows that I'm working on the case independently for my paper, so that he won't be surprised at my wanting to ferret out any additional evidence. That is one thing in your favour, Tim; you have got a friend on the inside. If the police do ever think of arresting you, we shall have due notice of the fact, since I'm pretty sure Shelley would tell me if an arrest was imminent. You see, in return for a few good turns which I have been able to do him, he has promised to keep me posted as to what he is doing in the matter."

"Well, that's one good thing, anyway," said Maya Johnson. "But it is a sort of negative virtue at the best. It's all very well to know when Tim is likely to be arrested. But what we want to do is to make sure that they don't arrest him at all."

"Agreed," I said. It seemed to me that we were arguing all around the point anyhow. We had to bring the thing down to earth, see if we could not get hold of some correct points of evidence which would point the suspicions definitely in one direction. And, as I had already said, the matter of the activities of John Tilsley was the crucial matter.

"Can't you think of anything more about Tilsley?" I said. "You told me that he was selling spare parts of cars—spare parts that were in short supply—and that he sold them at a price considerably over the price agreed on by the makers as fair and reasonable."

"That's right."

"Well, what sort of spare parts?" I asked.

"Mainly the small stuff—cotter-pins and pieces of carburettors," answered Tim. "They were the sort of thing that any competent mechanic could make. But if they were made by an ordinary mechanic they would take a long time, and would be very costly."

I seized on this. "Small parts?" I said. "Never things like a cylinder head or a radiator?"

"I think that he did let me have a radiator once," Tim said. "But as a rule it was the small stuff. And that was what made me think that they might be stolen. I thought, you see, that he might have a ring of men working in the factories of the various motor manufacturers, with a scheme whereby they could pinch small parts and bring them to him. After all, you could carry home a few small parts in your pocket, and, unless suspicion had been aroused, you would not be likely to be found out. But it wouldn't be at all easy to carry home a radiator or a cylinder head."

"Agreed," I said. I felt that this was getting somewhere, though just where it was not at all easy to decide. It was, at any rate, a slice of new information, different from what I had previously heard.

"I suppose that this couldn't have been a sort of decoy for something else," I suggested.

"What do you mean?" asked Maya Johnson.

"I mean that these spare parts couldn't have had something else hidden in them—some sort of contraband in which the man was dealing."

"Contraband? You mean some sort of smuggling?" Maya said.

"Yes."

Tim Foster thought this over. "I suppose it's possible," he said slowly. "Though I don't quite know what sort of goods could be smuggled in that way."

Maya Johnson sprang to her feet, her eyes blazing with the excitement of what she obviously thought to be a pure brain-wave.

"I know!"

"What do you know?" asked Tim.

"I know what might have been hidden inside those spare parts!"

"What?" I asked.

"Drugs."

This, I saw, was a brilliant suggestion. "That is a definite possibility," I admitted.

"Cocaine, hashish, and so on," she said. "Don't you see, Tim? He was using you to distribute the stuff. No doubt he would tell his clients that they could get the stuff from you by saying that they wanted a new cotter-pin or whatever it was. And the thing would be made hollow, the inside filled with the drug. And the payment would be made partly to you and partly to him—no doubt in advance of delivery."

I looked at the girl with admiration. This was an astonishingly brilliant idea. And it was, as I have said, quite a possible explanation of what had been going on.

"You said, didn't you, Tim, when I was talking to you yesterday, that the customers who got served were often complete strangers to you?"

"Yes."

"And that often things that you wanted for your regular customers were not available?"

"That's right."

I turned to Maya Johnson. "It seems possible that you've hit on the right explanation," I said. "I shall certainly pass this on to Inspector Shelley. It may be the very sort of thing that will lead him somewhere."

"And it might help to clear Tim from suspicion?"

"It certainly would if it proved to be true," I said. "No one, I think, would be likely to accuse Tim of having anything to do with a drug racket."

She heaved a great sigh of relief.

"We're not out of the wood yet, you know," I warned her. "This, after all, is only a sort of inspired guess—nothing more."

"Still, you agree that it is a possible explanation of what has been going on?"

"Yes," I said, and then another idea occurred to me. "It marries up, too, with what I have learned about Margerison," I said.

"In what way?"

"Margerison knew Tilsley as a dealer in gold and platinum," I said.

My companions looked puzzled, so I went on to explain what I meant.

"Gold and platinum are two very expensive materials," I said. "Anyone who buys some will be paying a lot of money for it. And the lumps of gold and platinum might be hollow. That, again, might mean that drugs were hidden somewhere."

So altogether I was more than satisfied with the outcome of my talk with Maya Johnson and Tim Foster. We had succeeded in getting somewhere. As I said, it might be no more than an inspired guess, but I felt sure that Shelley would greet it with pleasure.

CHAPTER XIX

In Which I Put a Theory Before Scotland Yard

WHEN MY SESSION WITH TIM FOSTER AND MAYA JOHNSON was over, I realised that it was too late to do anything with Shelley that night. I knew, of course, that the man from Scotland Yard was wont to keep all hours when he was busy on a case. The normal man's requirement of sleep did not seem to be in any way a necessity of his in such circumstances. But at the same time I thought it would be unfair to expect him to listen to a new theory at ten-thirty at night. Indeed I had no desire to interfere with his beauty sleep—or with my own.

I had had two difficult and trying days, and I knew that I needed sleep. But at the same time, when I had got back to my lodgings and gone to bed, sleep seemed to elude me for a long time. It was difficult to compose my mind for it; I found my thoughts going round and round in circles, thinking all about our arguments of the evening. Was it, I asked myself, indeed possible that Tilsley had been a drug-trafficker, disguising his business under the pretence that he was a dealer in car spares or precious metals, or something similarly harmless?

I was unable to find any flaw in the argument; but at the same time I thought that it would be very difficult to prove the truth of the allegation. Yet I knew that Scotland Yard had their methods. No doubt that they had a group of men whose job would be to deal with the traffic in dangerous drugs. They would deal with all those suspected of having any connexion with this horrid trade, and it might well be that they would have some knowledge of Tilsley's connexion with drugs, if such connexion really existed.

I could not sleep for a long time. These things were swimming around my brain. I found that I was repeating all the familiar arguments again and again, not getting any further forward but at the same time losing sleep which I knew would be of vital importance to me if I had to do any lengthy job of investigation in the near future—something which might well prove to be true in the next few days.

At last I did fall asleep, though it must have been about two o'clock in the morning. And then my sleep was disturbed by the most unpleasant of dreams, in which all those who were concerned in the case were stupidly muddled up. It was with considerable relief, in fact, that I woke up in the morning to find the bright sunshine streaming into my room. I glanced at my watch. It was half-past seven.

I heaved a sigh of relief. There would not, I told myself, be much competition for the bathroom at that hour of the morning. A tepid bath would be as refreshing as anything could well be, I thought. So I bathed, shaved, and dressed. Then I wandered downstairs. There was no one about—it was only just after eight o'clock. So, for the third morning in succession I went out for a stroll along the promenade. I felt a bit nervous, since for the last two mornings I had found a dead body in the Broadgate lift. I was scared that there might be a third murder.

Yet I was not going to give in to any feeling of nervousness. I was resolved to face up to whatever might happen. So I went along and sat on the seat nearby the lift. If there was anything to be seen I was resolved to see it, even though it might be a sight just as shocking as those which had met my eyes on the previous mornings.

Nothing of the kind happened. It looked as if the trouble was over for the time being. I didn't see Bender. That red-headed, limping figure did not put in an appearance. I wandered over to the little path leading to the lift. The padlock on the lift-doors had clearly not been tampered with, and the notice stating that the lift was out of order was still in position. I knew that the police had decided that the lift should be kept locked, until further notice. But I was in a way astonished that Bender had not turned up. I had expected that he would do so, if only in the hope that the police ban on the use of the lift might be raised.

He had told me, in fact, that he was paid a small wage, plus a fairly considerable commission on his takings. So it was a good thing for him to have the lift working for the longest possible hours.

Still, the fact remained that he was not there. So I wandered back to my lodging at nine o'clock, and ate a thoughtful breakfast. This over, I made my way to the Police Station. It was now half-past nine, and I knew that I would find Shelley in possession. Indeed, he seemed to have been at work for hours. As on previous occasions, he was surrounded by papers. I presumed that the reports on the various names in Tilsley's notebooks were now coming in.

"Busy?" I asked.

"Never too busy to see you, Jimmy," he smiled. "After all, I don't suppose that you've come here merely to pick my brains, for you've been able to give me some useful leads up to now, and it may well be that you've got something useful again. What do you say?"

"Well, first of all I would like to pick your brains, as you put it," I said.

"Why?"

"Well, I have an idea which I think is suggestive," I said; "but I shall be able to see better if it's likely to be any good if I know a little more about what Tilsley was doing."

"I've got some of the reports on the people in his notebooks, of course," said Shelley a little reluctantly. "They're not altogether as satisfactory as I should wish."

"In what way?" I asked. This was not quite the answer from Shelley that I had anticipated.

"Well, I thought that there would be some common factor between them, which would enable us to get some idea of just what the man was doing. But there seems to be little in common between his various business acquaintances."

"What do you mean?"

Shelley picked up a bunch of papers from the table, apparently more or less at random, and said: "Well, the materials in which he was apparently dealing seemed to vary. Here's a man who used to buy radio valves and other small parts. The chap was a radio dealer in Chiswick. And here's a chemist, who bought all sorts of patent medicines from him. And here's a man with a music shop in Hammersmith. He used to buy rare and out-of-print gramophone records from Tilsley. As you probably know, Margerison was a dealer in precious metals, and Tilsley used to supply him with gold and platinum, while your friend Tim Foster had a garage, and used to buy spare parts for cars. The different sorts of goods in which Tilsley dealt were so striking that I can't conceive that any one man could possibly be sufficiently expert to deal in them all. The whole thing puzzles me considerably, I don't mind admitting."

"Have you thought of the possibility that these deals might be a disguise, hiding something else?" I asked.

Shelley looked at me with a glint of surprise in his eyes. "What do you mean, Jimmy?" he asked.

"Well, you've got so obsessed with the idea that there was some black market racket behind this that I think you've overlooked any other possibilities," I said. "You found no evidence of the black-market petrol business that you originally thought lay behind it?"

"Very little," he admitted. "Though several garages were involved in whatever is going on."

I now played my trump card, almost with an air of triumph. "Do you think that the answer might be drugs?" I asked.

"Drugs?"

"Yes—cocaine, hashish, and what have you," I explained. "After all, it does seem possible. These other things might be mere disguises for dealing in drugs. And the garage proprietors, radio and music shops, and so on might be totally innocent of any connexion with the case—they might be innocent agents, distributing drugs without any knowledge of what they were selling."

Shelley slapped his knee with his hand. "By Jove, Jimmy!" he exclaimed, "I believe that you've got hold of something there. It might be an explanation of what has happened. All the things, except possibly the car spares, were comparatively small things; they might easily be vehicles for the passing about of drugs."

I was pleased. I had not thought that Shelley would greet this suggestion with so much enthusiasm. It was clear that it had struck him as a worth-while idea.

"No indication in your reports that such a drug-ring might be in existence?" I enquired.

"I don't think so," he replied. "But then one would not expect anything of the sort. After all, if one is dealing in, say, cocaine, one would not expect to have to advertise the connexion. But I will certainly get our drug squad working on this, checking up on all the names in the list and seeing if any of them have at any time been suspected of having anything to do with drug traffic in this country."

"How long do you think it will take before you can get a pretty comprehensive report on things from that angle?" I asked.

"Not more than a few days," said Shelley. "Of course, one can't make any sort of firm promise; it all depends on whether these gentry have covered their tracks effectively. If they have, it may take a long time to dig the facts out. On the other hand, if they've been a bit over-confident, and have taken things too much for granted, it may be fairly easy to get the information we are after."

"But you do think that it is a possible explanation of what has been going on?" I asked.

"I do indeed."

"Well, it came from Miss Johnson and Mr. Foster," I said, and went on to explain what had been said at our discussion on the previous night. Shelley listened, without comment, to what I had to say. And at the end he nodded solemnly. Naturally, I had omitted from my statement the fact that Miss Johnson was worried because she thought that Tim Foster might be coming under suspicion.

"What do you think of that couple, Jimmy?" Shelley asked.

"Miss Johnson and Mr. Foster, you mean?" I said.

"Yes."

"I think they're very pleasant people," I said.

"But you don't think that they know anything about the murders?" he persisted.

Here it was coming, I told myself. Now I should know if there was any truth in my idea that Tim Foster was to some extent under suspicion.

"I don't think that either of them knows a thing about it," I said.

"You know that accusations have been bandied about?" Shelley asked.

"I know that Mrs. Skilbeck thinks that Foster had something to do with it," I said.

Shelley grinned. "So you know where the information came from?" he said.

"Well," I replied, "I didn't quite give you all the story about last night. You see, Mrs. Skilbeck came on the scene once, and very nearly caused some trouble." And I went on to tell of the pale lady's intervention.

Shelley looked thoughtful. "Yes," he said, "when she left you, she came right around here and spilled her story. There was some pretty nasty stuff in it, too, you know."

"In what way?" I asked.

"Well, you know she was engaged to John Tilsley," he said. "She is, in fact, almost the only person we know as yet who had any connexion with Tilsley, apart from his business. And she was able to tell us a lot about his personal life—things which correspond with what we have known from other sources. And she swears that he was in mortal fear of Tim Foster—says that he told her many times that Foster was out after his blood, and that one of these days Foster would attack him. Of course, we have no evidence on this point apart from her word; and we shouldn't take action on that alone. But I tell you, Jimmy, if we get hold of any concrete evidence to support what she has said, things will look a bit sticky for your friend Foster."

I was grateful for this hint, and I said as much. Then I asked: "But what does she give as a reason why Foster should be out after Tilsley's blood? After all Foster doesn't strike me as being a particularly bloodthirsty type. And a man doesn't usually threaten another unless he's got pretty good grounds for it."

Shelley looked mighty serious at this. "She says that Foster accused Tilsley of cheating him over these deals in spares—said that Tilsley had sold him some useless stuff, for which he had to pay high prices. Oh, Jimmy, there's no doubt that her story hangs together all right. I think that, since Foster is a friend of yours, you should know what is going on. At the moment he's safe enough, but, as I said, if any new evidence crops up, he might be in quite a spot."

I thought it decent of Shelley to give me this word of warning. While I was still thanking him for this, however, the telephone rang. With a muttered apology to me, he picked up the receiver.

"Shelley here," he said. Then: "What?" came in a really startled tone.

"Where is he? On the promenade, near the bandstand? On one of the seats behind the bushes? All right. Ring the doctor, tell him to come around. I'll be there without delay. Try to keep a crowd from assembling if you can. It's in a pretty quiet spot, is it? Good."

He slammed the receiver down. "Surprising news, Jimmy," he said quietly.

"What is it?"

"It's our friend Bender."

My heart sank. "Murdered?" I asked.

Shelley shook his head. "No," he said. "Our friend the enemy has made a mistake this time, Jimmy. Bender isn't dead. He is lying unconscious on one of the seats by the bandstand—you know, those paths that run behind the bandstand, with bushes in front."

"I know," I said.

"Well, then, off we go!"

And off we went.

CHAPTER XX

In Which We Find that a Plot has Failed

A S WE HURRIED AROUND TO THE PROMENADE I IMAGINE THAT the thoughts flowing through Shelley's mind were not unlike those that flowed through my own. I was at last alert to the fact that something had happened which presumably our enemy had not reckoned with.

Previous events—the murder of Tilsley and that of Margerison, both taking place in the apparently impossible surroundings of the locked lift—seemed to have moved with a kind of fateful certainty. The murderer, or so it appeared to me, had such a control of the whole affair that all that we could do was to move in his wake, trying vainly to follow what he had done after it was over. The initiative, in other words, remained wholly with him. He was the attacker, whereas we were perpetually on the defence. But now, for the first time in forty-eight hours, it appeared to me that the murderer had made a mistake. This I assumed, not so much because Bender had not been killed, as because the attempt on him had been made on the promenade and not in the lift.

Shelley, in the course of many talks on criminology which I had had with him from time to time, had repeatedly pointed out that the criminal almost invariably carried out a series of crimes on precisely similar lines. The criminal, in other words, tends to be a specialist, repeating himself. And the fact that the deaths of Tilsley and Margerison were precisely similar showed that the plot was working according to a pre-arranged plan.

The death—or rather the attempt on the life—of Bender was so completely out of pattern that I felt that something that we had done had thrown the murderer temporarily off his balance. I said as much to Shelley as we hurried somewhat breathlessly along the street.

"I'm inclined to agree with you, Jimmy," he said. "This attempt doesn't ring quite true, somehow, though I'm not at all sure what is wrong. But it's no good for us to get too confident, you know. That is the way in which the whole scheme, as we see it, may well fall to the ground."

"But you agree that we may have thrown him off his stride, somehow?" I said.

"Either that, or this is deliberately out of pattern, in order to throw us off *our* stride," Shelley pointed out. "We're up against a pretty clever and original brain, Jimmy, and I wouldn't put it beyond him to do that, you know. The main thing in a case of this sort is to be a thought ahead of your opponent all the time."

"You think we are?"

Shelley smiled ruefully. "Up to now, we have been about two thoughts behind him," he admitted. "But I hope, now, that we are about drawing level."

By this time we had reached the promenade. I should, perhaps, explain that at Broadgate there is the usual wide promenade, with a bandstand in the middle of its broadest expanse at one end. But there is also a sort of back promenade, running behind the main promenade, and separated from it by a more or less continuous chain of decorative shrubs of one sort and another.

It was on this small back promenade that there are a ring of seats. And on one of these seats the unfortunate Aloysius Bender was lying. A constable stood by, and our old friend the police surgeon was in attendance.

"Well, Doctor?" asked Shelley as we approached.

The doctor was holding the man's wrist, his eye on his watch.

"He'll do," was the doctor's brief answer.

"Yes; you mean that he'll live?"

"Of course. Only a scratch," the doctor said. "I should think he probably fainted from shock. Certainly the wound was of no importance."

"Where was the wound?" asked Shelley.

"Left side. But it did not go in at all deep. I should say that the intention was to strike the heart—but probably the man was nervous, at carrying out his attempt in such a public place. Either that, or he was disturbed just at the crucial moment. Not my business, of course," the doctor added hastily, "to explain why things happened as they did. But I thought, Inspector, that you might care to have my impression of the thing."

Shelley duly considered these remarks. Then he said: "Would you consider that this wound was given by the same hand as that which killed Margerison and Tilsley?"

"Could have been," the doctor said. "After all, the circumstances were so different. Both the two murders were carried out in privacy of the lift. If the criminal had somehow lulled the men he was to murder into a sense of security, he could carry out his purpose more or less at his leisure. But this attempt on Bender was done in a public place, with no chance to pick the time. As a result, I think that he may well have made a more or less clumsy attempt. If he had had Bender in the lift well, the conclusion might have been very different."

"I'm inclined to agree with you, Doctor," said Shelley. "And you think that, if the other blows, on Tilsley and Margerison, showed signs of some knowledge of anatomy, this one was not in any way inconsistent with it."

This seemed to be as far as we were likely to get in this respect, and Shelley now turned his attention to the man on the seat. Bender was pale, though, in view of what he had gone through, that was in no way surprising. Doctor Duncan had put a bandage around his chest, as a bulge underneath his shirt showed clearly enough.

Shelley felt for the man's pulse. Then he looked at me. "I should think he would be O.K. in a few minutes, Jimmy," he said. "Will he be able to walk, Doctor?"

"With assistance, I should think so," Doctor Duncan said. "But my car is on the road at the back. Why not put him into that and take him around to the Police Station—since I presume that is what is in your mind?"

"Should we carry him there?" asked Shelley.

"If you like," answered the doctor indifferently. "But you will save yourself a lot of work if you wait for a few minutes. As you surmised, he's likely to become conscious at any moment now, and I think if two of us help him, he will be able to make his way to my car without much difficulty."

Indeed, I could see a flicker about Bender's eyes as the doctor was speaking. Now he stirred and made as if to sit up. Doctor Duncan hurried around and assisted him, holding him in position as he made the effort to get into a sitting posture.

Bender blinked. "What... what... what's happened?" he murmured slowly.

"Don't worry," the doctor reassured him. "Just come with us, won't you?"

I couldn't help admiring the skilful way in which Doctor Duncan slid Bender's feet off the seat, got him standing, and then, one arm around the man's shoulder, managed to start him walking. Bender was not altogether reluctant to walk, but his feet seemed to move like those of an automaton. I stood at the other side, and Bender put his left arm around my neck. Thus assisted by the two of us, he made his way to the car. Shelley followed at the back, and the little procession was ended by the constable who had found Bender and had first reported his find over the phone to Shelley.

The doctor's car was fortunately pretty roomy. It was an old-fashioned model, but we all got into it without any difficulty at all. Bender lay back in the seat and closed his eyes, as if he had found the effort of getting so far almost too much for him.

Within a matter of three or four minutes, however, we were at the Police Station. Now Bender had to be got out of the car and into Shelley's office. That was in some respects a more difficult matter than it had been to get him into the car, for there were some steps to be negotiated, and Bender's feet seemed to find steps not at all easy to get up or down. Still, with a little extra effort we made it.

Shelley hauled out a battered old leather armchair. In this Bender slumped back and shut his eyes gratefully, as if he had found the whole performance of the last ten minutes infinitely trying—as, indeed, he might well have done. Doctor Duncan thought that the man had lost some blood, which is always apt to leave the victim in a somewhat weary state.

However, the detective wasn't prepared to let the man get away with it. He frowned portentously on Bender. Then he spoke.

"Now then, Bender," he said.

"Yes?" Bender's voice was hoarse and strained.

"We want to know what happened to you."

"I don't think that I know much more about it than you gentlemen do," Bender replied.

"But you must know what happened, man!" Shelley exclaimed, looking definitely impatient.

"I was sitting on the seat out there," Bender said, "and I never gave a thought when I heard someone walking along the path behind me."

"What time was this?" asked Shelley.

"Just about nine o'clock, I should think. You see, I was at a loose end. Your people have not returned the keys of the lift yet. It's still not ready for use by the public."

Shelley nodded. He knew all about this, I could see. "You say that you heard someone approaching along the path behind you?" he remarked.

"Yes. Even when the footsteps stopped quite close to me, I didn't think anything about it. Then the man suddenly grasped me around the mouth with his left arm. I couldn't move or cry out. I was so scared I was just paralysed. I didn't struggle or anything, I was so frightened. Then I felt a sharp prick in my ribs, as if the man was pushing a sharp knife in there. I knew nothing more until I woke up, lying on the seat, with all you gentlemen around me."

Shelley grunted sceptically. I could see that he thought this a thoroughly unsatisfactory story, but I couldn't understand why the appearance of disbelief flashed over his usually friendly countenance. It appeared to me that Bender's story was eminently possible. He might well have been taken completely by surprise, as he had explained.

Shelley grinned savagely. "So that's all that you know about the attack that has been made on you, is it, Bender?" he said.

"Yes."

"You never caught the slightest glimpse of the man who tried to stab you?"

"No."

"Nothing at all that would give us the slightest clue to his identity?"

"No."

"H'm." I could see that Shelley was in no way satisfied with this tale. But at the same time it was not easy to see how the man could be shaken. Indeed, as I have already said, I was tolerably impressed with the way in which he had told his story. It struck me as having the ring of truth. I thought that Shelley, with his lengthy experience of cross-examining suspicious characters, might well have a sort of sixth sense which made him realise when a man was not telling the truth. But at the same time, even if he was not altogether impressed with what the man said, I did not see how the story was to be broken down.

"Well, I think that's all we can say to you at the moment, Bender," Shelley said. "We'll let you have a car to take you home."

Bender was assisted to the car, and Shelley slumped back in his chair in a brown study. Doctor Duncan had already left us, and I was alone with the detective.

"Not quite satisfied, Inspector?" I said slowly.

"Not a bit satisfied, Jimmy," he said. "But I don't see just what we can do about it. After all, we have no witnesses of what happened. And if Bender isn't telling the truth, I don't see what chance we have to prove that he's lying. After all, it's never easy to prove a negative."

"But you think he's lying?" I remarked.

"Yes."

"Why?"

"When you've been a detective for nearly twenty years, Jimmy," he explained, "you get an idea that a man is lying, without being able to say why. I think it's something about the look in his eyes. Very few liars can look you straight in the face; there is something vaguely shifty about the way they look at you. And I've rarely failed to detect a liar, though often there is nothing very concrete that I can lay my hand on."

I thought that this was not getting us very far. I thought likewise, that it was time to change the subject. I knew that I should have little need of extra material for my story to be phoned to the paper that evening. This attempt on Bender's life provided me with quite enough sensational material to justify splash headlines for the third day in succession. But at the same time I liked to get all the background material that I could; one never knew when it might be useful, on a day when the main story was at a standstill.

So I said: "Bender said that you had the keys of the lift?"

"That's true."

"Bender's own set, and the set that was found in the Council Offices?"

"Yes." I thought that there was a glint of slight amusement in Shelley's eye, as if I was now getting on to a point that had occurred to him long ago.

"Then that might be the reason why this attempt on Bender's life did not take place where the two murders occurred—in the lift?" I said.

"Yes."

Shelley's monosyllabic answers suggested to anyone who knew him as well as I did that I was getting warm in my questions, that I was getting hold of some information not obvious on the surface, and not precisely what Shelley was anxious to disclose to me. The detective, indeed, would not hide things from me—his agreement with me was something that he would, I knew, keep to the letter. But that was no reason why he should share with me every little suspicion that might enter his head. It was therefore up to me to see if I could solve the little mystery that he had obviously made about this affair of the keys.

"But Bender told a story about a man who had had copies of his keys made," I said.

"Yes." Shelley smiled.

"That's one of the things that makes you suspicious of Bender," I remarked.

"It's the main thing," Shelley admitted. "That man is hiding something, Jimmy. I don't know what it is, but I've got no doubt that there is something there. And it may well be that he is holding out on us, and perhaps on the murderer also. You see, if he really knows something about the death of Tilsley, while it may not be enough to make the murderer scared, it may be enough to make him feel a little unsafe. And a man who has already committed two murders is not going to allow himself to be unsafe because of Bender. He's going to put Bender out of the way without delay."

"Then you think Bender is in a spot?"

"I do."

"But surely you've just sent him home. He might be murdered as soon as he gets there!" I exclaimed.

"You don't credit me for much sense, Jimmy," Shelley said with a smile. "Why, it may even be that Bender may, without being conscious of it, lead us to the murderer."

"And what are you doing about it?" I asked.

"Putting a plain-clothes man on his tail," Shelley said. "From now on Aloysius Bender will be watched night and day. And I think that before many days are over we shall have the murderer."

CHAPTER XXI

In Which I Take Part in a New Council of War

U P TO NOW I HAD ALMOST FORGOTTEN MY PROMISE TO TIM
Foster and Maya Johnson. Those two young people were
going through a sticky time, I knew. I knew, also, that I should
have to do something to ease their uneasy minds. After all, they
had thought that they were in some degree under suspicion—as,
indeed, in a measure, they were. And I had promised to do what
I could to help them in their difficulty. And I had done nothing as
yet to keep that promise.

I made my way to the garage, therefore. Tim Foster was standing
in the doorway when I got there.

"Any news?" he asked eagerly as I approached.

"A certain amount," I replied. "Nothing very important, but
I thought that I should like to have a chat with Miss Johnson and
yourself. Is there a peaceful little café anywhere near here, where we
could have a chat over a cup of coffee, do you think?"

"Just down the road there's a place where we often go," he said.
"Shall I give Maya a ring and ask her to come along?"

"Do," I said.

He went inside and did the necessary work on the telephone. He
was with me within a few moments.

"She'll be here in five minutes," he announced at length, "so we'll
make our way down."

The café was a peaceful little place, as I had asked. In fact, it was so quiet that I wondered how the proprietors managed to make a living out of it. There wasn't a soul in the place when Tim and I entered. We made our way to the corner, where a small table was tucked away under a discreetly-shaded lamp. We ordered coffees and awaited Maya Johnson's arrival.

When she came I was struck as before by her appearance. Her beauty was as breath-taking as ever. I'm no good at describing clothes, but she was dressed in a pink-and-white frock of some silky material that suited her complexion admirably. I could scarcely resist a gasp of amazement at the way in which she swept into the room. Unlike most beautiful women she did not seem to be in any way conscious of her beauty. She made her way to our table, sat down, and asked the waitress, with an unconscious arrogance, for a coffee.

"Well?" she said quietly to me when the coffee had been delivered.

"I thought that I should report to you and Tim what I've found out so far," I explained.

"And what is that?" she asked with considerable eagerness. I could see that she was anxious to know what was being done. Her love for Tim Foster was so transparently obvious that it almost made me smile, and feel paternal. Such is the feeling of the man of forty when faced with young love—for I supposed that they couldn't be more than about twenty-five years of age, either of them.

"Well, the police are suspicious of Tim, but have no really concrete evidence against him," I said.

"Of course not," Maya Johnson said, with an indignant toss of the head. "Who could have concrete evidence against a man who is innocent?"

"Well, such things have happened," I said. "There was Oscar Slater. There was a man called Wallace in Liverpool about twenty years ago. He was actually found guilty of murder, though the verdict was reversed by the Court of Appeal. But the police don't often make mistakes of that sort. As a rule they don't arrest anyone unless they're pretty sure, or unless the case looks more or less cast-iron."

"But why are they suspicious?" Tim asked. "I don't think that I've done anything which is likely to arouse their suspicions."

"You forget Mrs. Skilbeck," I reminded him. "It seems that she had told the police a pretty convincing tale about you, and about the things she alleges Tilsley told her about you. She may be in a queer spot herself, or it may be that she has made up her mind that you did it. Then she would have told the police anything that she could think about which would be likely to put you in the queer."

"Surely no one would do anything so dreadful," exclaimed Maya Johnson.

"Don't forget that Mrs. Skilbeck was engaged to Tilsley," I said. "Put yourself in her place for a moment. Suppose that it was Tim, here, who had been murdered, and that you had suspicions of someone. Wouldn't you do anything you could to get that person under arrest?"

"Ye—es," she said, rather unwillingly. "I suppose that I should."

"And if you were sure that you knew the murderer, but were afraid that he might escape through lack of evidence," I went on, "wouldn't you even condescend to manufacturing a spot of evidence, if you thought that it might tip the scales?"

"That's possible," she admitted. I thought that Maya Johnson was one of the most honest people I had ever met. She had no capacity for self-deception, but forced herself to admit anything which was genuinely part of her feelings.

She looked at me now with wide-open eyes. "You have done a lot for us," she said.

"Only as part of my job," I said.

"Well," she went on, "I wonder if I could persuade you to do something more for us?"

"What is it?" I asked.

"Would you go to Mrs. Skilbeck again—you told us, I remember, that you had interviewed her once, a day or two back—and see if you can find out what it is that she has against Tim?"

I looked a trifle alarmed. After all, Mrs. Skilbeck had seen me with these young people, and, after that, it was a pretty tough assignment to expect me to get anything more in the way of information out of her. Yet the fact remained that she might know something that I had not yet found out. And, as I had thought when talking to Shelley, background knowledge of the case was something which I wanted, and which I could not get in too great a quantity. Besides, there was nothing which Maya Johnson asked me that I could refuse. That unearthly beauty simply made me helpless.

At the same time, however, I felt more than a little perturbed at what she was asking me to do. I thought that Mrs. Skilbeck would now take a pretty poor view of me, considering, probably, that I was a mere stooge of Tim Foster and Maya Johnson. And, indeed, she had every right to think that, since in effect I was acting on their behalf. Still, to the Charrington Hotel I certainly had to go.

I swallowed my coffee at a gulp, laid a shilling on the table in payment, and made my way to the door. In the street I blinked at the sudden sunshine, lit a cigarette, and made my way towards the Charrington. To any observer I must have appeared a very ordinary man on a holiday in Kent. If the passers-by had only known the thoughts that were coursing through my head they would have been astonished. I was, in fact, wondering if the true explanation of Mrs. Skilbeck's interest in Tim Foster arose out of the fact that she knew the true murderer and was shielding him by attacking Tim. That was a possible explanation, and if it were true, it meant that I was thrusting my head into a hornets' nest or a lion's mouth (choose your own metaphor).

Still, it was now much too late in the day to draw back. I had promised Tim and Maya that I would have another go at Mrs. Skilbeck, and have another go at Mrs. Skilbeck I must. The Charrington was not far away—nowhere in Broadgate is far away from anywhere else. I reached the door of the hotel in a matter of ten minutes or so, tossed away the remnants of my cigarette, and made my way into the vestibule. The place had not altered at all from the occasion of my previous visit. Its dimness remained, and Mrs. Skilbeck still sat behind the little reception kiosk.

"Good morning, Mrs. Skilbeck," I said as cheerfully as I could.

"Good morning," she replied, greeting me with a stony glare that did not suggest my mission of enquiry was likely to be very successful.

"You remember me, don't you?" I asked.

"I remember you," she agreed with what was almost a sneer. "I'm not likely to forget you, the man who posed as anxious to solve the mystery of John's death and then became friendly with John's murderer!"

This was the sort of attack that I had anticipated, and I thought that I knew the best way to deal with it.

"You're not quite fair, Mrs. Skilbeck," I said. "The matter is not as simple as you appear to think."

"It is perfectly simple," she asserted flatly. I quailed a little. This was not going to be so easy to deal with as I had originally hoped it might be. The woman was obviously very much embittered. She had a kind of savage intensity which was almost frightening.

"Do you think that you could grant me a few minutes somewhere not quite so public as this?" I asked indicating the hotel vestibule.

"I don't see why I should," she said. I felt a little impatient. This really was getting much more difficult than I had anticipated. But I had promised Tim and Maya to do my best, and I knew that I should have to go through with it, however unpromising it might appear.

"It is merely that we have a good deal to talk about," I explained. "You have misjudged me, Mrs. Skilbeck. I have to tell you that I am still as eager as ever to solve the mystery of John Tilsley's death. It is merely that I think you are mistaken when you consider that Timothy Foster was responsible for it. But I think that we should talk it over."

"All right," she said. "Come this way, please." Her dead white face was expressionless, and she led the way to an inner sanctum which was presumably her private room. It lay off the vestibule, on its inner side.

When we had come into this room—a cosy little room with a window overlooking the hotel garden, which lay at the back of the building—she waved me into an armchair, sat herself on a high chair facing me, and folded her hands on her lap. Her face was still as expressionless as ever.

"Now, what did you want to say, Mr. London?" she asked quietly.

"I wanted to tell you, first of all, that you have completely misjudged my attitude in this case," I said. "I'm not trying to clear the guilty person."

She jumped in at this remark. "Then why did you hobnob with him?" she asked.

"I meant that I don't accept your suggestion that Timothy Foster is guilty of the crime," I said.

"I am sure that he is." Her mouth shut almost with a snap, as if she thought that this was the last word to be said on this matter.

"Can you give me some indication of why you think that?" I asked. Somehow, I told myself, I had to get on better terms with this woman. And the only way in which I could do it was to get her talking about it, to allow her to have her head, and see if what she said was good sense. After all, she must have some reason for her emphatic belief that Tim was guilty. For I was prepared to back my belief that he was not guilty.

"I knew John Tilsley better than anyone else," she announced. "And I know that he was in mortal fear of Foster. He often said so to me."

"Did he give any reason for his fear of Timothy Foster?" I asked.

"Yes." The monosyllable came like a shot from a gun.

"And what was his reason?"

"He used to say that he had done a smart deal which Foster had resented. He said that Foster had always disliked him, and that now he had got the better of Foster in a business deal that dislike had got a lot deeper. In fact, he said that it had turned to hate. He often said to me that he was sure Foster would try to kill him one of these days. And that is why I say that now I am perfectly sure that Foster is the murderer."

This was, of course, more or less the story that Shelley had told me. I wondered how much truth there was in it. The malice in Mrs. Skilbeck's tone was obvious; but I didn't know how much of that might be derived from her mistrust of Tim, and how much might be due to her genuine belief that what she thought of Tim was the simple truth. She had clearly been very fond of John Tilsley, and if she really thought that Timothy Foster had been responsible for Tilsley's death she would naturally want to see him brought to justice.

I had often prided myself on my insight into human nature, but I couldn't for the life of me decide whether this woman was lying out of pure desire to be avenged on the man whom she thought responsible for the death of the man she loved, or whether she was telling what she sincerely believed to be the truth. I was, in fact, getting thoroughly involved. It seemed to me that whatever I did I was now deeper and deeper in the mire. Every brainwave that I had seemed to lead nowhere. I was just having arguments and discussions with the people in the case, and seeing those arguments and discussions peter out into nothing.

I wondered what Shelley was doing, and whether his investigations had got him any further forward than mine had got me. The way in which this case was working out was, indeed, curiously different from what one had anticipated. The detective stories which I had read never presented this aspect; nor did those books on criminology which had come my way. But I thought that such volumes portrayed the case at the finish. I was in the middle of this one. Perhaps in a few days' time this case might look more complete; perhaps all the pieces of the jigsaw puzzle would fall neatly into position. For the moment I thought that there could be little doubt that I was bogged in the mud of surmise.

Still, I had to deal with Mrs. Skilbeck somehow, so I tried to get some more information about this supposed hatred of Tilsley which Tim Foster was alleged to have felt. Surely, I told myself, there was something that I could do to elucidate the thing.

"What was the business deal in which Tilsley was supposed to have got the better of Foster?" I asked.

She shook her head helplessly. "I don't know," she said. "As I told you when you were here before, I knew nothing of the details of Mr. Tilsley's business. All that I know is that he got the better of Foster somehow, and Foster resented it—resented it to such a degree that he threatened John Tilsley's life."

"Threatened his life?" I asked. This was the first time that threats had been mentioned.

"Yes; he said that Foster said he would see that Tilsley would regret having done him down."

"That's not exactly a threat on his life," I pointed out.

"No; but John interpreted it as such."

And from that position I was totally unable to move her. She was, I thought, completely obsessed with the idea that Foster had killed Tilsley. Every statement, every fact, was viewed from that idea. If you've ever dealt with a person suffering from a genuine obsession, you will realise the total impossibility of arguing. Nothing penetrates into the mind of the person which tells in any way against the obsession. Only one side of the case makes any kind of impression.

And yet Mrs. Skilbeck was in many ways a sensible, rational woman. But on this one point rationality was suspended. I hoped that Shelley would read her character as I was reading it; otherwise it was a poor outlook, I thought, for Tim and Maya. As I left the Charrington Hotel I thought that this had been, on the whole, about the most unsatisfactory of all the interviews which I had so far undergone.

CHAPTER XXII

In Which More Surprises Occur

I WAS IN NO WAY SATISFIED WITH MY INTERVIEW WITH MRS. Skilbeck. I think that you will understand that. I had hoped that something might come out of it which would lead me to definite proof of Tim Foster's innocence. Instead of that, all that I had managed to secure was a repetition of the vague accusations that Shelley had told me about, without a vestige of proof in any shape or form.

Mind you, I was not accusing Mrs. Skilbeck of lying. I did not now think that she was telling lies. I merely thought that she was so hopelessly biased against my friend Tim that she was entirely unable to look at the matter of his guilt or innocence with anything like an open mind. And the witness who is, albeit unconsciously, biased is the worst possible witness to deal with. It is difficult to account for the bias without oneself acquiring a bias in the opposite direction.

I was quite prepared to admit that I had a pretty considerable bias in Tim's favour. Indeed, Maya Johnson's belief in him was in a way enough to convince me that he could not be a murderer. But I did not know whether I should say that my bias in his favour had been increased by all that Mrs. Skilbeck had said. I knew that Shelley would have said that it was. And Shelley, after all, was the genuinely unbiased observer. The police, in spite of all that has from time to time been said against them, do genuinely want to get the guilty man. They have no desire to arrest a man who is innocent. Apart from everything else, there is the very severe danger that they may arrest an innocent man, and then go through the trying ordeal of seeing that man's counsel drive a coach and four through their case when it comes up for trial.

So when I made my way back to the lodgings for lunch I was feeling a bit dismal. I had enough material, it was true, to phone another pretty sensational instalment to *The Daily Wire* that evening. But, while my main job was as a journalist, the fact remained that I had set my heart on solving the mystery, on presenting Inspector Shelley with a cast-iron case on which he could make an arrest. And I thought that there now seemed to be less and less chance that I should be able to do anything of the sort.

At the end of lunch I took a cup of coffee and went to drink it in the lounge. I wanted to think, and I knew that the dining-room would be a buzz of conversation—no doubt mainly concerned with the murders. That went without saying. These mysterious deaths now provided the main topic of conversation in Broadgate, and one couldn't go anywhere without hearing them discussed. I was utterly fed-up with the most fantastic theories which I had heard quite seriously advanced by people who in actuality knew nothing at all about the case.

As I was sipping my coffee and smoking my cigarette—without much pleasure, I must admit—I heard the telephone ring outside. I didn't give it a thought. Then Mrs. Cecil came into the room, looking rather puffed and hurried.

"Oh, Mr. London, I'm so glad that you're here," she said with an almost comic sense of relief.

"Why, Mrs. Cecil?" I asked.

"Because you're wanted on the telephone."

"Who wants me?"

"A Mr. Foster. He said that it's very urgent, and that I was to get you at once."

"Thank you, Mrs. Cecil," I said. But I still felt fed-up, wondering what on earth Tim Foster could have to say to me that he couldn't have said earlier in the day. Still, I made my way to the telephone.

"Hullo," I said.

"Jimmy London?" queried the voice at the other end of the line.

"Speaking."

"Tim Foster here," he said.

"Yes, Tim, what is it?" I asked.

"Can you come round to the garage at once?" he asked, a suppressed eagerness in his voice.

"I should think so. Is it something very urgent?" I asked.

"Very urgent. I think that we've got some evidence that might well support the theory we were discussing earlier. I can't say much on the telephone, but I think that if you come around here, you will be as excited as I am."

He certainly sounded excited enough. He even infected me. I said "I'll be with you in a few minutes, Tim," slammed down the receiver, rushed up to my room to get a hat, and was out of the door within what could not have been more than a minute.

I hurried along the street. The sun was boiling hot, but I was quite prepared to run, should running appear to be in any way necessary. What on earth, I told myself, did Tim mean by the theory we had discussed earlier? Did he mean the theory about drug-peddling? Or did he mean some theory with regard to Mrs. Skilbeck which we had formed? I ran over in my mind what we had said, but I couldn't make up my mind what he had meant.

I had intended to go and see Shelley after lunch, to try once more to pick the brains of the man from Scotland Yard. But Tim had sounded so insistent that I thought I must go and see him first. After all, if he had succeeded in getting some sort of concrete evidence, that would be all the better. I should have something worth while to hand on to Shelley when I did see him—and I didn't intend that meeting to be far ahead.

Within the promised few minutes I was at the garage. As I came to the end of the road I could see Tim. He was in the street outside the garage, pacing up and down the pavement as if he could not contain himself in patience anywhere indoors. He waved wildly to me as he spotted me, and I waved back as sedately as I could.

Still, as I have already said, he had infected me with his excitement, and I found it very difficult to maintain my equanimity. I was sure now that Tim had got hold of something really worth while.

"Thank God you've come, Jimmy," he said as I drew near. He grasped my arm with an iron grip and drew me near to the outer door of the garage.

"Here, easy does it, Tim!" I expostulated. "My arm's not made of steel, you know. No need to do a lifelike imitation of a vice when you see me."

"Sorry," he replied. "But I'm so excited, Jimmy, that I scarcely know what I'm doing."

"Keep yourself under control," I advised him. "Whatever it is that you've found out, it'll keep for a few minutes longer, you know."

"I'm not sure that it will," he said.

"Well, I'm the best judge of that," said I. "Lead on, my lad, and let me see what it is that you've found that you think is so very important."

Without a word he turned on his heel and led the way in. I followed as speedily as I could. He led the way into the inner office of the garage, where I had first seen him. Then he shut the door as soon as I had entered, and swung round to face me.

"You know," he said, "that Maya suggested that the solution of this problem might well be something in the nature of the smuggling of drugs?"

"Yes," I replied, "and I passed the suggestion on to my friend Inspector Shelley."

"What did he say?" asked Tim Foster with much eagerness.

"He was very interested, and promised to put the drug squad from Scotland Yard on to the matter. He said that they could easily check up on all the addresses from Tilsley's notebook and find if there was anyone mentioned there who has been known or suspected of having any connexion with the traffic of dangerous drugs," I explained.

"Any results yet?"

"I don't know. I was just going to see Shelley, as a matter of fact, when you phoned, and it sounded to me as if your message was more urgent than my going to see Inspector Shelley."

"It certainly was," Tim said. "In fact, it may well be that what I have found will be of some use to you—and to Inspector Shelley, if he's really anxious to get to the solution of this business."

"Well," I said impatiently, "what have you found, Tim?"

He pulled open a drawer of his desk. "Do you know anything about sparking-plugs?" he asked.

"Nothing at all," I said, "except that they are the things that go wrong when you're driving a car, and leave you stranded miles from anywhere, down a lonely lane when it's pouring with rain on a pitch-black night."

Tim grinned. "I suppose that is the ordinary man's opinion," he said. "Well, it so happens that a few months ago sparking-plugs— good ones of the well-known makes—were very difficult to get hold of. And Tilsley provided me, from time to time, with quite a number. They were very useful to me, though I once fitted one to a car of my own and found it no good at all. Just refused to spark, in fact."

"Well, get on, man!" I snapped irritably. Tim Foster seemed to be taking a terribly long time to get to the point of what he was trying to say—seemed, indeed, almost to be trying deliberately to spin the yarn out as long as he could. I found it all most tiresome.

"Sorry. I was just allowing my thoughts to ramble a bit," he explained, "so that you should have some chance of getting straight the background of what I was trying to tell you."

"Well, don't let the old thoughts ramble any more," I advised him. "I'm only anxious to know what it is that you've found. If you take such a long time to tell it, I shouldn't think that it can be all that important."

"It's important enough," he said, and, diving into some papers in the drawer which he had opened, produced a small tin, containing a sparking-plug. At least, it bore on its lid the name of a well-known make of plug, and I presumed that it contained one of these plugs inside.

He opened the tin and took out the little plug. "This, in fact, is the plug which I fitted to my own car and which was so poor," he said. "I cleaned the points and did all the usual things that one does, but nothing happened. The thing just completely failed to work."

Now I thought that I was beginning to understand what he was getting at. We had heard a lot about the business connexions of John Tilsley, but this was the first time that we had actually been able to lay our hands on something which was part of the stock-in-trade in which the dead man had been dealing. It was clearly of some importance, and I again began to feel nearly as excited as Tim Foster.

"When did you think of this?" I asked.

"Only after leaving you this morning. You remember, Maya had suggested that there might be some possibility that Tilsley was using his various deals as a sort of blind for some other material—material which was illegal. I wondered whether we couldn't lay our hands on something. I had nothing, I thought, which he had sold me—and then I suddenly remembered this plug. It had actually been intended for a customer of mine, but it had happened that just when he brought his car in I had had a consignment of half-a-dozen sparking plugs direct from the makers. So I fitted one of them on his car and shoved this away in a drawer. Then, some time later, when I had plug trouble, I remembered having this one and got it out. I was in a hurry—going to meet someone at the station, and when I found it was defective I hauled it out and put another one in."

"And that's the last time you handled it?" I suggested.

"Yes. Until today. Then I remembered it again, and I thought it would be a good idea to examine it with the greatest possible care, to see if there was anything in the suggestion that Maya put forward."

"And was there any?" I asked.

"Wait!" he cautioned me. Then he unscrewed the top of the plug—it was a very neatly made little piece of apparatus, I thought—and removed it. He spread a large sheet of blotting-paper on the table and tipped up the inner part of the plug on it. A small amount of white powder emerged on to the blotting-paper.

"There!" he said with an air of triumph. And I really could not find it in me to blame him for his moment of excitement.

"What do you think it is?" he asked, after a few moments' silence.

I dipped my finger in it, took up a few particles and placed them on my tongue. There was not much taste about it, but there was a queer tingling sort of sensation about my tongue afterwards.

"I would be prepared to guess that it's cocaine," I said. Tim Foster sat back in his chair with an air of absolute triumph.

"Maya was right!" he exclaimed.

"Maya was right!" I echoed.

"Do you think that your man from Scotland Yard will be satisfied with this?" he asked.

"I'm sure that Shelley will find it very interesting," I said. "It certainly seems to provide the proof that we were after, with regard to the job that our friend Tilsley was doing."

"And do you think that it lets me out of the soup?" asked Tim.

I looked serious. "I wouldn't altogether say that," I warned him. "In fact, I wouldn't say that it doesn't put you deeper in the mire."

"In what way?"

"Well," I explained. "Look at it through the detective's eyes. His view would be that he thought you had some sort of connexion with this man. Tilsley was dealing in drugs, and here you are—with drugs in your possession. I know that your story is true, and Shelley might think it probably true. But he has to remain sceptical about everything that happens. And the obvious explanation is that you were in with Tilsley on his deals in drugs. And that might in some way provide the motive for the murder. See?"

Tim Foster saw. I have seldom seen a man so taken aback. But I thought that, after all, I had been wise in not allowing him to fill his mind with a false optimism which the events would not justify.

CHAPTER XXIII

In Which Shelley Makes a Move

O F COURSE, IN ACTUALITY I SAW THE VALUE OF TIM FOSTER'S discovery. I knew that what he had found out was likely to be a clue of great importance. But he thought that it was a kind of magic touchstone, which would enable him to prove his innocence of any connection with the murder. I just had to disillusion him on that score.

But at the same time I knew that Shelley would greet this new clue with real joy. It would provide him with the very sort of concrete evidence which he had constantly been complaining was absent in this case.

So I shook off Tim as quickly as I could, telling him not to worry overmuch, but that I would put things right with Shelley. That this was advice easier to give than to follow I knew. But I was now working on Tim's behalf, and, even if he did worry for the time being, it was better to worry in a garage in Broadgate than in a cell at the Old Bailey—and the Old Bailey was what I was trying to save him from.

When I got to the Police Station the old, unpleasant sergeant was there in charge.

"I suppose you want to see Inspector Shelley again?" he said with a sneer.

"Yes," I said, restraining my impulse to punch him on the nose.

"You can't."

"Why not?"

"Because he's not here."

This was a bit of a facer for me. For the first time I had secured what I thought to be really important evidence, and for the first time Shelley was not on the spot to receive it in person when I arrived.

"Where is he?" I asked.

"Is there any reason why you should get an answer to that question?" the sergeant asked.

"I don't know that there is, except that I have an important piece of evidence to give him," I said.

"You wouldn't consider giving it to me, I suppose?" the sergeant said with another sneer.

"I certainly wouldn't. I am working with Inspector Shelley," I said. "And I have promised to keep him informed of anything that I may find as a result of working for my paper."

"You'd better come in and see Inspector Beech," the sergeant remarked, leading the way to an inner room.

This was unexpected. It was not altogether welcome, either. I hadn't seen Inspector Beech since the very beginning of the case, but I knew that I had taken a pretty dim view of the local man. I suspected, too, that he had taken a pretty dim view of me. But I couldn't very well refuse to enter the man's presence, merely because we had taken an instinctive dislike to each other from the start. So I followed the sergeant, hugging the tin with the sparking-plug in it. This was in my pocket, and I didn't intend to take it out if I could possibly avoid it. The knowledge that I had I intended to share with Shelley and with no one else.

Inspector Beech looked up sharply as I came in.

"Well, London?" he snapped.

"I wanted to see Inspector Shelley," I explained.

"I have already been told this," answered the local inspector. "But I fail to see why you should be prepared to hand to him any information which you are not prepared to hand to me. After all, as Inspector Shelley has so often said, he and I are working together on this case. We share our discoveries and our opinions, and the fact that he belongs to the staff of Scotland Yard and I to the staff of the Kentish Constabulary makes no difference to our collaboration."

I thought he was a pompous ass; but I couldn't very well let him see what I felt. I cast about in my mind to think of some way to stall him off until such time as Shelley should arrive. It was an awkward situation.

To think out, on the spur of the moment, some excuse was not at all easy; but I knew that I should have to stall somehow. The main thing was to find out what Shelley was doing, and when he would be back. If, for instance, he had gone to London to carry out his enquiries, I could not expect to hold off Beech until Shelley's return. If, on the other hand, Shelley was merely doing some sort of routine enquiries in Broadgate, I might possibly be able to hold things off while I awaited his return.

"I know that Inspector Shelley and yourself work in close collaboration, Inspector," I said as smoothly and equably as I could. "But it so happens that I have promised him—not as a policeman but as a man—to tell him whatever I may be lucky enough to discover. And, while I am sure that you and he do not keep any secrets from each other, I should be a good deal happier to await his return than to tell things to you, and to have you hand the information on to him." Then I thought that this sounded a trifle distrustful, so I added hastily: "It's not that I want to withhold information from you, Inspector; it's merely that I want to keep a promise given in all seriousness to Inspector Shelley a day or two ago."

Beech, I thought, looked a bit taken aback at this. He was, naturally, not too pleased at the attitude I had taken, but there was little that he could do about it. I was not a criminal; I was not even a hostile witness, whom he could argue into submission. There was little, I thought, that he could legally do to force me to give him whatever information I had in my possession. For a few moments he frowned in an angry manner. Then his brow seemed to clear suddenly.

He said: "Inspector Shelley should be here shortly, Mr. London and I presume that you would then be prepared to hand over whatever it is that you have in the nature of evidence."

"Certainly," I replied.

"He is in Broadgate. He has gone to take a statement from someone involved in the case," the Inspector explained. I was not at all sure that I liked this change in attitude; but it got me out of what might have been a nasty hole.

"Mrs. Skilbeck?" I asked. It was a shot in the dark but it went home. There was a sudden change in expression which seemed to me to indicate that he had decided that I knew more about this affair than he had first thought.

I wasn't at all sure whether I had really impressed him, or whether he was merely making the best of a bad job. But I had no need to think this over any more, as at this moment Inspector Shelley came in.

"Good-morning, Inspector," he said to Beech. "Hullo, Jimmy!" This with a friendly nod to me, which I was sure did not pass unnoticed by Beech.

"Any luck?" Beech enquired.

"A fair amount," Shelley said. "I think that we have got hold of a statement that will lead us somewhere useful. The trouble is that we have no concrete evidence as yet to support it. And we still haven't solved the most awkward problem of the whole case—the problem of how those bodies got into the lift without the locks being tampered with. That is something that I'm still absolutely stumped over."

"Mr. London here has some evidence which he wants to give you," Beech explained. "He said that he preferred to keep it and hand it over to you in person."

There was a touch of annoyance in Beech's tone. I saw that, in spite of the man's changed attitude, he still rather resented my refusal to give him the information.

"Well, shall we all adjourn to my room?" Shelley suggested. I thought that he would probably have preferred to have had his talk with me without Beech being present, but as things were he had no legitimate excuse for getting me away from this local man.

Anyhow, we all moved down the corridor to the office that had been allotted to Shelley. Here the Scotland Yard man settled down in his armchair, filled his battered old briar with his favourite mixture, and clearly intended to make a long session of it.

"Who speaks first?" Beech asked, when we had all installed ourselves in chairs.

"Well," said Shelley, "provided you remember that this is not for publication until I give the word, Jimmy, I think that we might give you an outline of what has happened since I saw you last."

I nodded. "You know that you can trust me, Inspector," I said. "I don't give my paper anything that you may say off the record. All I want is to get the background material right; then I can deal with the more confidential stuff as you release it for publication."

"Good." Shelley puffed out a cloud of pungent smoke and resumed. "You know that Mrs. Skilbeck has been saying nasty things about Timothy Foster," he said, "flinging about accusations in the most wholesale way."

"She repeated her accusations to me," I remarked.

"Yes. Well, I thought that it was time that she was asked to give us an official statement that would give us something really concrete to build on."

"You have been to see her?" I asked.

"Yes."

"Did she give you anything which seemed likely to be in any way useful?"

"Yes... and no," Shelley said doubtfully. "She gave me a good deal of information which tended to confirm what I'd previously suspected. But she didn't give anything that would prove what she has been saying about Timothy Foster. In fact, I rather think that her accusations of murder against Foster are pure hot air. I think that she has, for some reason, got her knife into Foster and that she is prepared to say anything at all that will hurt that young man. It may well be that she genuinely thinks that he is the murderer, and that in consequence she is prepared to accuse him of it, even to the extent of telling lies, if she thinks that those lies will tend to make us feel more suspicious about him. She is, in other words, that dangerous person who has made up her mind about the case from the start, and is prepared to twist her ideas to meet those prejudices."

This was almost exactly what I had thought about Mrs. Skilbeck, and I said as much to Shelley, "And you don't think Foster is guilty?" I asked.

"I wouldn't go as far as to say that," he replied. "But I would say that I don't think that Foster is guilty for the reasons that Mrs. Skilbeck advances. He may be innocent and he may be guilty; but I don't think that what she has to say has any real bearing on the question."

I could see that Beech was getting impatient at this exchange of opinion. It appeared to me that the discussion seemed to him to be of merely academic interest. And, like most purely practical men, Beech had an extreme distrust of theoreticians.

"But you said," Beech now broke in, "that Mrs. Skilbeck had given you some valuable information. What you've said up to now seems to suggest that the information she gave you—if it was information at all—was of no value."

"She told me the truth about Tilsley," replied Shelley. "She had no concrete clues to support what she said, but I had already come to the conclusion that what she told me was true, and her statement was therefore in a sense collaboration of my ideas."

"And what was that?" I asked eagerly. At last, I told myself, the case was coming round to a solution.

"That was that Tilsley was working for a gang, mainly concentrated on the south and east coast, which was distributing cocaine."

Beech whistled softly. I saw that, in spite of his assertion that he and Shelley were working so closely together, he really had little idea of what had been in the mind of the man from Scotland Yard.

"No evidence for it?" he asked.

"None," said Shelley. "But what we had found out previously about Tilsley's activities had made me suspect something of the kind. You will remember that he was dealing in all sorts of things; the one quality they all had in common was that they were fairly small and that they could be sold at a price much above their normal value."

"That's true," Beech admitted. "But we shall have a devil of a job to prove it, you know."

I thought that it was time that I sprang my bombshell on the two policemen. I fished in my pocket and produced the sparking-plug in its little tin.

"You see this plug, gentlemen?" I said.

They both sprang from their chairs and made their way over to my side of the table. It was really quite impressive to see the two men waiting for my revelation. I chuckled gently to myself.

"Watch," I said. I took the plug out of its tin, fiddled with it until I managed to get the screw that Tim Foster had undone. Then I gently unscrewed it, tipped the body of the plug up on a sheet of paper, and made a gesture, demonstrating the white powder that came out of it.

"Where did that come from?" asked Shelley.

"Tim Foster's garage," I said.

Shelley looked puzzled. "But I thought that you were convinced of Foster's innocence," he remarked.

"So I am," I explained. I went on to describe how the plug had come into Tim's possession, and how it had been left behind because it was, as Tim thought, faulty.

Shelley touched the white powder with his finger-tip and put a tiny portion of it gingerly on his tongue. He moved his tongue around his mouth, and then grinned.

"This is just what we wanted, Jimmy," he said.

"You think it's cocaine?" I asked.

"Not a doubt of it."

"And it gives you the concrete evidence that you want, to connect Tilsley with the cocaine deals that Mrs. Skilbeck mentioned?"

"Quite right."

Beech held out his hand. "I should like to apologise, Mr. London," he said. "I admit that I didn't trust you, but now I see that Inspector Shelley, here, was correct in his judgment of you."

I smiled. "That's all right, Inspector," I said. "The more or less hardened newspaper man is pretty well accustomed to being mistrusted and misunderstood."

"But don't forget, Jimmy," said Shelley, "this leaves some of our worst problems still unsolved."

"Such as…?"

"Well, first of all, the fact that the bodies were found inside a lift with locked doors. That is the worst problem of the lot."

"But what do you think happened?" asked Beech.

"As I view it, Tilsley was a comparatively minor figure in this drug-distributing scheme. Probably he was doing a bit of blackmail on the side. The chief of the gang thought that he was finding out a bit too much about what was going on, and therefore decided to deal with him. Margerison suspected what had happened, and maybe did something to hold the man up to ransom in some way. So he too had to be dealt with. Those two murders are all of a piece, and the whole thing hangs together well enough. I'm a little bit less satisfied with the other business—the attack on Bender. He clearly knows very little if anything about what was going on in Broadgate; but the criminal may have thought that Bender knew more than he actually did, and have therefore decided that he had to be dealt with accordingly. The only thing that really puzzles me there is why that attempted murder was done so differently from the other successful crimes. Why was Bender not attacked in the lift? That's what really puzzles me most. I think that if we could solve that mystery we should have the solution of the whole case."

And there, certainly, Shelley had uttered what was perhaps the wisest remark he ever made.

CHAPTER XXIV

In Which We Try to Find the Chief

I KNEW WELL ENOUGH THAT WHEN ONCE SHELLEY HAD GOT ON the scent of a case he was not a man to let go until he had got the whole thing thoroughly and finally solved. But at the same time I realised that he had now got something difficult to do. The general outline of the problem, as he had given it to us, was no doubt correct enough.

Personally I could not see how the question of the lift could be solved. The thing seemed to me to be fantastic and impossible to straighten out. How a body could be found in a locked lift, the locks clearly not having been in any way tampered with, seemed to me to be such a nightmare problem that any rational solution appeared absolutely impossible. I was, indeed, not at all surprised that Shelley thought this of really vital importance.

In fact, it seemed to me that Shelley had now succeeded in solving the case in its broad outlines; he had not, however, settled one not unimportant part of it—the identity of the murderer. That the chief of the drug-peddling gang was the man responsible for the deaths of two members of the gang seemed to be certain.

But who was the chief? That was the great problem. After all, if he was someone outside those we had already met in the case it would not be at all easy to get hold of him. We should be working completely in the dark. If, on the other hand, he was one of those we had already met, who could it be? I assumed that Tim Foster and Maya Johnson were not implicated in the crime; and somehow I couldn't see Mrs. Skilbeck as one of the great figures in a drug racket. Bender had no brains, and, while there were a few others who had entered on the fringes of the case, I could not readily envisage them as drug-kings. The whole thing was, it seemed to me, as puzzling as ever.

I looked back at that morning when I had seen Bender staggering over the promenade. Many things had happened since that moment, and, while I now knew a lot more about the background of the case, I was really not much further forward in my knowledge of its fundamentals.

I wandered into another little café after I had left the Police Station, ordered myself a pot of tea and some toast, and sat back, in a brown study.

Then I suddenly became conscious of the fact that a familiar figure was sitting opposite me. It was Shelley.

"Where did you come from?" I asked in some surprise.

"Deep in thought, weren't you?" Shelley said with a broad grin. "Well, Jimmy my lad, I thought that I'd like to have a few words with you away from the estimable Beech. He is a perfectly respectable officer, for whom I have a good deal of admiration, but he doesn't possess one of the vital necessities for the good detective."

"What's that?" I asked.

"That little touch of creative imagination which is needful if you are to get to the heart of a case from the start," Shelley said. "You see, I had to apply a considerable amount of pressure to our friend Mrs. Skilbeck before I got her to admit the connexion of Tilsley with the drug racket. Her main aim now seems to be to keep his memory sweet. And if for a moment she was prepared to admit that he was a peddler of cocaine it would make him a bit of a disreputable individual—not at all the sort of person whom she wants to remember. But at the same time she gave way when I pressed her hard. And I don't think that Beech would ever have got to that point. The idea that the man might be selling cocaine is the sort of idea that only comes to a man with a trace of creative imagination."

I smiled. Shelley seemed to have forgotten that the idea had come from me—or rather from Maya Johnson originally. Still, as long as the idea seemed to be leading somewhere I didn't mind all that much if my part in it was rather overlooked.

"The greatest problem, I suppose, is finding the identity of the chief," I said.

"Yes; that was why I followed you here, Jimmy," Shelley said. "You see, our branch at Scotland Yard have sent me some details that I think may lead us to the man we're after. They're a bit too vague to be immediately valuable, but I thought that if you did some unofficial snooping around you might be able to lay your hands on what we're after."

"You want me to become a detective again?" I remarked with a grin.

"Something like that. Mind you, there will be a bit of danger attached to this, Jimmy," he said. "I'm not questioning your personal bravery, but I think that you should be warned before you shove your head into the lion's mouth."

"I'm not braver than the next man," I said. "But if I'm allowed eventually to publish what I find out, I don't mind taking a chance on it."

"Good man!" Shelley answered. "I thought that was what you would say."

"What do you want me to do?" I asked.

"Well, it's a bit of a long story," Shelley explained. "If you'll listen I'll see if I can make it clear to you."

Fortunately the café in which we were sitting was practically empty. We could talk quietly without much chance of being overheard.

"Our men at the Yard usually have a fair idea of the gangs that are involved in this drug business," the detective went on. "They may not always have enough evidence to convict them, but they keep a pretty close watch on them, and are ready to jump at any moment if it seems likely that a conviction can be obtained. I hope you understand what I mean, Jimmy."

"I think I do."

"You see, there's a fairly constant amount of illegal cocaine in circulation in this country. If some new source of supply becomes available we usually learn about it pretty soon. And then the job is to run this new source down. If we can do that, we're happy."

"And a new source has become known lately?"

"Yes. And it centres on this bit of the coast. The idea they were working on at the Yard was that it was being smuggled in."

"Smuggled?" This surprised me somewhat.

"Yes; there still is a certain amount of smuggling of one sort and another going on, and it seems at any rate possible that drugs are being smuggled in from a continental port," Shelley explained. "You see, it is almost impossible for the coastguards to protect the whole of the English coast. The coastguards, in fact, are spread out pretty thin, and there are bound to be spots where little guard is kept. I don't suggest that this corner is in any way worse protected than the rest; but it is here, in Kent, that our drug squad suggest a new source of supply of cocaine has become available in recent months. It's not at all difficult to decide just where the stuff is centred on, you know."

I followed this pretty well. It was clear that the drug experts at Scotland Yard would have a fair knowledge of what was going on. If cocaine was being smuggled into the country and was then being distributed from some spot on the east coast, it might well be that Scotland Yard would become aware of that fact. But Shelley had asked me to help him in the case, and I couldn't for the life of me see just where it seemed to him that I should be useful in the present set-up.

"But what is to be my job in all this?" I asked, rather puzzled.

"I was coming to that in a moment," Shelley said. "You see, as I have explained, our people get some idea of what is going on; they know, with some degree of accuracy, just where the drug comes from. And sometimes they have a fair idea, too, of where it is going to and how it is distributed."

"They have that in this case?" I asked.

"Well, I don't know that I should say that they know all about these things," Shelley admitted. "But they have some idea, and those ideas lead them to some particular spots which need close investigation."

I began to see what the detective was getting at now, and I said as much to him.

"They know," Shelley went on, "that the centre of distribution is somewhere not very far from Broadgate. They have a suspicion that one or two local people are in some way connected with the business of distributing cocaine. But, in general, this was one of the cases that I was describing to you just now—a case in which suspicions may be quite strong but in which it is not possible to go into any definite legal action, since the direct evidence is lacking."

"You think that I could get that direct evidence?" I asked.

"Yes."

"What have I to do?" I asked.

"Don't forget what I said about the dangers involved in this business," Shelley warned me.

"I haven't forgotten," I assured him.

"Right. Then I'll give you the details, as they were given to me on the phone from the Yard this morning," Shelley said.

You may be sure that I awaited this with some eagerness. I felt in my bones that this was the last lap. Even though there might still be something to do, the fact remained that if I could do what Shelley was suggesting, I might well lead them to the end of the chase. Thus I might be leading to the final proof of the innocence of Tim Foster and Maya Johnson. If I could bring that off, I should have no complaints. I should think that my intrusion was in every way justified, and I should be finally putting myself in the running for almost every special job that Fleet Street might have to offer me.

"Our people at the Yard," Shelley continued, "have no idea who is the leader of this conspiracy. Various names have been mentioned, but none of them convey anything to me, or to any of the others at the Yard. In fact, they are almost certain to be false names. Few people in this racket sail under their true colours, you know."

"I didn't expect that they would," I commented.

"So, unless the names they use are in some way already moderately familiar to our people," Shelley said, "we can't depend on getting much out of them merely from their names."

"But you have to start the investigation in some way," I objected.

"Usually by finding a place which is important," Shelley said. "You see, people like this gang may work out a most elaborate way of distributing the drugs to the unfortunate folk who are slaves of the drug habit. That's all right. What I may call the secondary distribution may be brilliantly organised. But what about the primary distribution?"

For the first time I was a little puzzled. I didn't quite see what Shelley was getting at, and I told him so, saying that I wasn't able to appreciate just what he meant by primary and secondary distribution.

"Well," Shelley said, "let me explain. If you smuggled some illegal drug, like cocaine, into this country, and had to get rid of it, selling to a lot of drug addicts in various parts, how would you set about it?"

"Get some sort of legitimate business as a screen, I suppose." said I.

"Yes; that is what I call the secondary distribution," the detective said. "You see, if the thing is done on a fairly big scale, it is necessary to have a number of sub-agents, who may be bad lots, like Tilsley, or may be perfectly innocent folk, as you assume Tim Foster to be. But the reception of the drug in this country must take place at a sort of headquarters somewhere. And it is probable that the same headquarters will be the place where the stuff is distributed to some of the principal agents. Now do you see what I am getting at?"

"I think so."

"And you also see what it is that I am asking you to do, Jimmy?" There was an almost eager tone about Shelley's voice as he said this, a tone which seemed to indicate that he thought I presented him with the best possible chance of finding out what he was after.

"You think you know where this distribution centre is?" I asked.

"Yes," he nodded.

"And it's in this neighbourhood?"

"Yes."

I looked at him rather curiously. "Don't think that I'm trying to wangle out of this, Inspector," I said. "But there is one thing that strikes me as a little odd."

"What's that?" he snapped.

"If you are pretty sure that you know the place where the gang meet, why don't you have an ordinary police raid, and pull them all into the net? You could easily sort them out afterwards, surely, and decide which of them were the birds you are really after. I should have thought that would have been the normal course of action."

He grinned cheerfully. "Of course it would, Jimmy," he admitted. "That would have been the normal course of action, but then, you see, this is not quite the normal sort of case. That's why I'm suggesting something different."

"What is abnormal about this case?" I asked.

"The murders," Shelley said, and there was something impressive, I thought, about the very quietness of his voice as he said this. "This gang won't be so easy to deal with. You see, if a man is found guilty of dealing with dangerous drugs, he may have to face a heavy fine, he may even, if it is a bad case, have to face a stiff term of imprisonment. But this is a murder case, and if a man is found guilty of murder, he may have to hang! And that is something that makes every criminal sit up and take notice. If we raided the place, we might have a shooting match that would end in a shambles; and the man might succeed in getting away. Then we should have to begin all over again."

"But what makes you think that I could do any better?" I asked. I wasn't trying to get out of things; I was merely curious.

"You can go there, Jimmy, as a stranger. You can get into conversation with people, and you can let us know the results of your conversation. You may even be able to let us have the name of the chief villain. That's what we want."

"All right," I said, "when and where do I begin?"

"Good man!" he exclaimed. "You begin as soon as you like, and the place you go to is the Smithy Inn, not far from Deal."

CHAPTER XXV

In Which I Visit an Inn

I HAVE HANDLED SOME TICKLISH ASSIGNMENTS IN MY TIME—WHAT man who has spent some years in Fleet Street has not?—but I anticipated that this business at the Smithy Inn would probably be as tricky as anything that I had ever tackled. You see, it was pretty sure, if this was the meeting-place of a gang of drug-smugglers, that they would be suspicious of anyone who came, however outwardly innocent. Also there was the fact that if, as Shelley clearly suspected, the head man of the gang was someone from Broadgate and someone with whom we'd already got into contact, he would at once realise that I was there for no good purpose.

And I hadn't needed Shelley's warning to realise that there was a lot of danger in the situation. Not that the dangerous aspect worried me over-much. I had been in the R.A.F. during the war, and had got through some unpleasantly sticky spots. But I did not really fancy the idea, as Shelley put it, of sticking my head in the lion's mouth without at least knowing who the lion was. And yet to find out the identity of the lion was my real reason for coming here. I hope that I haven't mixed my metaphors. Even if I have, I hope that my meaning is reasonably clear.

Anyhow, I went on to the promenade at Broadgate that evening, close to the bandstand, where the pleasant little string orchestra was already tuning up for the evening concert. I looked at the lightly dressed couples making ready for their pre-dinner walk. And I saw the tired children being brought home from their last paddle or bathe. It seemed to me that there was a queer contrast between their activities, so harmless and enjoyable, and the way in which I was to spend the evening.

I had warned Mrs. Cecil that I should not be home for the evening meal, and had added that I was going to see a friend at Deal. I told her that it was possible that I might even spend the night with him, so that she was not to worry if I did not arrive back that night.

I waited at the bus-stop near the bandstand. I knew that there was a bus for Deal and Dover about every half-hour, and I guessed that I shouldn't have long to wait. As the bus swung around the corner and came towards me, the orchestra struck up its opening number, the overture to "William Tell." I thought of the legend which had inspired that bright and cheerful music. I remembered Tell's great accuracy in shooting the apple off the boy's head, and I thought that the task that lay before me was possibly more difficult than that which Tell had performed.

As the bus moved off the music died away. Before I had been plunged into this mystery I had often spent an enjoyable hour listening to that orchestra, and now I wondered if I should ever hear it again. I gave myself about a fifty-fifty chance of getting out of this thing alive. But at the same time it was something that I would not have missed for the world.

It was a fairly short run to Deal. Here and there the bus stopped, people got on and people got off. Some of them were people who had been doing their shopping. Some were merely holiday-makers out on the spree. I saw that most of the latter got off at one or other of the numerous little country pubs that we passed on our way.

I had dressed myself to suit my pose of a man out to enjoy his evening. I wore an old pair of flannel slacks, an open-necked shirt, and a blazer. I thought that the line to take was that I was out for an evening's drinking. Then, if my friends the enemy turned out to be too curious about me, I could feign drunkenness. I knew that this might not be effective, and I was well aware that my plans might have to be changed at a moment's notice. But at the same time it was as well to have a general plan of campaign worked out, so that I should be well prepared to take up a particular attitude, should the curiosity of the other side turn out to be too pressing.

Not far from Deal the bus stopped. "Smithy!" the conductor rapped out, and I was glad to see that a considerable number of my fellow-passengers alighted. This was a popular pub, that was clear. It was good. It meant that I could submerge myself in a crowd. And in my present lonely task to be one of a crowd seemed to me to be the ideal state of affairs.

I made my way into the saloon bar of the Smithy. It was a small room, with a low-built ceiling, and it appeared to be absolutely packed with a seething mass of humanity. I looked around me with some curiosity. I couldn't at first see anyone I knew—not that I expected to be able to do so. After all, that little room, about ten or twelve feet square, must have contained not much short of a hundred people, and it would have been a miracle if I had been able to recognise any of them.

Still, my first instinct on going into a pub is to get a drink. I had nearly to tear apart those who stood between me and the bar. Still, by using shoulders and elbows, I made my way to the counter.

"Half of bitter, please," I said to the tired-looking barmaid who was serving there.

"Tenpence," she snapped, pulling at the handle of the beer engine.

I put down a shilling and got my twopence change. Then I made my way back to the side of the room. I thought that if I stood at the bar I should get intolerably bustled by others in search of beer. And I wanted to fade away into the background. I knew that the last thing that I should do would he to push myself into the forefront of the crowd in that bar. The main thing was to remain as inconspicuous as possible.

I looked around me. The crowd in that bar seemed to be the typical sort of holiday crowd that you would find in almost any sea-side pub in England between June and September. There were the middle-aged gentlemen who thought that a holiday without plenty of beer would scarcely be worthy of the name of holiday.

There were the people who had merely come out to escape the problems of life at home—these were the local folk whom one sees in almost any pub anywhere.

There were the young people—too young, one would have thought, to have acquired the taste of alcohol. But no doubt they got quite a "kick" out of the swirling life of the saloon bar which surrounded them.

I sipped my beer and looked around me. I tried to make my glances look careless. Actually, however, I was doing my best to see if there was anyone present whom I had already come into contact with in Broadgate. That there must somehow be a connection seemed to be obvious from what Shelley had learned from his people in London.

There was, however, no one whom I knew. At least, I couldn't see anyone at a first glance. The whole crowd was, to all appearances, out to enjoy itself. There seemed to be nothing that I could do for the moment.

I thought ruefully that I might be engaged on a wild goose chase. Even if the people I was after were meeting here, it might be that they were meeting in some quiet room upstairs, far from the saloon bar. The pub was a fairly big place, and there must, I thought, be a lot of rooms out of sight, rooms to which the ordinary public never gained access. But somehow, if I was to get anywhere, I had to find out where this room was, and what was going on there.

Then I spotted something a little odd. Every now and then one or other of the crowd would silently detach himself from the rest and would melt away somewhere at the back of the bar. Sooner or later he would return, but he would be missing for a good ten minutes or so. It was not a matter of going to the toilet rooms, since these were in the opposite corner of the bar.

I went up and bought myself another half-pint of the really excellent bitter; then I edged myself into the direction of the corner from which the various individuals I had been observing had disappeared. I thought that if I still stayed inconspicuous I might perhaps see what was going on.

I soon realised what had happened. In that corner of the room, almost invisible in the press of people, was a little door, covered by a chintz curtain. As I stood not far away, half hidden by a hilarious crowd of youngsters, I saw a man's head emerge from the curtain, glance around him swiftly as if to make sure that he was unobserved, and then the man came out.

The man moved quickly towards a pint of bitter standing on a table. He picked up the glass and took a sip, looking around him in such a way as if to make sure that no one had noticed his manoeuvre. I swiftly turned my head away, before his roving gaze had come in my direction.

Then, when I thought that I had been looking elsewhere for long enough to destroy any suspicions which he might have entertained, I looked back at him. He was an odd-looking fish. Tall, gaunt, almost emaciated in features, his complexion was almost dead-white. What colour there was in it was a kind of sickly grey. I thought that here, at any rate, was a tie-up with Shelley's suspicions. Unless I was very much mistaken this man had the typical colour of the drug addict.

I glanced again at the curtain that held behind it the entrance to the more secret part of the building. I really felt that at last I was getting somewhere. The trouble was that I didn't know how many of the apparently harmless crowd in that room might be in some way involved with the drug-smuggling gang we were up against. And if I went into the room that I was now sure lay behind the curtain, I might be attracting to myself the very attention I was so anxious to avoid.

Yet I knew that I had to get there somehow. I continued to watch the curtain. Now a girl, pretty but with anxious wrinkles in her forehead, approached the curtain. She glanced nervously around, as if she didn't want to attract any sort of attention from anyone. Then, with a sudden whisk of the curtain, she was in there. I thought I had the secret now. I stood quite still, doing my best to efface myself behind the hilarious group, and kept watch.

It was a good quarter of an hour before the girl came out again. Now the anxious look had gone. Her face was serene and peaceful. I was sure of what had happened. She was a drug addict, probably in the early stages of the habit, since her face had not shown the typical degeneration of the man I had previously seen. And she had gone behind that curtain to get a supply of the drug that she was after. Her anxiety had doubtless had its origin in the fear that it might not be available. And now that she had secured the new supply that feeling of desperate anxiety had suddenly disappeared.

Shelley had been right. I thought that the machinery of Scotland Yard was really rather wonderful. How on earth they had stumbled on the information about this apparently innocuous little pub I couldn't say. But there seemed to be no doubt that it was a centre from which dangerous drugs were being distributed.

What I had to do was to choose my moment so that I slipped behind the curtain comparatively unobserved. Just what I should do when I got there I didn't know. I should have to improvise, let the moment bring its own inspiration.

There must, I thought, be some sort of signal which the regular customers gave each other—either that, or they had some sort of regular time-table, which ensured that they should not overlap in their visits to the room beyond. For as I watched I came to the realisation that there were never two people going through at the same time. Within a matter of a minute or so of one person coming out, another would go in. The decision which I now had to take was just how to slip between these people who presumably had definite appointments.

A man had just gone in—a fat, rosy-cheeked individual who seemed to me to be the very reverse of what one generally understood by a drug addict. But he was only in there about a couple of minutes, and when he emerged he was smiling all over his cheery face. He had not looked exactly worried when he went in, but he certainly looked more cheerful when he came out.

I thought that they must be doing good business in that inner room. There was a regular procession inside there. I had now been quietly and unobtrusively watching that curtain for nearly an hour and there had been seven people in and out. They were all types and classes. One or two of them had seemed ordinary working folk, almost out of place in the comparatively luxurious surroundings of the saloon bar. But one and all had been marked by a change in expression from the moment when they went in to the moment that they came out.

Anxiety disappeared, wrinkles were ironed out. There was some-thing very striking about this. I didn't think that it was in any way due to imagination on my part, derived from my suspicion that this was a centre of drug distribution. I was sure that this was the place that I was after.

Still, I had somehow to penetrate. By this time I was drinking my fourth half-pint of bitter. I had made the beer last as long as pos-sible, for I knew that I should have to keep my wits by me for the ordeal that lay ahead, and I was only too conscious of the fact that it would be no good to go in there in a half-fuddled condition. Yet if I didn't have a glass of beer in my hand, and if I didn't take a sip from it fairly regularly, I knew that I should attract undue attention to myself. And to attract any attention at all was about the last thing that I wanted to do.

I looked at the curtain irresolutely. Another young girl had just gone in. I was making up my mind that when she came out I would just take my courage in both hands and go in there to see what was going on. As I said before, I could scarcely make any sort of plan as to what I was to do when I got there, until I saw what was hidden. But I knew that I should probably have to put up some sort of fight.

Shelley had given me a small automatic pistol. This was in the pocket of my blazer, and the feel of its cool butt in my hand gave me at any rate some sort of courage. I still watched the curtain. I saw the girl come out, glance around her, and make her way to a table where an obviously untasted glass of gin and lime was standing. She picked this up, tossed it down her throat at one gulp, and made her way swiftly to the door. In her case it was only too clear that the drink had been a mere excuse. She had deliberately come to the Smithy for whatever it was that was obtainable behind that curtain.

I made up my mind. I put my now empty glass down on a nearby table and strolled apparently carelessly over to the curtained doorway. I pushed the curtain on one side, and made my way in. Well, I had burned my boats with a vengeance!

CHAPTER XXVI

In Which I Penetrate Behind a Curtain

I KNEW NOW THAT I WAS ENTIRELY DEPENDENT ON MY OWN efforts and my own ingenuity. But that didn't worry me overmuch. I don't think I'm an unduly conceited man, but I *do* know my own worth and my own qualities. I knew well enough that I should need some luck. But, given reasonable luck, I thought that I could get away with it. I don't look like a typical policeman, and it was the police that the gang we were up against would be looking for.

I peered down the corridor that lay behind the curtain. It was dim in there. The windows, such as they were, were heavily curtained. It was clear that whoever was responsible for this place was taking no risk to anyone seeing anything from outside.

The corridor looked a long one. There were a number of rooms running off it on either side. I thought that this was a tougher business than I had anticipated, since one could not tell which of half a dozen or so rooms was the one that I was after.

And at any time, I told myself cheerfully, I might be interrupted by some plug-ugly who would ask me what I was doing. There might well be some pass-word, which was unknown to me, and my ignorance of which would land me in real trouble. The whole proceeding was a most hazardous affair. Still, I did not worry. My life was now on the laps of the gods, and all that I could do was to carry on and hope that I should not make too many foolish blunders.

I hesitated opposite the first door on the left. I put my ear close to it, but was unable to hear any sound. I turned the handle very gently, but the door did not give to pressure. It was at once obvious that this was a locked door, and I could do little about it. Unless there was some special code of knocks which would open it, there was nothing that I could do in the way of dealing with a locked door. Just opposite to it was another one.

This time it turned and the door gave slightly. Inch by inch, almost millimetre by millimetre, I opened the door. Inside the room it was dim—almost as dim as the corridor in which I stood. I glanced inside. The room was furnished like an ordinary lounge, but the curtains were drawn. There were a couple of leather-covered armchairs and a settee. A table stood in the middle of the room. On it was a picture. I tried to see, from the doorway, who was in the picture, but I was too far away to see in that dim light. I didn't think it was really important enough to merit spending time on it. And I had a lot more to do than explore rooms that, superficially, looked harmless enough.

I slipped out into the corridor again, glancing swiftly around me. No one was yet in sight. I congratulated myself on having managed things well enough as yet, though I knew well enough that this was not due to any brilliance on my part. It was, I knew, due more to the fact that luck up to now had been on my side.

A little further on was another door. This was likewise unlocked, as I found on turning the handle. And this looked as if it might be a bit more promising. At one end, underneath the window, was an open bureau. On it there was a pile of papers.

I was not silly enough to think that these gentry would commit to paper much of what they were doing, but at the same time I guessed that some details of their business must be written down—if only some sort of financial account. And I thought that here might be something worth while.

I shut the door gently behind me. I couldn't afford to have anyone else snooping into what I was doing. I knew that it would now not be at all easy to get back into the corridor unobserved; but this was the sort of risk that I had anticipated I should have to take.

I glanced at the mass of papers on the bureau. At first glance it did not seem a very promising source of information, since the papers seemed to be inextricably muddled up. But it was, I thought, probably here that I should find something valuable.

There were a lot of letters. Mostly they were typewritten, and they came from addresses scattered all over the east and south coast, from Herne Bay to Eastbourne and Brighton. They seemed for the most part to refer to deals in something totally unspecified. They merely said this sort of thing: "I was very well satisfied with the last consignment. I enclose five pounds in cash. Will you please send a repeat order, and arrange for delivery as before?" That was one of the letters, from an address in Hove. It might, on the surface, look harmless enough.

Anything at all in the way of raw materials or other goods might, indeed, be covered by the letter. But equally possibly the letter might refer to cocaine or hashish or some such dangerous drug.

I realised, of course, that I could not expect to find here a letter which said, in as many words, that the money was paid for a drug. But I thought that the gentry we were up against had obviously worked out a sort of formula for the letters. They were almost all couched in practically identical terms.

There did not seem to be much to learn here. Apart from these letters there was nothing really suspicious. There were a few letters that seemed to be purely personal—references to holidays, relations, weddings, and all the other usual adjuncts of personal correspondence abounded. I had hoped that there might be something in the nature of account books, but there was nothing of the kind. No doubt these would be kept somewhere safely under lock and key.

I had not time to spare, otherwise I would have gone very carefully through the business letters and noted all the names and addresses involved; but these would have taken a long time, and in any event Shelley would no doubt be able to get hold of them when he wanted them.

I edged my way towards the door again. This time I knew well enough that I had a rather dangerous move ahead of me. I put my hand on the door-knob, turned it silently, and opened the door just a crack. Then I paused. It was just as well that I did so, for I could hear footsteps coming down the corridor.

I stood still, as if rooted to the spot. Just what I should do if the stranger came into the room I was in, I did not know. I just hoped that he would pass by... and pass by he did. The footsteps, firm and decisive, went on past the door. I hadn't opened it widely enough to be able to look out—indeed, if I had done so, I should probably have invited the attention of the man outside. But I could listen, and when I heard those firm footsteps I was sure in my own mind that this was the big white chief we were after. Certainly the steps were not those of one of the drug addicts we wanted to save.

I was pretty sure that the steps of a man or woman in any way under the influence of drugs would have been halting and uneven, very unlike those of the man I had heard.

The footsteps went some distance along the corridor. A door opened and then closed with a slam. Then all was silent once more. The man had gone into a room further along, though, of course, I had no way of determining which room it was.

I thought that this was in some ways satisfactory, in some ways totally not so. Still, I was now more or less at liberty to get out into the corridor again.

Inch by inch I edged the door open. Soon I was outside. I shut the door gently and looked around me. There was no one in sight, and no indication that the corridor had in any way changed while I had been exploring in the room. But I thought that I was becoming aware of a change in the psychological atmosphere, almost as if I knew that I was being watched.

I looked about me more or less apprehensively, but could see no one. Nor could I see anywhere which could be a possible vantage point from which anyone could be watching me. It was all most annoying, but I didn't see that there was much that I could do about it. It might, of course, be that my nerves were feeling the strain of this dangerous work of exploration, though as a rule I am in no way a nervous person. But I certainly felt that I was under observation from somewhere, though where the watchful eyes might be I was unable to say.

I tried another door—opposite to that of the room from which I had just emerged. No luck there. This was locked. I wished that I had provided myself with some sort of pick-lock or skeleton keys; but I hadn't and there was nothing that I could do without such implements. After all, I was not an expert burglar, who would no doubt have been able to get those doors open with a penknife and a pin. I had to give up the locked rooms as totally impossible.

So I moved a little further along, in the direction which those firm footsteps had taken. I had tried to estimate just how far the man had gone, but had found it impossible to achieve anything more than the roughest of rough guesses. And that guess told me that as yet I was nowhere near the spot at which he had gone into a room.

Several more doors, in fact, awaited me before I came to the spot where I considered the man had left the corridor. The only way I could get on with my work of exploration was to work steadily along the rooms as I passed them. This I proceeded to do, though now without much confidence that they would lead me to anything really worth while in the way of information or evidence that Shelley would find useful.

Many of the doors were locked. Here, as before, I was completely stumped. Those which were unlocked opened into rooms that seemed to be innocuous enough. One was a lounge, not unlike that which I had seen at the beginning of my excursion down this corridor. Another was a dining-room, with a fine old round oak table, set out ready for a dinner for four—and a dinner which was intended to be a pretty big meal, judging by the array of cutlery and the sherry, port, and brandy glasses which flanked the knives and forks.

I wondered who was intending to dine there that night. I wondered, too, if we should manage to get hold of them before that dinner took place.

I was still working my way along the lengthy and silent corridor. I was, indeed, more than a little surprised that I had been allowed to get that far without any sort of interruption. When I remembered that previously there had been almost a continuous flow of customers, in and out of the curtained doorway that now lay some distance behind me, it seemed to me queer that none—except the one man I had heard, and I was sure that he was not a customer—had come into the corridor since my first entry.

I was suspicious about it, actually. I thought that they must somehow have seen me, and were just giving me enough rope to hang myself, while turning off the tap of visitors, so to speak, so that I should get deeper and deeper into the recesses of this odd old pub.

This feeling of suspicion tended to deepen my previous feeling that I was being watched. I shrugged my shoulders, as if to rid myself of the feeling of nervousness; but the nervousness would not be forced away.

Shelley had certainly given me a tough assignment. I wondered if, when he had cheerfully invited me to take this on, he had realised how tough it was. Still, there was no way to back out of it now. If I made my way back into the saloon bar, which was my way to freedom, and took the next bus back to Broadgate, I should be admitting ignominious defeat.

To admit defeat is something that no one likes to do. Besides, there was the undoubted fact that this might be the only way that I could get the information that would save Tim Foster from the gallows. I knew that my own life was now probably in danger, but, having come so far, I didn't see that I could help matters by being unduly cautious.

I reckoned that by now I should be somewhere near the spot at which the man I had heard had gone into a room. Just opposite me was a door. Was this the room that hid the secrets we were after? My heart thumped in my chest. This was, I thought, almost certainly the climax to which the events of the last two or three days had been building up.

I put my hand on the doorknob and paused. Everything was silent. From the saloon bar that I had left I could hear a faint sound of laughter. It was not easy to envisage the happy cheerfulness that I had left behind. I had ventured into a nightmare kind of world, from which there was no way out.

I turned the handle and put my ear to the door. Not a sound came from inside. I pushed the door gently. The hinges creaked slightly as the door opened.

I looked inside. The room was a rather cosy little study. Bookshelves lined the walls, and in one corner there was a curtained alcove which no doubt hid the window. The room was in complete darkness save for a solitary desk-lamp which stood on a table on the far side. No one was there, but I could smell the smoke of a Turkish cigarette which had very recently been smoked in there.

I took a pace forward. My nerves were tingling now. That consciousness of being watched had increased until I thought it was a practical certainty. But I could still see no one. That, indeed, was not surprising. The room was so dim and distant that it was not easy even to imagine that it was ever light and airy.

I shut the door quietly behind me. This was the crucial moment, I told myself. I made my way over to the table on which the desk-lamp was standing. With every pace my apprehension increased, though I could still see no one who might be watching me.

On every side there seemed to be advancing shadows. I looked around with each step. It did not appear to be possible that, if anyone was going to attack me, they would be able to do so without my knowledge. I grasped the cold butt of the revolver in my blazer pocket. That weapon gave me the only touch of reassurance that I had.

On the table there were some papers, kept in place by means of a stone sphinx. I lifted the sphinx silently and put it on one side. I lifted the top layer of papers and glanced below. I was very surprised to see that they consisted of newspaper clippings—and clippings of my contributions to *The Daily Wire*. This at once resolved all the doubts that had been in my mind. There could be no question that this was the place where the murderer had been hiding. He was reading what I had written about the crimes. I felt subtly flattered that he had thought it worth while keeping my hastily-telephoned material. It looked as if he had thought that I was on the track of something.

Then… a hard metal tube, no doubt the barrel of a weapon of some sort, was pressed into the small of my back. I had, in glancing at those press clippings, for a moment relaxed my vigilance.

"Put your hands high into the air, Mr. London!" said a pleasant voice.

I obeyed. There was nothing else that I could do. A hand reached into my blazer pocket and removed my pistol. I was caught like a rat in a trap.

CHAPTER XXVII

In Which I Talk to a Murderer

"KEEP THOSE HANDS RIGHT ABOVE YOUR HEAD STILL, IF YOU don't mind, Mr. London," said the voice. I still did what I was told. Indeed, I had no real alternative. I was helpless in the control of this man, and I felt annoyed that I had so allowed myself to be caught. Yet I did not really see what other precautions I could possibly have taken.

He prodded me in the back. "Just move this way, please, Mr. London." There was a sort of ironic politeness about the man's voice which at once annoyed me and amused me. He led the way—or rather indicated the way in which he wanted me to go. This was towards a chair at the other side of the room.

"Sit down," he said when I reached it.

Again I obeyed. He produced a cord from somewhere and tied me down in such a way that I could not move. I was really in a most ignominious position, but there was literally nothing that I could do to improve matters. In a trice I was fastened so that I could scarcely move a muscle. My feet were fastened to the legs of the chair, and my hands, twisted behind my back, tied to the chair-back.

"That, I think, is eminently satisfactory," he said in a suave manner. "Now all that we have to do is to arrange the lighting in a way which will be what we want."

He crossed the room, and I watched him. I could see nothing of his features, since he kept his back to me. And he tilted the desk-lamp so that it shone directly into my eyes, while he remained so deeply in the shadow that I could really see nothing of him—not enough to get anything approaching a detailed idea of what he looked like, anyhow.

He was obviously a man of something over the average height, and when he walked across the room I noticed that he had a long stride and a firm step which I thought was clearly what I had heard when I was listening inside the room further back the corridor. This was certainly the man who had passed by. He clearly knew me, and I wondered if he had been observing me the whole time that I had been investigating things. Almost as if in answer to my thoughts, he spoke.

"You thought that you were so very clever, Mr. London," he said, and now there was something like a sneer in his voice. "You thought that you could do something to defeat us, didn't you? Well, you see, we are a little brighter in the intellect than you thought. No stranger comes to the Smithy without being duly noted and pigeon-holed, and you were so obviously in search of something that your arrival was reported to me without a moment's delay."

This didn't seem to require any answer from me; so I said nothing.

My companion laughed. It was a humourless laugh, not at all pleasant to hear. I did not know what would be my fate in his hands, but I was sure that it would not be anything enviable to undergo. Still, I managed to keep my pecker up. I thought that I should find some way out. And there was one thing that I had to do—keep from them, if it were at all possible, the way in which I had come here. For that was the secret which would enable them to kill me and make a quick getaway before the police arrived. Whereas, if I could stall and play for time, it was possible that Shelley might get a bit anxious and arrange a raid in time to save me from whatever fate this man might be hatching for me. All that went through my mind in a much shorter time than it takes you to read it.

"Who do you think you are?" I asked, making an effort at bluster. You must remember from this point onwards I was mainly concerned with spinning out time, and I thought that to make him a bit annoyed with me might be the best way of playing for time, since he was probably as conceited as most criminals and would therefore be concerned to justify himself in my eyes, even though he was already planning to kill me as soon as the interview was finished.

"I should think the more crucial question is who do you think I am?" he returned. He was not a scrap annoyed, which riled me a little. Nothing, in fact, is more annoying than the man who resolutely refuses to be upset by any sort of insult which one may hurl at him.

"Is that important?" I asked.

"We will return to that question in a few minutes, if you do not mind, Mr. London," he said. "I have some more important matters which you can help me to deal with. I should therefore be very much obliged if you would just answer a few queries which I am going to put to you."

There was something very odd about this. The man was talking as if this was an ordinary business conversation. The fact that I was tied to a chair and half-blinded by the light that was shining directly in my eyes seemed to have no influence at all on the way he was speaking.

"Ask away," I said, "though, of course, I can't guarantee that I shall answer all your questions."

A kind of silky malice crept into his voice as he replied to that. "Somehow I think that you will, Mr. London," he said. "You see, we have methods of making people talk, methods that have rarely failed. But I hope that there will be no need to use the more drastic methods against your good self. In fact, I am sure that there will not—you have too much good hard common sense to be under the necessity of driving us to any inordinate lengths in these matters."

I didn't altogether like this. During the war I had heard a few things about the more unpleasant refinements of the Gestapo torture camps. I had no doubt that it was something of that sort at which he was hinting. I hoped that somehow I should be able to stall him off until Shelley arrived—but I knew that to do that would mean wasting a considerable amount of time.

"I hope that we can get together on these things, too," I said. "But I can't really tell about that until you start asking your questions, can I?"

"Well, my first question is this: who told you about this place, and suggested that it might be worth your while, as a newspaper crime investigator, to come out here?"

"No one," I answered.

"No one? What do you mean?"

"Well, if you must know, it was a fellow-guest of the boarding-house in Broadgate where I am living," I said. "But he did not for a moment suggest that it would be of any interest or value to me as a crime investigator."

"What did he say? And what was his name?" These queries were rapped out like shots from a gun.

"His name is Sam Weldon," I replied, making up a name on the spur of the moment. I knew that they would take time to check up on such points, and I was also aware that if I played my cards correctly, by the time they had found I was not telling them the truth, Shelley would be dealing with them, and therefore I should have no need to do anything about it.

"And what did he tell you?" snapped my opponent.

"I was saying to him that I was at a bit of a loose end this evening, that I was getting a little tired of the Broadgate pubs, and that I thought I'd like to drink somewhere else for a change. He told me that this was a pleasant little pub, where the bitter was first-rate, and that he thought…"

The other man interrupted suddenly: "Are you trying to tell me that you merely came to the Smithy for an evening's amusement, just to have a few drinks in a new pub which you had not visited before?"

"That is exactly what I am trying to tell you," I agreed.

"And you knew nothing about this place apart from that?" he demanded with a kind of savage intensity.

"Nothing at all."

"It was never suggested to you by anyone that the place might have some features of interest to you in your other capacity as a crime reporter?"

"Never."

He rose to his feet. Yes, I reflected, I was quite right. He was a tall man—six feet two or three, I reckoned. I still couldn't make out any details of his features.

"I'm sorry, Mr. London," he announced in tones that were almost comically reluctant. "But it won't wash."

"Won't wash?" I said.

"No; I frankly don't believe you."

"I don't know how I am to convince you that I'm telling the truth," I said in what I hoped was a satisfactory imitation of a man thoroughly aggrieved and disgruntled by the way in which he is being treated.

"Nor do I," he snapped, sitting down again.

"Yet I had no idea that there was anything odd going on here at the Smithy," I said, "and even now I'm not at all sure what it is. The fact that you've got me tied up like this convinces me that there is something here in some way connected with the crime that I am engaged in investigating on behalf of my paper. But what the connexion is I don't know. You have completely mystified me—and that is something that happens very rarely in my life."

"I don't expect that it will happen again in your life, Mr. London," he said smoothly, and this time there was no doubt about the innuendo.

"That's something to be thankful for, anyhow," I remarked, pretending not to see what he was getting at.

He suddenly faced me with another question, obviously intended to take me completely by surprise. "Are you sure that you were not put on to this place by your old friend... what is his name?... Inspector Shelley," he said.

"Inspector Shelley is merely a man with whom I have been inevitably in contact over my work for *The Daily Wire*," I tried to explain. "He has been very good to me, helping me with some information which has provided me with useful background material for my stories in the paper."

"Indeed?" This time the sneer was not disguised. There wasn't even an attempt to disguise it.

For almost the first time since I had come into that room I felt a spasm of fear. Did this man know too much? Had he some inside source of information? It was not pleasant to think that he might merely be laughing at me, thinking that I was a silly blundering fool, who had pushed my head into a hornets' nest without even noticing that the hornets could sting? Or did he really not know as much as he pretended? Was he really only bluffing after all? It was impossible, of course, for me to say which was the correct analysis of the position into which, with Shelley's aid, I had got myself. But I felt, as I say, a definite twinge of fear when I thought that it was possible that I had put myself within the power of a man who knew all about me, had, perhaps observed my work in Broadgate with a smile on his face, knowing that before long I should fall into his hands, to be dealt with at his leisure, and as he thought fit. But, I told myself, it was no good giving way to any sort of despair. I had to face the situation as best I could. If my opponent was bluffing—well, I could bluff also, and maybe I should be able to bluff my way out of this situation, as I had, in the past, bluffed myself out of others that had seemed, if not as awkward, every whit as difficult as this.

"Anyhow, sir," I said, as politely as I could, "what do you propose to do with me? You can't keep me a prisoner here. I should be missed before long. In fact, I might easily be missed by now, since I have not arrived back at dinner."

"I'm not as easily taken in as that, Mr. London," he said, with a chuckle in his voice. "I am aware that, like so many journalists, you are a trifle erratic, shall I say, over the matter of mealtimes. I am quite sure that if you did not turn up for a few hours at your boarding-house the good Mrs. Cecil would be in no way perturbed."

Here again there was the suggestion that he had a deep knowledge of my general background. The name of Mrs. Cecil came from his tongue so readily that it at once suggested to me that he had kept me well under observation for some time. The mere fact that he knew her name, in fact, shook me somewhat.

"But the fact remains, that I shall soon be missed," I said. "People knew that I was coming here for a few hours."

"People?" He at once took up every point, I noticed.

"My friend Weldon," I said hastily, trying to cover up what had undoubtedly been a verbal slip. "And I have no doubt that he will have mentioned it to others. We are a group of friends in the boarding-house, you know." I thought that I sounded rather like a radio comedian in saying this, but it was the best way, on the spur of the moment in thinking a way out of the difficulty into which my careless talk had landed me.

The man laughed out loud. "My dear Mr. London," he said. "You must realise that we are not quite as simple as all that."

"No?"

"No. You were no doubt seen to enter the saloon bar here, but we shall have plenty of witnesses prepared to swear that you stayed for an hour only, that you were then slightly the worse for drink, and that when you left you were seen to stagger down the road towards the bus-stop. Once that is satisfactorily established there should be very little difficulty in proving that you stumbled, when half-drunk, beneath the wheels of a passing lorry, or into the bed of one of the nearby streams that you have no doubt observed passing underneath the road at fairly frequent intervals."

This was said in a perfectly friendly fashion. The man might have been discussing the prospects of the cricket season instead of describing a way in which I might be brought to an unpleasantly sticky end.

I must confess that it took me aback a bit. I tried, however, not to show this, and kept my voice as steady as I could when I replied to him.

"Then what do you propose?" I asked.

"I propose to leave you to yourself—shall we say for about half an hour?"

"And then?" I asked.

"And then I shall return and ask you if you have come around to a more sensible view of things. In other words, my dear Mr. London, I shall want to know if you have decided to tell me the truth about what brought you here."

"And if I can tell you no more than I have told you up to now?"

"Then I shall be compelled to apply to you those rather more drastic methods at which I hinted earlier."

He melted into the dark distance. I was alone.

CHAPTER XXVIII

In Which I Think All is Lost

M Y POSITION NOW WAS ABOUT AS DESPERATE AS IT WELL
could be. I felt pretty grim. I tried, of course, to tell myself
that Shelley would soon rumble that something had gone wrong.
But at the same time I knew that he might come to this conclusion
too late.

After all, Shelley had said to me that he thought it would be dangerous for him to embark on a full-scale police raid on the Smithy
Inn. He thought that in that case there was a considerable danger
that these people might escape. And if he had been thus hesitant
when he was briefing me for the job, he would not be at all likely to
make the raid when he thought that I was engaged in investigating
the place. He would, in other words, tend to hesitate until he was
sure that I had either succeeded or finally failed. And final failure
might well descend on me before I was able to get in touch with the
detective—if, indeed, I ever got in touch with him again.

Yes; I was a pretty dismal creature in the first few moments after
the villain of the piece had left me to think about my problems. He,
no doubt, intended that I should go through the mental torture of
seeing where everything had gone wrong. He hoped that by facing
these facts I might be led to tell him everything that had happened.

Personally, I was convinced that there was little that I could do
about it. To begin with, I was not disposed to tell, but in any event, I

knew that if I did so I should gain nothing. The man I was up against was, I knew, in no way scrupulous; the way in which events had gone was enough proof of that. And if I gave him the most exact and truthful account of what had happened, the only result would be that he would kill me at the end, just as he would kill me at the beginning, did I merely refuse to say a word.

In fact, as I have already said, my position was as grim as possible. I couldn't see any way out of it. At the same time I thought that there must be some way. Human nature is so resilient that few men will ever admit themselves to be utterly defeated. The eternal obstinacy and optimism of human nature is enough to overcome anything.

Then there was something which gave me a little basis for my irrational optimism. I had, as I have said, been tied to the chair in such a way that I couldn't move. I had wriggled and writhed, but not a movement had I been able to make. But now, all suddenly, I felt the ropes that held my hands slip; the man must have tied me not quite as securely as he thought. One of the knots must have given slightly. It made my heart suddenly thump with excitement. If I could get out of these bonds it would mean that I should be able to take the man by surprise when he came back into the room!

At first I was tempted to pull madly at the ropes that bound me; but a sudden stab of pain from my wrist made me see that this was no way of getting free. My captor had been cunning enough to tie me up so that any sudden jerk would merely tighten the rope around my wrist.

I therefore moved in a gingerly manner. I could move my right wrist about an inch, I found. I wriggled it very carefully. Of course, I did not know quite what I was doing, since I was totally unable to see just how my hands were secured. Still, I thought, as I twisted the wrist, that the bonds were getting slowly looser. Something had happened that enabled me to loosen the rope still further.

The sweat poured down my forehead as I struggled. The pain in my wrist was excruciating. Still, I was sure that I was now getting near freedom. That put real joy into my heart. At last, I told myself, my opponent had made a mistake. I did not, at this stage, make up my mind exactly what I was going to do when I had escaped from my bonds. But at the same time I knew that I was a bit nearer to liberty, and, in my desperate position, that was quite enough to make me feel very much heartened.

More wriggles, more struggles. Now there was a good two inches of play in that loosened rope. It was good to know that I was now on the right lines.

I persisted, though the muscles of my right arm were already feeling very weary from the unaccustomed effort. Soon I gasped with delight. My right hand was free!

It was then only a matter of moments before I had freed the other hand. Then the bonds which tied my feet to the legs of the chair were undone.

I rose to my feet, and nearly collapsed on the floor. I sat down again suddenly, and massaged my ankles. They had been so tightly tied that the circulation had been interfered with. Still, it took only a matter of a few minutes before my feet and ankles felt somewhere near normal. I stood cautiously up, rested my weight first on one foot and then on the other. It was all right. I felt some slight weakness— the sort of feeling you get when an ankle is slightly sprained—but I thought that I was now in sufficient form, if not to win a hundred yards' sprint, at least to tackle most things that might come along.

Then I thought it was time to look around me. After all, the man who was responsible for my imprisonment would soon be back. He had said that he was going to leave me for half an hour or so to think things over. That half-hour would soon be over. And I had to work out some way to get the better of him.

The trouble was that I was not at all sure he would be alone. If he was on his own the matter would be comparatively simple. I should merely have to stand behind the door and clout him with the proverbial blunt instrument as he came in.

If, on the other hand, he was accompanied, I might find myself faced with the question of how to tackle two or more men at the same time. After all, I was not yet a hundred per cent fit. There were various muscular stiffnesses which I had to overcome, and I didn't expect that they would wear off by the time the man came back.

Still, I told myself, it was no use thinking of too many awkward things before they happened. I would work out a scheme that would suffice to deal with the main villain. If it proved that he brought assistance with him, I should have in some way to temporise and hope that the moments as they passed would bring some inspiration.

The obvious way, as I have already said, to deal with the one man if he came alone, was to dot him over the head, either as he came in, or as he wandered around the room. It would certainly be no good for me to sit peacefully in the chair where he had tied me, for then he would never give me a reasonable chance of hitting him, since he would certainly face me throughout the new interview.

No; I should have to hide in some way that would give me a chance of taking the fellow completely by surprise. I glanced around me. There was, of course, one obvious place to hide, and that was behind the curtain—the place where my opponent had clearly hidden when I came in. But I thought that was so obvious that he would jump at it as the probable place where I should be—that is, when he saw that I was no longer tied to the chair as he had left me.

The rest of the room was more or less bare. There were few if any places which looked in any way possible as hiding places. Behind the door. That was about the only spot that seemed to hold out any promise of success. I stood behind it and mentally pictured the man coming in. Yes; that was what I would do.

Of course, it had the very real objection that if he came in with some of his assistants, I should be at once exposed to their attentions. But I thought that I could lie more or less doggo, at any rate for those first few crucial seconds when their eyes would no doubt be riveted to the chair where they had been expecting to find me.

The next thing was the choice of a weapon. He had taken away my pistol, or the butt of that would have been ideal. I have had little experience of so hitting a man across the back of the head (that was what I proposed to do) in such a way as to knock him out noiselessly. But I guessed that what was wanted was something heavy and not bulky. One couldn't expect to hit him at all effectively, for example, with a chair. It would have enough weight, but it would be so unwieldy that it would not hit him in the necessarily vulnerable spot.

A poker would have been the sort of thing indicated. But there was no poker in the room. There was, indeed, no coal fire. In the empty grate stood an ornate electric fire. I looked at the grate carefully, as I thought that there might be something else in the way of fire-irons. But there was absolutely nothing at all that was likely to prove in any way a satisfactory weapon.

I was getting more than a trifle worried now. After all, the man would be coming back very soon. And if he came back before I had managed to get hold of a weapon of some sort I should be completely sunk.

Then I saw what I wanted. On the desk, alongside the pile of papers which I had been examining when the man had challenged me, was a small statuette. It was a representation of a nymph, poised on one toe, obviously about to dive into a river. It was a pretty little thing, and in better surroundings I might have appreciated it as a work of art. But all that I was now concerned with was its value as a weapon.

I picked it up and balanced it in my hand, trying to estimate its weight. It was made of metal, and, unlike many of its kind, it was solid. It weighed a good seven or eight pounds, I reckoned. Wielded with all the strength that I could put behind it, I thought that it would certainly be heavy enough to knock out any man who had not a thick skull.

If, of course, the man's skull was too thin, it might be that I should, in my ignorance, hit him so hard as to fracture it. That might mean the man's death. But my conscience did not assault me too violently on that score. If I killed my opponent I should regard it as being the clearest possible case of justifiable homicide. For, given the opportunity, he would quite certainly kill me, as he had already killed Tilsley and Margerison and attempted to kill Bender.

It may, in fact, strike you as a little odd that I was, up to this time, not consumed with curiosity as to the identity of the man in whose power I had been. But I am not the fellow to worry about something which I am unable to solve. And the man I was up against had so cleverly arranged the lighting of the room that it was not possible for me to get any sort of suggestion as to who he was. His features, I have already explained, were so hidden in darkness that I couldn't see them.

The main thing, in fact, was that I should get him under my control as soon as he came in. The matter of his identity was something that could then be dealt with at leisure.

I stood behind the door, the little statuette grasped firmly in one hand, and listened. I knew that he might be back at any moment, and that the only real danger was that I might allow myself to be lulled into a false sense of security, so that I did not do the necessary hitting at the precise moment that it was needful.

The wait was, in fact, quite a boring business. Shelley had often said to me that the long periods of waiting were the worse parts of a detective's life. And while I had been concerned with these calamities in Kent I was beginning to understand what he had meant.

There was, in fact, nothing that I could do as I stood there. I had to keep my mind concentrated on the job in hand. I had to listen to every sound that might come from the other side of the door.

The fact was that for the moment no noises came. And yet I still had to stand and listen. The statuette got very heavy in my hand, and for a time I rested it at my feet, where I could pick it up at a moment's notice. I leaned against the door, with my ear almost touching it. I had no idea, of course, of how long this ordeal of waiting might go on.

I had a plan of campaign, but that plan was dependent on a first move being made by my opponent. I guessed, however, that he was in many respects a shrewd psychologist, who would do his best to keep me in suspense for what he regarded as being the optimum time. The trouble was that I had no way of reading his mind, and so I did not know what he would regard as the optimum time in my case.

Then I pricked up my ears. I heard a firm footstep in the corridor outside. I was sure that it was the footstep that had previously heralded the approach of my opponent. Yes; he was coming!

I picked up the statuette and grasped it firmly in my hand. The footsteps stopped outside the door. There was now no doubt about it. My opponent was about to enter.

I heard the scratch of the key being inserted in the lock. I took a firmer grasp of the statuette. I was holding the nymph by the head, intending to hit the man with the solid base on which the statuette stood.

The handle turned and the door opened. I raised the statuette above my head, swung it and brought it down on the back of the newcomer's skull.

It went home with a kind of dull thud. He fell flat on his face before me in the doorway. I rapidly grasped him by his shoulders and dragged him hastily into the room. I had no desire to run unnecessary risks, and I knew that if any of his underlings had seen what had happened they would be after my blood without delay.

Then I did what took more sheer cold-blooded courage than anything that I had done before. I knew that it would be no good to leave the key on the outside of the door. Anyone might come along and think that it was queer to find the key there. Therefore it was now necessary to regain that key.

I knew well enough that there might be someone in that corridor. The man had not made much noise in his fall, but there had naturally been some sound. The sound might therefore have been enough to bring someone down in investigation. Well, there was only one thing to do—I should have to get that key. I did my best to squint around the door. I couldn't see anyone, so I rushed around the door whipped the key out and rushed back into the room.

It was done! I had at any rate won a round in the fight.

CHAPTER XXIX

In Which the Mystery is Solved

I CAN'T THINK WHY I WAS SUCH A FOOL AS NOT TO LOCK THE DOOR behind me. I was, I suppose, so elated at getting the key without, as I thought, being observed that it never occurred to me that my action might have been seen. Anyhow, I went back into the room, and was bending over the man whom I had knocked out, when I was suddenly conscious of a sound behind me. It was the merest rustle of clothes, as if someone was moving gently towards me. I sprang to my feet and had half-turned towards the source of the sound when something descended on my head. Instantly unconsciousness overcame me, though I think that in the moment that consciousness was going, I cursed myself for having been so absurdly careless as to let the whole course of events change to my disadvantage—and that was putting it mildly enough in all conscience.

From the blackness of unconsciousness I slowly came to myself. My head ached abominably, and I was conscious of the fact that it was bandaged. I was lying on what seemed to the touch to be a leather couch of some sort. I opened my eyes and frowned in the effort to focus them. At last the room which had been swimming round, came into focus, and I realised that I was still in the same place as that in which I had earlier been imprisoned. I felt a sinking at my heart to think that I had been so near to victory, but had, it seemed, lost the last trick. Well, I supposed that I could put up with defeat as well as the next man.

Then I gasped. A man was seated at the desk, steadily working through the pile of papers there. And that man—I gazed at him with astonishment—was Detective-Inspector Shelley! What was the meaning of it?

"Inspector," I said. My voice was stronger than I should have expected, in view of what I had gone through. Shelley looked towards me.

"How d'you feel, Jimmy?" he asked.

"Terrible," I said. And it was true.

"I'll bet that the man you hit feels worse," he commented.

"Why? Did I hit him hard?" I asked.

"The doctor said that he's very lucky to escape without a fractured skull," smiled Shelley. "You've merely had some bad bruises."

"But what has happened?" I asked.

"Well," answered Shelley, "it's rather a long story. I'm not sure that as yet you are in a fit state to listen to it."

I sat up. My head swam about almost intolerably, but I thought that if I did not at once get a complete description of what had happened I should soon die with curiosity. I managed somehow to control myself, though I felt as if I might faint at any moment. Still, I called into service every scrap of will-power that I possessed, lay back against the cool leather back of the settee, and said: "I'm all right. I want to know what's happened. You see, Inspector, the last thing that I remember was being slugged in the back of the head. I thought that I'd lost the whole thing through carelessness, and then the next thing that I know is that I find you here, and, I suppose, our friends the enemy under arrest."

"They're under arrest all right," said Shelley with a grim smile. "And you will be an important witness at the trial, Jimmy, if we can patch you together in time."

I grinned. "I'll be only too pleased to put in an appearance at the Old Bailey," I said. "I suppose that I'll be allowed to write about it afterwards?"

"Still the journalist, eh, Jimmy?" Shelley smiled. "Well, I must say that I cannot but admire the way you sailed into this job, even though in some respects I feel that you made a bit of a mess of it. Still, all's well that ends well, the old proverb says, and I think that this is going to end well."

"But can't you give me a bit of an explanation?" I pleaded. "I know that I ought to get some sleep, but I shall never sleep without some sort of explanation of what has been going on."

Shelley fished in his hip-pocket and produced a flask. "Have a swig of this, Jimmy," he advised. "But don't drink too fast. It's brandy."

And that brandy was very welcome. It put new life into me. I felt its warmth coursing through my veins. The headache improved in an almost miraculous manner, and I was at once much more fit to discuss the case.

"Let me give you an outline of what lay behind the case," Inspector Shelley said. "It concerns, as we thought, drug-smuggling. The gang, under the control of a chief who lived at Broadgate, were bringing into the country supplies of cocaine, made in a secret factory in the north of France. It was brought out into mid-channel in fast motor-boats, and transferred to what were supposed to be harmless fishing-boats from various ports along this coast. They caught some fish, and hid the small packets of cocaine underneath the fish."

"And distribution?" I asked. My head was fast clearing now, and I found no difficulty in following the story that Shelley was telling me.

"Distribution was carried out under various disguises. There were a chain of agents all over the south and east coasts, and extending up to London," the detective went on. "They all had some small business of their own, which gave them an ostensible reason for travelling about the country. They were supposed to be dealing with various things, as we suspected, from motor spares to precious metals. All that we said about it was correct."

I smiled, though it hurt my head to do so. Shelley still pretended to forget that the original idea had been mine—or rather Maya Johnson's.

"This inn was the headquarters of the gang. It was here that the smuggled cocaine was brought, and distributed to the various agents."

"But the murders?" I asked.

"Tilsley was one of the principal agents. But he thought that he was not getting enough out of it. He was threatening to give away the head of the gang, if he did not get some better pay. Therefore he had to be got rid of. And so he was killed."

"Margerison?" I asked.

"He had rumbled the way that the first murder was committed. In fact, he suspected it was coming. He wrote, in a disguised hand, a postcard warning Tilsley—the postcard you found at the Charrington Hotel. He had pretended to be a doctor when you met him, but merely in order to hide his identity. He thought that if he gave a totally fictitious identity we should find it difficult to trace him. And so, indeed, we might well have done if he had not applied the screw to the murderer, and himself been killed in turn."

"It all sounds very simple," I said. "But you haven't solved the problem of how the bodies were in the lift."

"What do you mean, Jimmy?" Shelley asked.

"Well," I frowned. My head was now aching again, and I found it difficult to formulate what I was trying to say. But I knew that unless I got an answer to the question I should be so consumed with curiosity that I should be unable to sleep.

"Don't worry, Jimmy," Shelley said. "You mean that you can't understand how it is that the bodies got into a locked lift without there being any signs of the locks having been in any way tampered with?"

"Exactly."

"Well, Jimmy, there is no such thing as a crime committed in a hermetically-sealed compartment. That is the first thing to remember. And you will recall that when Bender was injured—not in the locked lift—both sets of keys, Bender's own and the set in the council offices, were in the possession of the police."

"Yes," I said.

"That means that there was nothing supernatural about the way in which the murders were committed. They were definitely done with the assistance of one set or other of the keys. In other words, the murderer was either someone connected with the council offices or someone connected with Bender."

"Agreed."

"I had come to that conclusion when the people at Scotland Yard told us about this place, and I had the idea of setting you on to it. I thought that you had a better chance of finding out something than an obvious policeman would have. I owe you an apology for giving you such a rough time, Jimmy. But we had a police guard not far away. In fact, we had a plain-clothes man from Scotland Yard in the bar. He saw you slip through that curtain, and when you didn't come out he phoned us, and we staged a full-scale raid. I came down the corridor just as Arthur Banbury's second in command hit you on the head."

"Arthur Banbury?" This was an unfamiliar name, I thought. But then, I told myself, I might not be able to think straight after the smack on the head that I had received.

"He's the chief of the gang, the real brains behind the whole set up, which was very brilliantly planned," explained the detective. "Of course, you don't know him under that name, though you've come across him under one of his numerous aliases."

"Arthur Banbury." I screwed up my eyes and did my best to think hard. But it was no good—the slugging that had come to me had, for the time being, destroyed my power of coherent thought.

"Yes. But cast your mind back to those lift murders," Shelley said. "You see the bodies were found in a locked lift, and found by Bender. We suspected all sorts of things, we tried to find out who could have got hold of the keys in the council offices. But for a long time there was one man we overlooked as a possible murderer."

"Who was that?" I asked.

"Aloysius Bender," he replied.

"Bender?" This puzzled me. I recalled the man, his unintelligent manner and his limp. He bore no resemblance to the firm-stepping, masterful, intelligent man who had questioned me in this very room.

"Aloysius Bender or Arthur Banbury. The initials are the same," Shelley said. "That struck me as soon as I got the name of the chief of the gang. You see, he could put on a limp, he could brush his hair in such a way that it looked unkempt and untidy. He could pretend to a general lack of intelligence."

"And he continued to work as liftman?" I asked.

"Yes. The lift was very useful. It was actually used in the night, when the coastguard was far away, to transport smuggled goods. They were landed on the beach at high tide and taken up the lift to the promenade, where a fast car would be waiting to bring them to this inn. Oh, the whole thing was very well organised," Shelley said.

"But... Bender!" This was a staggering discovery to me. "But what about the time that he was stabbed?" I asked.

"He did that himself, after telling you a lying tale about a man who had a set of keys made," Shelley said. "You will recall that he was only superficially wounded. The business about shock was ingeniously done. But I have found that a few years ago there was a promising actor called Alfred Bailey—same initials again, you see. I suspect that he was the man. That, of course, is why he was so convincing in the rôle of Bender. He was a practised actor."

"And so he merely arranged to meet these people in the lift," I said.

"Yes. He killed them there, and locked the lift and went home. Then the next morning he came back, 'discovered' the body, and everything was all right," said Shelley. "Still, he is safely under lock and key now, and I forecast that his trial will be a sensation."

I leaned back, feeling very tired. Now that the mystery was solved I had only one real urge—to get some sleep. I felt as if I hadn't slept for a month.

"There is one other thing," Shelley said.

"Yes?"

"There are two people who want to thank you for what you have done," he said.

"Who?"

Shelley made his way to the door, opened it, and stood aside, to let Maya Johnson and Tim Foster come in.

"You're all right?" Maya said, as she came towards me.

"I shall be when I've had a bit of sleep," I said.

"Well, I don't know how to thank you," she murmured.

"Don't try," I advised her.

"But Tim and I are getting married next month," she said. "If it hadn't been for you that might never have happened."

"Forget it," I said.

"I'll never forget it," she replied.

"Thanks, Jimmy," said Tim, holding out his hand.

And if I ever regret that slug on the head—well, the memory of the gratitude in the eyes of Maya Johnson and Tim Foster will be enough to overcome my regret.

Murder in the Museum

When Professor Julius Arnell breathes his last in the hushed atmosphere of the British Museum Reading Room, it looks like death from natural causes. Who, after all, would have cause to murder a retired academic whose life was devoted to Elizabethan literature? Inspector Shelley's suspicions are aroused when he finds a packet of sugared almonds in the dead man's pocket; and a motive becomes clearer when he discovers Arnell's connection to a Texan oil millionaire.

Soon another man plunges hundreds of feet into a reservoir on a Yorkshire moor. What can be the connection between two deaths so different, and so widely separated? The mild-mannered museum visitor Henry Fairhurst adds his detective talents to Inspector Shelley's own, and together they set about solving one of the most baffling cases Shelley has ever encountered.

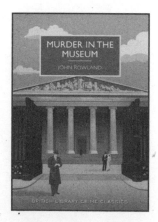